First edition published in the United S

by Light Investments & Publishing LLC

Copyright © Light Investments & Publishing LLC 2021

All rights reserved

No part of this book may be reproduced, stored, or transmitted,
in any form by any method without the prior written permission of
the publisher, nor be otherwise circulated without a similar
condition being imposed on the subsequent purchaser.

All characters, companies, organizations, events and
circumstances in this book are completely fictitious, and any
resemblance to existing organizations or real persons,
living or dead, is purely coincidental.

Photos and images are stock photos posed by models, and are
being used for illustrative purposes only.
Any person depicted is a model.

ISBN 978-1-7361078-5-0

www.lipublish.com

The Dryer

Chapter 1

Sailing around the Caribbean Sea on Phil's yacht, renamed 'Freedom', for more than twelve months really slowed life down, giving the five friends a new appreciation for the small pleasures of relaxation, sunbathing, fishing and diving. The random, short and infrequent stops for fuel and supplies, coupled with whatever they could catch from the sea, has allowed them to survive on water for long periods of time and, they hope, continue to remain far enough of anyone attempting to track them down.

Phil, Paul and Tiago have conditioned their bodies for increasingly longer morning swims and, as a result, are leaner than they have been in years. Bianca loves Phil's new 'swimmer body' and stays glued to him in their small cabin for ten hours straight every night. Phil had been worried that spending every minute of every day with Bianca would create old couples' habits, but he is quite happy with their continued love birds' manners. In fact, the whole crew has been enjoying their adventure with no apparent cabin fever behavior or drama. For all the doubts and disappointments that Bianca had after meeting Phil and having to help him launder money in order to survive from the grip of Norrid's criminals, she is now so happy and thanks Phil every day for having taken her out her boring accountancy career back in Australia.

Notwithstanding daily workouts in the water, without access to a proper fitness facility, Tiago's muscle mass has shrunk by at least twenty pounds. He is still very muscular and ripped, but not as scary as before, according to Bianca. More importantly, he feels better than ever, with significantly less stress and pressure than what he faced, working with the criminals of Norrid. Tiago's mood has also steadily improved as Phil helped him fight the addiction to the various performance enhancing drugs that he was required to take as part of Norrid's Enforcement Division's regimen. He is now completely clean and has vowed to a healthy and low stress lifestyle.

After three weeks of rough weather, they are excited to finally set foot on firm ground. It is also the first time that they are back to Grand Turk since they picked up Phil a year ago, after he collaborated with the police to take down Norrid and its puppet master Henry, who had been hiding in plain sight by being the CEO of one of the largest multinationals and simultaneously running the most powerful criminal cartel in the world. Until Phil made him reveal his dirty secrets, nobody had suspected that Henry, a self-proclaimed master of ethics and behavior would risk a very lucrative career by associating himself with criminals. Henry had been using the laundered fruits of the Norrid's drug operations to prop up any deficient part of Kexcorp, the century old company that he had been known to brilliantly lead.

During their last visit to Grand Turk, Bianca and Linda had befriended Maria, one the dock attendants at the pier, while waiting for Phil. They had tried to match her up with Tiago but he was too focused on recovering Phil, and escape to open waters, to pay sufficient attention to Maria. During this upcoming visit, however, Bianca promised to track Maria down and see if they could leave with an additional sailor-passenger on board, and perhaps form a third couple to continue their journey.

Tiago has softened up a lot since his first encounter with Phil, and secretly entertains some sweet conversations with Maria. He remembers her dark Latina features and perfect female attributes when she was sporting a red bikini top with tight jeans shorts. Tiago doesn't let his infatuations show though, and just sports a lopsided smile whenever the others tease him about his possible upcoming encounter with Maria. During those moments, Bianca likes to hug Tiago and tell him that they are going to take care of his heart to ease him into a happier and balanced life that include the right amount of love and tenderness. To keep his tough guy appearance in those instances, Tiago usually taps Bianca on the back and tells her "thank you for your support and encouragements… can I go back to work now?", which makes everyone laugh.

Despite being out at sea, Phil has kept up with the news, downloading articles with his satellite phone, and stocking up on newspapers whenever they dock somewhere. Consequently, Phil was able to learn that after his collaboration with the FBI to help arrest Henry, his former boss at KexCorp Industries, the companies were unwound, sold in pieces and lengthy trials ensued. Several executives were sent to prison for white collar crimes or involvement with drug cartels and money laundering operations. Also, all actors of Norrid known to Phil were convicted. Including, to Phil's disappointment, Dr. Debo. He was extradited to the U.S. by the Singapore government, but received a reduced sentence for helping the authorities understand the extent of the document forging employed by Norrid and

KexCorp. Phil wishes that he could have done more to keep such a great person out of prison.

Henry himself is still on trial and house arrest, facing life in prison, with grim prospects of ever going back to his celebrity CEO life. The legal team of Norrid escaped gracefully, invoking that their employers, law firms based in major metropolitan cities around the world, were merely providing legal advice to Norrid. The lawyers even denied having any knowledge of criminal activities at Norrid and refused to help Henry in his defense against U.S. Government prosecutors. Phil suspects that the legal team became extremely worried when he saw them argue with Ernesto, the Norrid executive that forced Phil to design money laundering schemes, presumably for having to vote the Goang proxy votes in favor of KexCorp's offer. The lawyers must have destroyed massive amounts of evidence. They must have realized, as Phil and the FBI agents did, that KexCorp's involvement with Goang would expose everything. It remains unclear to Phil, however, how much Ernesto and the legal team really knew of Henry's intentions. Their actions had seemed so disjointed over the handling of Goang. Perhaps Henry's tendency to keep a lot of information close to the vest backfired on him.

Most agonizing though, is that Li and all of his operatives are still at large despite a series of arrest warrants issued by authorities around the world for drug trafficking, money laundering, racketeering and kidnapping charges. Given Li's determination and recklessness in previous encounters, Phil believes that the chances of coming across him again are rather high. Li is probably aware that Phil, Bianca and Tiago have cooperated with authorities, so Phil hopes to avoid any encounter with him.

The feeling of perpetually having to look over his shoulder does not sit well with Phil. Moreover, worrying that Bianca could be kidnapped at any time by Li's thugs, or anyone impacted by Phil's cooperation with the FBI, is not something that he wants on his mind. Plus, the relative safety from roaming around the Caribbean Sea may not last forever. To clear his mind and make sure that he does not let his guards down too early, Phil would like to test the waters and stay on land for increasing amounts of time to see if any suspicious operatives are following them.

The night before docking at Grand Turk, with everyone lounging in different areas of the yacht, taking advantage of the first calm water in days, Phil joins Tiago on the front part of the boat. He offers him a beer and asks if he can sit with him to chat for a few minutes.

"Beautiful night. This sea can be so peaceful whenever the weather cooperates," says Phil as he sits down.

"Yeah, it is quite relaxing. And I'm really enjoying my time with you guys. Thank you for taking me onboard. You've made an extraordinary difference in my life. I hope we can work together for years to come," says Tiago, in an unusually soft voice.

"Of course, we love having you with us. We make such a good team. And we're more like family now," says Phil as he wraps one arm around Tiago's large shoulders. "Hey, I need to get your thoughts on something. Don't you think that we should try to determine if anyone is actually after us?" asks Phil.

"I've been thinking about the same. And if someone is after us, we probably need to know what we're up against so that we can prepare a good defensive strategy," says Tiago.

"Yeah, as long as it does not involve too many weapons... Listen, perhaps Grand Turk would be the right place to initiate this, since this is where I flew in from New York a year ago? The jet's registered flight plan might have left a trace and there could be people stationed there, just waiting for us to show up again," says Phil.

"That's a good idea. Let me devise a plan tonight that will allow us to stay a step ahead of anyone trying to come after us. And we can share it with the others in the morning, before we dock," says Tiago.

The following morning, while the group is having breakfast, Phil announces that they will dock for two nights in Grand Turk. The ladies scream of joy and immediately assume that the objective is to give Tiago more time with Maria, so they turn to him with huge smiles. Tiago just sports a small grin and shakes his head, makes everyone laugh for a few seconds, and gets his serious look back. He explains the plan to bait any operative in the area and to potentially follow them around, so that they can determine the extent of any threat.

Chapter 2

With Paul sailing the yacht near the sparsely inhabited Turks and Caicos Islands, a British Oversea Territory, the whole team is sitting on the deck to watch this paradise on earth come in front of their eyes. Turquoise water, beautifully preserved landscape and unlike during the era of pirates' regimes that its history suggests, Turks and Caicos is nowadays well governed and ruled under Common Law.

Mid-afternoon, Maria is waiting on the pier in a sexy summer dress and smiles flirtatiously at Tiago as Freedom approaches the dock at Grand Turk's cruise ship pier. With his trademark half smile on display, Tiago turns to Bianca and raises one eyebrow to express that it's very obvious that she arranged this in advance. Bianca turns the palm of her hands upwards and says: "What? I just called Maria to make sure that we could dock here for two nights. That's all, I promise." Phil shakes his head with a smile and jokingly tells Bianca that she should only use the satellite phone for emergencies, to which she answers that it was an obvious emergency – in some sense.

While Phil and Paul refuel and handle the paperwork for their stay, Tiago discusses with Maria the supplies that they will need to bring onboard over the next day or so. Bianca and Linda, whose only responsibility as part of Tiago's master plan is to guard the boat, are sipping champagne and watching the situation unfold, perched on top of the yacht.

The ladies whisper to each other the awkward words that a tough guy like Tiago would use with Maria in this situation.

"What do you think he's saying to her?" Bianca asks, sipping her drink.

Linda straightens, pushing out her chest. "Hey, gorgeous, anyone bothering you that you'd like me to beat up?"

Bianca snorts into her drink. "Or, would you like to come back to the boat to see me flex my biceps?"

Linda bursts out laughing splashing champagne in front of her when Bianca imitates Tiago's low voice. Tiago turns to them with a disapproving look for a moment, prompting Linda to hide her face, and Bianca to wink at Maria with limited subtlety. She waves, shouting from the deck. "Don't worry honey, he doesn't bite… too hard," says Bianca in Maria's direction, lightening the moment for Tiago to continue his smooth talking.

Since the pier is meant for cruise ships with nearby shops mostly selling touristy souvenirs, Maria offers a ride to Tiago in order to run his errands at establishments near the center of the island. Tiago hesitates for a few seconds because this is upending his Seal Team Six plan to bait anyone looking for them. But he does not want to disappoint Maria after just five minutes, and frankly doesn't want to lose the opportunity to spend a few hours with her running errands, so he agrees gracefully to go along with her suggestion. Conscious that spending time with Maria will distract him from safely guarding the rest of the crew, Tiago huddles with Phil and Paul, orders them to remain on Freedom until his return and tasks them to use the binoculars to spot anyone out of the ordinary.

Tiago immediately likes Maria's choice of car; an old Jeep Wrangler, with a soft top, which she removes before they get on the road and start driving towards the main part of town. On the way, Maria offers to stop for lunch at her favorite place: Sandbar Restaurant, an unassuming little place by the beach. According to her, it's the best place to relax, drink and enjoy some local fried delicacies. The place is packed with locals, who all seem to know Maria. She turns somewhat shy and giddy when she introduces Tiago as her new friend.

In sharp contrast to Tiago, Maria is very talkative and asks a million questions about his background, interests and hobbies. Without lying to her, he remains vague regarding his years of security work for Norrid and says that he now much prefers to work and travel with Phil and Bianca. He keeps turning the conversation back to her life story to avoid sharing too much information, but Maria sees this as caring, unassuming and humbling. When she speaks, Tiago stares at her beautiful brown eyes and the most amazing smile he has ever seen. She looks so happy. And in spite of the few tropical drinks already ingested, he remains disciplined with his eyes, not wanting to look down at her revealing top, in case that would make her uncomfortable. He would like to just reach across the table and kiss her. But he holds back. After all, they barely know each other, and this wasn't even officially a first date.

Three hours sitting at this beach side bistro pass by so quickly that when Tiago looks at his watch, he realizes that he may have left his friends exposed for too long.

He looks up. "I've been so enjoying your stories that it looks like we've lost track of time."

Maria looks at her own watch. "Oh my goodness! Good food and good company sure does make the time fly!"

Tiago grins. "No worries. I've really enjoyed myself. I can't remember the last time I had this much fun."

Maria's smile dazzles. "Me neither. I'm glad we decided to stop."

Tiago nods. "But unfortunately I think we need to head back, and handle the errands tomorrow."

She stands. "Okay, but only if you let me come with you again."

Tiago tries to hold back his grin. "If you insist, your wish is my command."

Back to the yacht, Tiago helps Maria out of the Jeep. "I'm sure that everyone would like to talk to you. How about you come onboard and see our little boat?" He smiles, knowing the yacht is far from little. Maria becomes somewhat hesitant for a moment, looks around as if she was about to do something wrong.

Tiago holds up his hands. "Only if you want to, and there are no preconceptions about coming onboard." He lowers his hands, rustling up his best grin. "I've just had so much fun, today, I'm not ready for it to end."

She smiles. "Me, too." She sighs, looking at the boat. "You know what? Why not. I need to learn to live a little." She grabs Tiago's hand firmly as she jumps onto Freedom.

Tiago is relieved to find his friends alive and well, napping in the living room middle section of the boat, but a bit disappointed that no one is surveilling the surroundings and that they have let their guards down, contrary to his strict instructions. What if it had been a Norrid assassin coming onboard, and not Tiago and Maria? They'd be dead, and be none the wiser. They all really needed to take the threat more seriously. With all they'd been through, they should know better.

Maria smiles, looking through the window out over the water.

Of course, Tiago had been no better, running off and having lunch for hours with a beautiful woman. Maybe he needs to cut his friends some slack. They had all been running for so long, they all needed some time to relax and believe they were not in danger.

This needs to be the last time, though. One thing his SEAL training had taught him was that any moment distracted could be your last—as in it might leave you dead.

Maria raises up on her tip toes and whispers to Tiago to avoid awakening the rest of the group. "How about we go back outside." She looks up, fluttering her lashes. "Or maybe back to one of the bedrooms?"

Tiago gapes at her, almost speaks, but stops himself in case he said something dumb to make her change her mind. He locks the main door, grabs a half-filled bottle of champagne and Maria's hand, and takes her to his cabin. First sitting, then lying on

Tiago's small bed, they continue to chat for hours until Maria yawns a few times and rests her head on Tiago's shoulder. He breathes a few times, finally taking in her perfume from up close, and without hesitation, Tiago gently places his hand behind Maria's neck and moves in to kiss her. Acting a bit surprised and reserved with Tiago's move, Maria freezes for a few seconds but quickly gives in to the temptation, and slowly moves her hands over Tiago's upper body's cut muscles. "Impressive," she whispers with a smile, pausing their intense kissing for a few seconds. "You too," says Tiago, while he places a hand on Maria's tushy.

At seven o'clock the following morning, Maria slips into Tiago's shirt hoping to quietly go to the bathroom. When she opens Tiago's cabin door, however, the two other couples are having an early breakfast, primarily because they napped through dinner the night before and drunk slept on the couches for most of the night. They all stop eating and burst out laughing when they see Maria with seemingly nothing other than an oversized shirt on.

Linda almost chokes on a piece of fruit and places her hand over her chest. "Goodness, we didn't even know you were here!"

"Oh! I'm so sorry to intrude!" Maria says.

"No no no!" Bianca stands. "Not at all. We're all thrilled to see you!"

Maria blushes. "I…I need to get ready for work."

Bianca stands up to hug her warmly and asks Phil to prepare coffee and juice for her. Maria takes a few sips, then rushes to the bathroom, while the other enjoy another chuckle at her expense.

When Maria is in the shower, Paul jokes that she might have had little sleep, but at least her morning commute should be lighter than usual.

Phil raises his coffee cup. "I'm sure our 'Head of Security', Tiago, will not mind if she comes in for a nap during her break." He laughs into his mug. "That would be a great midday stress reliever for them both!"

When Tiago finally wakes up at nine o'clock, everyone keeps silent as he sits at the breakfast table. He assumes that no one saw Maria come in and out of the yacht, but everyone is unusually quiet. So, Tiago decides to break the silence.

"Anything out of the ordinary around the yacht yesterday?" asks Tiago.

"Well, yah, we had a visitor," says Paul.

"Really? Who was it?" asks Tiago.

"I don't know, but you should. She was in your bed!" says Paul as everyone start laughing. Bianca and Linda jump on Tiago to hug and congratulate him.

"Oh... I thought you guys would be asleep this morning and notice nothing. What time did she leave?" asks Tiago.

"She got up at seven and left around seven fifteen. She is probably less than 50 feet away if you need to talk to her," says Phil, with more laughs from the group.

"No need for now but I'll finish the errands with her this afternoon. Meanwhile, we need to get back on our mission," says Tiago, knowing full well that this is not the time for serious talks and his friends are going to continue to roast him a little bit longer.

"Well, we don't have to hurry that much anymore, because I convinced the captain that we were staying here for a week," says Bianca provocatively looking at Phil.

"You did?" Phil asks.

Bianca nods. "Yes you did." She points at his nose. "And don't you dare try to get out of it."

Phil rubs the bridge of his nose. "Darn Jamaican rum." He lowers his hand. "No fair preying on a man blinded by liquor," says Phil looking back at Bianca with a jokingly reproaching look. "But in any case, we indeed have to give you guys time to get to know each other a bit," continues Phil as he turns to Tiago.

"I appreciate it, but we really have to be on our guards. No more excessive drinking," orders Tiago.

Mid-morning, they all head outside to lounge on the top deck for the rest of their hangovers to pass, watch the surroundings and smile at Maria when she passes by to attend customers at the dock. Tiago offers to help her a few times when she seems tired or overwhelmed, but she refuses categorically by shaking her head, opening her eyes wide opened and tightening her lips, in an apparent effort to hide their burgeoning relationship.

An hour before the end of Maria's shift, Phil proposes that they all walk around the shops near the cruise terminal before Tiago leaves with Maria. They stay close together as they go into touristy clothing and jewelry stores. As planned, for the first time in more than a year, Phil uses a credit card to make a purchase, to purposely provide a location to someone potentially watching over their financial transactions. On the way back to the yacht, Tiago spots a few suspicious individuals and spends time studying them, but he concludes that they are not a threat.

Tiago then joins Maria in her Jeep to run the errands that were meant to be done yesterday. Uncomfortable with people watching her leave with Tiago for a second day in a row, Maria doesn't display any affection until they hit the main road. Waiting at a red light, however, Tiago turns to look at her with a teasing smile, and she leans towards him for a kiss. Tiago has always been annoyed at couples kissing and slowing traffic down from their reduced attention to the road. But he just cannot resist Maria's beauty, so he lurches over for a quick touch of their lips.

"Everything ok? Sorry I was sound asleep when you left this morning," says Tiago with an apologetic tone.

"Oh, no worries, I didn't want to wake you up. I've been feeling quite tired all morning. And sorry that I didn't give you much attention in front of my boss and colleagues. I'm just not too comfortable displaying affection in public, especially with the dozens of dating offers that I've received and turned down in the two years that I've been here. I've managed to stay single the entire time because I just feel like the first guy I date will get targeted by all the others," explains Maria.

"Ouch, should I be watching my back now?" asks Tiago, in a boastful tone given the remote possibility that an untrained suitor would stand a chance against a former Navy Seal.

"Yes, maybe. But you're only here for a few days, so it shouldn't be too bad," Maria says with a smile.

Tiago laughs it off, knowing that he is twice the size of any other man on this island. But he doesn't quite like how she made it sound like their encounter would be just a fling for a few days. He intends to fully leverage the whole week that Phil agreed to stay in Grand Turk for. But he knows that any conversation of a relationship with Maria could be perceived as premature. Especially since it might lead to the difficult decision of letting go of her whole life in Grand Turk to hop on a yacht for a long adventure with people that she barely knows. Tiago decides to leave these thoughts for later and to try to enjoy their afternoon together without asking any questions that may seem too committing.

They continue their incessant chatter throughout the afternoon. Maria describes how she grew up in absolute poverty in Columbia, and since her teenage years, had wanted to leave Bogota for a peaceful life, away from the violence and crimes. Her parents had always described Columbia's issues as being the result of Americans' thirst for narcotics and the United States' enforcement agencies wanting to lead the war on drugs in their poor country instead of on America's streets. These negative opinions of Americans have kept Maria away from the U.S., where most of her friends had sought political asylum or just entered as illegal immigrants. Consequently, she restarted a life in Grand Turk, where she actually learned to appreciate many foreigners, including Americans. But she also misses her family back home immensely.

After Maria yawns a few times, Tiago offers to drive her back home.

She agrees that he drives her Jeep but completely refuses to be away from him for the night.

"Okay." She smiles. "But how about we go back to your cabin?"

Tiago's heart almost leaps out of his chest. "Are you sure?"

Maria nods. "I've never been more sure about anything."

When they walk onto the yacht, the table is already set for dinner and an amazing smell of roasted meat fills up the entire interior of the boat. This time, everyone is awake and excited to get to know Maria better over a meal to be washed down with plenty of alcohol. Bianca made sure that champagne bottles were on ice and French red wine would pair with the meal.

Chapter 3

For better or for worse, Tiago's concern about whether Maria would commit to a long-term relationship vanished a week later. When he wakes up alone at six o'clock, he wonders whether Maria had an early shift at the dock. So, he immediately gets out of bed in case she is still on board, and perhaps he could convince her to have breakfast with him before she goes to work. Although not an expert at charm offensives, Tiago wants to ensure that Maria understands the way he feels about her, especially that Freedom's planned departure is today at eleven o'clock.

When Tiago steps into the kitchen, he is surprised to find Bianca holding Maria's hair as she is throwing up in the sink. Bianca looks at Tiago with a faint smile while rubbing Maria's back. Tiago is petrified. He knows what the smile is about. And Maria's vomiting cannot be from a hangover because she barely drank half a glass of wine the night before.

After Maria's natural colors come back, Tiago helps her to slowly sit and relax on the couch, and passes his fingers through her hair, near the neck area, to pacify her. Tiago tries to hide his own worries as much as he can. He thinks about the potential responsibility of bringing a child to the world. While he sees an opportunity for a strong bond with Maria, part of him hopes that it's only a case of bad mayonnaise.

Linda, awakened and surprised by the early movements in the kitchen, also comes by to attend to Maria. She pours some ginger ale, and gives her some nausea-avoiding advice. Before Paul made a fortune during the Internet Bubble, Linda had been a registered nurse, so, as far as medical advice at the present moment, she's unparalleled. Linda also knows that they must take Maria to a doctor before sailing again. Irrespective of the group's travel plans, which may or may not include Maria, determining whether she is in fact pregnant from Tiago, and ensuring that she has access to proper care, are absolute imperatives.

After making Maria call in sick for work, which is inconsequential because there will apparently be limited activity at the dock today, Linda sends Tiago to buy an over-the-counter pregnancy test. He grabs Maria's car keys, kisses her on the forehead and leaves.

Bianca goes back to snuggle with Phil, who is still sleeping and slightly hungover. He smiles when Bianca awakes him with the news that Maria is probably pregnant. He is sincerely happy for Tiago, who has become a really close friend and confidant. The two of them spend most of their daylight time together and have come to appreciate each other's reliability.

Phil tells Bianca that they will stay in Grand Turk for a couple more days to figure this out, and let Tiago and Maria decide if they want to stay here, continue on Freedom, or go elsewhere. Bianca is relieved to have such an intelligent and understanding man in her life. He really makes fundamental life issues take precedence over whatever other priority or need, including safety from people potentially chasing them.

Around eleven o'clock, Phil finally gets out of bed and notices Tiago and Maria chatting on the sofa with the pregnancy test result in their hands. Phil quietly heads outside to let them discuss their next steps. He sits down with everyone else on the top deck. They all stare at Phil as he rubs his temples.

"This is why it's called an adventure. And at least this time, we're dealing with nature at its best, as opposed to thugs chasing after us," says Phil as he puts on his sunglasses to help sooth his headache.

"Yes, indeed. And I wouldn't trade this adventure for anything else in the world. I'm really glad that you guys are so supportive – especially you, Phil, even letting us stay on the ground for more than a few hours. We should celebrate!" says Linda with a funny grimace towards Phil.

"Yeah, we've been here more than a week, that's a record," says Paul.

"I know... let's buy some more champagne today," says Phil sarcastically, with a hand on his forehead, his brain still pounding from yesterday's over-consumption.

"It's funny though, I must admit, that it happens to Mr. *Plan Everything*," says Paul with a laugh.

Bianca grins. "Well, maybe he actually planned it that way. And I wouldn't blame him. She's a great girl, beautiful and so sweet. She really deserves a guy as protective and caring as Tiago.

Behind the tough guy shell, there is a genuinely outstanding man. I honestly hope that Maria can join our family, we will all be better for it."

The group is interrupted when Tiago shows up on the deck and asks Phil if he has a minute to join him for a conversation in the yacht's living room. Phil follows Tiago inside and sits with Maria and him. Maria is sobbing quietly.

"Maria, what's wrong? This is a beautiful moment. There is absolutely nothing to be sad about," says Phil.

"I know... it's just that I am from a Catholic family, you know? I'm supposed to be married before becoming pregnant," says Maria, with tears rolling down her cheeks and feeling melancholy.

"Well, I'll have to let the two of you figure out the marriage part, but meanwhile, you're welcome to stay with us. We would be delighted to help in whatever way you would like," says Phil.

"Really?" asks Maria, looking at Phil with her puffy eyes.

"Of course. Tiago is like my brother, so you're also family now. We'll support you guys no matter what. Here in Grand Turk, sailing around the Caribbean Sea or back to your home in Columbia, if you'd like. You're our new priority. We won't let you down, I promise," Phil says.

"I would be so delighted to see my family again," says Maria. She then turns to Tiago for his approval, which he immediately gives. "But I cannot afford my way back to Columbia."

"We can sail there! It's not that far. And we would love to meet your family! Next stop: Columbia. And if you guys decide to get married, we'll be standing right by you. Everything will be alright. You guys will bring a beautiful baby to this world," says Phil, as he embraces both of them in a tight hug and whispers some more encouraging words. The three of them have tears in their eyes as they lock their heads together for a few minutes.

In order to avoid parading Maria in-and-out of the yacht, potentially in front of her boss and colleagues, Phil asks Paul to move the boat north, closer to the town center, and drop the anchor 100 feet from the shore. While Paul remains on the yacht, the rest of the group uses an inflatable dinghy to reach the beach, which gives Maria more nausea, but she holds it together for the short ride. Meanwhile, Tiago drives Maria's Jeep from the cruise terminal to the beach where Phil, Bianca, Linda and Maria landed. They drive together to the local general practitioner doctor.

Phil sits down in the corner of the clinic's waiting room, breathing normally for the first time since the morning. Still affected by hangover, he places his fingers on his temples as he stares at Bianca walking towards him.

"Seems like you have increasing difficulty to handle your liquor," says Bianca as she sits beside Phil, who just offers a quiet nod. "Well, it might be a good thing this time around, because your usual sixth sense for danger hasn't yet lit up," she continues. Phil turns to her, eyes wide open.

"I guess not... what did I miss?" asks Phil.

"Interesting," says Bianca. "Should I keep the suspense for you until you sober up?" She rubs her hands together slowly while

Phil's eyes narrow. "Honey, you agreed to go to Columbia. Don't you think that it's a hot bed for old remnants of Norrid?"

"Gosh, you're absolutely right... I guess it's too late now. We would crush her morale if we changed our minds," says Phil.

"Well, I guess things are about to get interesting," concludes Bianca as she stands up to check on Maria.

Chapter 4

Maria's simple life in Grand Turk made it quite easy for Tiago to wrap everything up in a few hours and load her few possessions onto the yacht.

While Tiago continues to analyze every single person that they come across, the group goes for one last shopping excursion for supplies to potentially last them for their entire journey to Columbia, as well as medicine and vitamins that Linda believes are needed to support Maria for the next few weeks. Finally, under Phil's instructions, Maria's Jeep is lent to her boss at the dock, with the arrangement that they can have access to it whenever they are back to the island. Who knows, this vehicle could prove useful in the future.

As Freedom leaves Grand Turk and starts sailing south, Phil, Paul and Tiago gather around the navigation's console to strategize on their route. In case of medical emergency, mechanical issues, bad weather or refueling needs, they decide to remain relatively close to land at any point during the journey to Columbia. Maria and the unborn child's health might at some point depend on a fairly quick access to a clinic or hospital.

Therefore, they will first sail south east, loop around all the Caribbean islands and finally head west, parallel to the Venezuela coast. Their last stop before arriving in Columbia could be the beautifully developed and touristic island of Aruba, often referred to as the Dutch Caribbean because it is part of the Kingdom of the Netherlands.

Maria's morning sickness finally abates after ten days of navigation, thanks to Linda's prescribed diet of bland food in the morning: crackers and cereal. The nausea, however, has not impacted Maria's romance with Tiago. The two of them are almost inseparable. A lonely man for practically his whole life, Tiago is now enjoying the many conversations with Maria during which he learns to share his feelings, thoughts, dreams and profound desires to grow old along Phil and Bianca's side.

Weeks into their journey, Phil takes advantage of a quiet night when everyone is relaxing on the yacht's deck to ensure that Maria is briefed on the risks faced by the group. He sees no way around some leveling of knowledge of the group's activities, and the reasons why they had to move around so much over the last year.

"Maria, I'd like to say that we're really looking forward to meet your family, and excited to attend your wedding," says Phil.

"It means a lot to me. You guys are being so nice," replies Maria.

"I'd like to take this opportunity though to make you aware of risks that, unfortunately, you've unknowingly accepted when you became part of our family," says Phil as Maria immediately turns anxious. Tiago starts rubbing down her back to attempt to relax her.

"You're scaring me now. Is this a dirty secret?" asks Maria.

"It's not a character flaw. You see, Tiago, Bianca and I were coerced into criminal activities a few years ago and…" starts Phil, before being interrupted by Maria.

"Have you killed people?" asks Maria as she stands up and pushes Tiago's hand to the side, disgusted by the thought that Tiago might have hurt people in the past, especially with the crimes and issues that she witnessed growing up in Columbia.

"Oh no, we were only involved in money laundering. And trust me, we didn't want to be part of it, but it was the only way to save our lives," says Phil, referring to Bianca and himself, not really sure how Tiago started with Norrid, and whether he has ever been part of violent crimes. Phil finds that, given Maria's reaction, speaking in high-level terms might suffice for the time being. "And the three of us collaborated with the FBI to send as many of those thugs to jail as possible. But some are still out there, especially in Columbia, which I suspect was a place where production was taking place. Some of these thugs may be after us for snitching. That's why we must constantly be on our guards and move around," says Phil, as he grabs Maria's hand in a way to plead with her for compassion and understanding.

Tiago remains silent to avoid aggravating Maria's concerns. And while he agrees with Phil that she needed to be briefed on parts of their situation, he knows that this topic will occupy most of his time with Maria over the next few days, instead of the amazing romantic flow that they have been sharing. Tiago also doesn't react when Phil mentions the heightened risk associated with Columbia. He had of course been thinking that he might encounter former Norrid operatives in Columbia but feels confident that he can safely protect the group since Maria's parents live in a remote area.

In spite of her simple upbringing, Maria is very smart and inquisitive about Norrid and its activities, especially Tiago's involvement with the organization. She wants to make sure that he was not involved with drug activities, given her disgust with the cartels' operations in Columbia. Phil smoothly handles most of the explanations by giving honest and balanced information about how they operated various money laundering schemes in Asia, and that Tiago was there to protect them. And on that, Phil explains that Tiago overdelivered. To prove his point to Maria, Phil even gives the example of when Tiago hid Bianca in a piece of luggage, allowing her to escape to safety, while surrendering himself to torture, in the most unselfish and protective way. Maria is touched by the recounting of these events, and she sits on Tiago's lap and hugs him warmly. Even Paul and Linda are learning more than they had previously heard from the Norrid adventures.

Phil also reassures Maria that any wealth that she has seen or will see from Phil, Bianca, Paul and Linda has nothing to do with Norrid's criminal activities. Phil of course continues to keep the real source of his wealth away from everyone, but he wants to make sure that Maria does not hold some form of disdain over the relative luxury that the group indulges while traveling. And anyway, Phil explains that he just does not see how they could remain safe without his transportation assets, namely the yacht and the jet.

With Maria's blood pressure back to normal, Phil explains how the next few days will unfold. Once they reach the city of Santa Marta in Columbia, Sergio and Claudio, Phil's personal pilots, will pick up part of the group in Phil's jet, which had been mothballed in Brazil for a year, to take them to Bogota.

"What do you mean 'part of the group'? Why would we separate?" asks Bianca with an attitude that Phil has not witnessed in a long time.

"Because I would like Paul and Linda to take Freedom back to the Bahamas. As soon as they safely dock the yacht, we'll send Sergio to pick them up with the jet," says Phil, as everyone else turn to Paul and Linda, like if they had become the abandoned children of the family.

"It would be better that we all stay together, for safety purposes," says Tiago.

"I agree. And trust me guys, you're all that I have for family, so I hold you all close to my heart," starts Phil in a soft voice. "But we might need the yacht as an escape mechanism in the future, and Columbia, sorry Maria, no offense, is not necessarily the safest place to leave it," continues Phil. Maria nods in agreement.

"Linda, are you ok with that? Do you feel safe?" asks Bianca, with a sad tone, giving no consideration to Paul, knowing that she will be without her primary drinking buddy for a few weeks.

"Of course. Paul and I have sailed together many times before. And I'm sure that we're not the primary targets here. As long as you guys promise to take good care of our Maria until we're back together, it's a deal," says Linda, as she moves her eyes multiple times between Paul and the rest of the group. Paul is not as convinced as her, but he does see the value in safeguarding Freedom in the Bahamas, as opposed to Columbia.

Everyone stands up for a group hug that lasts at least five minutes, and during which Phil praises each of them for their courage. He also explains that they will dock in Aruba for a day or two, while the jet is being put back into service, and Sergio confirms that he has landed in Santa Marta. Tiago lightens up the emotional moment by telling the group that he will take the opportunity of the stopover in Aruba to teach them some covert communication techniques, which they will use during their time in Columbia. They all smile at how Tiago is able to bring up such serious thoughts in a moment like that. "Maria, you'll have to get used to the 'Tiago Way' military style. But don't worry, Linda and I will more than compensate with fun stuff", says Bianca.

Chapter 5

Finally in Columbia, Sergio meets the group at the Marina Internacional in Santa Marta, on the coast of Columbia, with a rented minivan. Tiago takes with him a few concealed weapons and leaves the rest of his artillery stowed away and locked in a false floor of the yacht. He explains to Paul that he should only retrieve the weapons in case of absolute emergency because, despite having licenses to carry weapons onboard, potentially corrupt authorities could use the discovery of the equipment as a way to inflict misery or obtain bribes.

"I can't believe that you're finally letting us set foot on land for a couple of weeks. We're gonna go shopping and hang out in all the best places," says Bianca with a wide smile while wrapping her arms around Phil's neck and bringing her mouth close to his. "And in Columbia too. What happened to your concerns about our security?"

"Yep, don't get too comfortable, we'll likely be on the run again soon," whispers Phil. "We just need to find out what Tiago and Maria want to do."

"Don't take this personally honey, but we need Tiago for our safety. For better or for worse, we're all staying together," says Bianca, releasing her hug with a charming wink and an affectionate spank on Phil's butt.

"Yes, my captain," replies Phil with a smile.

Phil asks Paul and Linda to start sailing immediately, but to remain near the coast of Columbia for half a day in case the team needs be re-extracted quickly. "If anything happens, just dock on the nearest island and we'll send Sergio to pick you up," says Phil with a paternal voice.

Onboard the jet, Maria calls her parents to announce that she will be home in a few hours with her fiancé and will be getting married within weeks. A long and emotional conversation in Spanish ensues. Phil has to ask Sergio to delay the take-off in order for Maria to finish her conversation. Although born from Brazilian parents, Tiago's Portuguese is limited because he grew up in the US, which only allows him to pick up a few words from Maria's conversation in Spanish. The words seem to flow out of Maria's mouth so quickly that Tiago wonders how he would ever be able to communicate with her family.

Bianca senses the distress in Maria's voice, grabs her hand and kneels in front of her. "It's okay, we're here for you," says Bianca but Maria continues the intense back-and-forth with her parents. Bianca thinks about the time she had to explain to her family back in Australia that she wanted to stay with Phil in South East Asia. Given the pregnancy and the upcoming wedding, Bianca hopes that Maria can smooth the relation with her parents.

When Maria hangs up, she is in tears. While unsure whether the wedding plans are still on, Phil, in his usual self-confidence, breaks the awkward silence by ordering the jet's departure through the cabin intercom. Phil figures that, at this point, they need to fly to Bogota, no matter what. Maria needs to see her family.

Tiago is rubbing Maria's back as she calms down and is ready to start talking after a long twenty minutes during which everyone is looking at each other, not knowing which part of Maria's story was the most difficult to discuss with her parents. The sound and vibration of the jet's engines on takeoff seem to sooth and calm everyone.

"I'm sorry guys. I didn't mean to break down like this in front of all of you. My father is very traditional. And learning that I am coming home with my new fiancé was not easy for him to hear," says Maria as she looks at Tiago with pity eyes.

"Oh, don't worry, I'm sure Tiago can sum up a few Spanish words to officially ask your dad's permission to marry you," says Bianca, faintly smiling at Tiago, who is uncomfortable but offers an approving nod.

"I agree, and we can all contribute to soften up the situation. Your parents must have been happy to hear that they will be grandparents, right?" asks Phil.

"Oh, I didn't tell them about the pregnancy. Let's leave that part of the conversation for after the wedding," says Maria, rubbing her belly, wondering whether there is any chance that someone could notice.

"Of course, anything else we should know before one of us puts a foot in his mouth?" asks Phil.

"Well, I asked them to respect our desire to keep the wedding very private and only invite close family members," says Maria, generating an approving look from Tiago.

"Everything is in order then!" says Phil as he stands up to grab drinks but stops halfway when he sees Maria's face change back to sadness.

"Wait… My father became angry at the thought of limiting the size of his baby girl's wedding. He said the invitation list is his decision," says Maria as she tightens her grip on Tiago's hand to ensure that he doesn't disapprove.

Tiago had wanted a smaller, more controllable crowd at the wedding for security reasons. He knows that as the groom at the reception, he will not be able to surveil people or any of their potentially unsafe actions. Tiago and Phil look at each other with the same thoughts. Tiago's name and perhaps picture will be published and distributed widely in a country where Norrid must have had operations. The chances of attracting undue attention have now multiplied.

Phil offers and insists that Maria and Tiago lie down on the retrofitted bed in the jet cabin. Maria is emotionally drained and falls asleep immediately, her head on Tiago's chest. Bianca sits on Phil's lap at the back of the airplane, looking worriedly at Maria.

"I wonder whether Maria's fatigue and body language will give away her pregnancy to her family members. We could be in for some drama," says Bianca, with a train of thoughts completely different from Phil's security concerns.

"I'm sure Maria's family will love Tiago and everything will be perfect. Without imposing ourselves, let's try to stay with them at Maria's parents' house, so that we can smooth things over if necessary," suggests Phil.

"That will be weird... all of us in the same house. Let's first see if we get invited. I can't see how any of us can make that request to her parents, especially in the current state of affairs," says Bianca.

"It's important that we stay together – you said it yourself an hour ago. With Tiago's name floating around on wedding invitations, we may be overly exposed," says Phil as he closes his eyes to catch some sleep during this short flight. Phil keeps his comments short of resurfacing to Bianca that Columbia might have been a key supply location for Norrid. He doesn't want to stress her out further and since she had brought it up herself as they were leaving Grand Turk, Phil hopes that the danger of Columbia is sufficiently engraved in Bianca's mind for her to be precautious.

"And until Linda is back from the Bahamas, we also need to make sure that Maria receives the proper care. We might have to sneak her to a Doctor's office," says Bianca, but Phil is already asleep.

Upon landing, Phil arranges a jet hanger for the week before going on the hunt for a rental car large enough for the four of them, and Maria's many luggage. Her belonging had seemed limited in the yacht and the plane's luggage compartment, but in a car, it seems too much for a group that is used to traveling light for quick and easy escapes, if needed. Phil offers to keep Maria's things on the plane for her, but she insists on bringing all of her things to her parents' place.

Before driving off, Phil turns to Sergio and Claudio, but before he has time to even say a word, Sergio says "we know the drill, we book a nearby hotel room and stay with the jets in alternating shifts". Phil smiles and hands over some cash. "I'm glad that we're reunited with you guys. I missed you. I'll call you when it's time to get Paul and Linda from the Bahamas," says Phil.

Sergio and Claudio are excited to continue their journey around the world with Phil and his increasing crew. They had limited work back in Brazil for the past year and are happy to log hours in Phil's beautiful private jet. Sergio also secretly loves the 'James Bond' lifestyle and Ironman toughness of Phil and Tiago. Despite not knowing the extent of the legality of the group's operations, Sergio finds hanging around Phil quite addictive.

Chapter 6

Maria is very emotional as they approach her family's house, a small bungalow in a dense suburban town on the periphery of Bogota. Phil drives slowly, through the many shirtless kids playing soccer on the dirt roads. Maria rolls down her window to wave at them. She has changed most of their diapers when they were infants. Maria basically babysat the entire neighborhood. The children scream and run after the car. Bianca tells Phil to be careful and smiles at Tiago, not surprised at Maria's popularity given her beauty and charm. Phil wonders if he should stop, so that Maria can chat with the kids, but she asks Phil to keep going – the neighborhood kids can wait after she reconnects with her family.

They barely pull into the driveway before Maria jumps out of the car and starts running towards her mother. They embrace for long minutes. Phil, Bianca, and Tiago get off the car, start unloading the luggage and tentatively walk towards the house. Maria, full of tears, releases the long hug with her mother and introduces Tiago as her fiancé. He says a few pleasantries to Maria's mother in Spanish and turns to introduce Phil and Bianca as friends who are traveling along.

As they enter the house, Maria enquires about her father. He is sitting in the backyard, sulking. But Maria knows how to unlock his emotions. She turns to Tiago and asks him to stay in the kitchen and only come outside to meet her and her father in five minutes. Then, she runs to the patio behind the house and clutches tightly to her father while sobbing heavily and letting out volumes of tears.

In an attempt to break the awkward silence with Maria's mother, Phil asks her questions about the vegetables and herbs that she is growing by the kitchen window. He speaks to her very slowly and with basic words. Albeit with a strong accent, she answers with a decent English, which is a relief for both Phil and Bianca, as they had wondered how difficult and isolating conversations would become over the next few days while they finalize the wedding preparations.

After a few minutes, per Maria's instructions, Tiago stands up and takes a deep breath under the watchful look of Phil and Bianca. He walks over to the backyard. He approaches Maria's father with a warm handshake and a pat on the shoulder. Maria makes some basic introductions, stands and walks back into the house to join everyone else, closely observing the two men from the house. "I hope he knows what he's doing. Maybe I should've briefed him," says Bianca, looking at the scene from the kitchen window.

Tiago first sits in front of Maria's father, shares some information about his Brazilian family and upbringing in the US. Shortly thereafter, he drops to a knee and uses a limited mix of Spanish and Portuguese along with some English words to explain how he cannot imagine his life without Maria, and it would mean absolutely everything if he could marry her. Maria's father talks to Tiago for long minutes while alternating between pointing a seemingly reproaching index finger towards Tiago and gentle rubs on his arms, shoulders, neck and hair. Maria nervously bites her nails, unsure which man she would have to choose if her father did not agree to the marriage.

"Maybe he wants to give Tiago some form of physical punishment by making him stay on one knee, for making wedding arrangements before his formal approval," says Bianca.

"I'm sure Tiago's body has been through worse punishments during his days as a Navy Seal. If a few additional minutes of pain can help secure an approval, it seems like acceptable torture," says Phil with a smile.

"Forget the Seals, his body has been through a lot for us. Phil, see if you can lend a hand," says Bianca. Phil looks at Maria for an approval before venturing in a situation that he is pretty certain he has no business butting into.

"Hum, no. It's better to let daddy get his way," replies Maria, knowing that Tiago is willing and able to endure whatever is necessary to secure a life with his beautiful Maria.

Maria's father finally stands up, grabs Tiago's hands and they tightly hug. Tears of joy are running down Maria's cheeks. Phil looks at Tiago's large muscular body embracing this frail and practically bald old man and is so happy that Tiago is now part of a welcoming family. Maria runs toward Tiago and her father and jumps in Tiago's arms. He catches her with just one hand and uses his other arm to wrap around his soon to be father-in-law.

"What a relief," says Phil as Bianca slowly comes in for a hug, and with a wide smile. Phil wonders whether Bianca is also expecting the big question soon. He never pictured her as wanting to settle down and get married, but the emotional scene that they just witnessed is certainly fertile grounds for such expectations to grow in anyone's mind. Perhaps meeting Bianca's parents in Australia would be a good start.

Without even having to ask whether they will be house guests for the upcoming days, Phil and Bianca are setup in the guest bedroom by Maria's mother. Tiago, however, knows full well that he will be sleeping on the couch, as far as possible from Maria's bedroom. The nature of the words, and warnings, used by Maria's father before agreeing to allow the marriage, are a clear indication of the family's Christian beliefs. Tiago is not even sure if they can hold hands in front of her parents. One thing is certain: no discussion of the pregnancy. Tiago is happy that Maria's morning nausea has not re-surfaced in days.

Adventurous as ever, Bianca wakes up the next morning with declarations of wanting to stroll the streets of Bogota to sightsee and find proper attires for everyone to attend the wedding. Still in bed, both in their usual birthday suit sleepwear, Phil asks her to slow down, so that they can safely get the lay of the land before risking any unfortunate encounters. Unhappy about Phil's overly careful comments, Bianca starts getting out of bed to execute her plan, but Phil pulls her back, hold her tightly against his body and kisses her romantically. She fights back, but only for a few seconds, before easily agreeing to a few more hours lost in his embrace.

Despite that her movements are being partially restricted; Bianca is actually quite happy to see that the fascination for each other's body is still so strong. She wraps her hands around Phil and plants her fingers in his back for some playful scratching. Phil raises his head and smiles. He asks her to wait for a moment, stands up and steps out the bed to lock the door. However, he notices that the old door handle does not include such privacy option. He looks around the room for a prop to block the door. Unfortunately, the only items available are the suitcases that they brought in. He looks back at Bianca's amazing body and decides that a luggage prop will have to do for now. Phil slowly crawls back into bed to rejoin Bianca, who is laughing at the sight of Phil's slow and awkward naked movements around the room, trying to avoid revealing noises.

A few hours later, Phil is startled out of sleep by the smell of fried bacon, only to realize the Bianca is not by his side anymore. Worried that she left to explore the surroundings, he quickly dresses in the clothing left at the foot of the bed. As he pulls up his jeans, he looks outside through the bedroom window. Bianca and Maria are sitting in the middle of the dirt street, with at least a dozen kids around them. Two toddler girls are playing with Bianca's hair, making and undoing different styles of braids. They seem completely fascinated with her perfect long blond hair.

Phil walks down to the kitchen to find Tiago cooking with Maria's mother. Her father is sitting in the corner, reading his newspaper, barely acknowledging anyone.

"Buenos Dias everyone," says Phil as he exchanges profound smiles with Tiago, who shakes his head to communicate that he would rather be assigned to tasks other than cooking.

"Good morning sir," replies Maria's Mother.

"I'm glad that you are making yourself useful, Tiago," says Phil as he sits at the table and Tiago puts a plateful of bacon, eggs, and potatoes in front of him. "Thank you, this looks delicious."

Bianca and Maria, reenter the house in an intense chatter, which relates to wedding preparations: flower arrangements, dresses, pictures, etc.

"Good morning ladies. I'm glad we're on the topic of clothing because I wanted to ensure that we agree on how to safely shop around Bogota," says Phil, drawing a puzzling look from Maria's father, but he quickly goes back to his newspaper.

"I have already drawn up a shopping plan for today and tomorrow," says Tiago with confidence but has to soften his eyes after Maria quickly turns towards him, in a sign of disagreement.

"You can't supervise my wedding dress fittings," replies Maria.

"Don't worry, I'll make sure that our overprotective men bake under the sun outside the shops," says Bianca, with wide smiles directed at Phil and Tiago.

Chapter 7

Two weeks after departing from Columbia, Paul and Linda finally approach the Nassau Yacht Haven Marina, near the famous Atlantis resort in the Bahamas. Phil had chosen this location due to the heavy tourist presence, which he thought would help keep the curious and, more importantly, the criminals away.

Early morning, winds are calm and the water is like a mirror. The vibration of the engine was keeping Linda sound asleep. She wakes up when Paul shuts off the engine and comes out of the cabin to the sound of chirping birds and faint distant voices.

All the time spent with Phil and Tiago over the past year has helped Paul improve his flair for evaluating risky situations. Therefore, he thoroughly thinks through and limits the information that he discloses to the manager of the Marina. Paul pays for three months' worth of docking but claims that he will be in and out frequently, perhaps even every day. He believes that the mere possibility of his presence may help to keep prying eyes away. Also, Paul turns on the surveillance equipment hardware that Tiago had meticulously prepared in order to monitor the activity in and around the yacht.

As previously agreed, Sergio is waiting at a nearby coffee shop to take them back to the jet. Paul and Linda casually enter and sit with Sergio. Seconds later, two Hispanic men with tattoos all over their arms enter and sit directly beside Paul.

"We hadn't seen that yacht around here for over a year," says one of the men while looking at the ceiling, but with the clear intention of engaging into a conversation with Paul.

"And renaming it Freedom is very catchy. Would you happen to be the owner?" says the other men as he turns to Paul.

"Oh no", says Paul, surprised of getting quickly accosted by the strangers. "We just rented it for a couple of days. I could put you in contact with the owner if you would like. He lives in Miami and is some kind of famous basketball player. He has security guys around here. I'm sure we can find one of them to help you, if you're interested," lies Paul, trying to intimidate the men by pretending that there could be a lot of attention around the yacht, hopefully keeping these suspicious fellows at bay. Sergio, still wearing his mirror coated aviator sunglasses, crosses his arms and looks at the two strangers to show annoyance with their impolite intrusion.

"Interesting, because we were told that it belonged to some corporate guy from New York," replies one of the Hispanics, referring to Phil.

"Apparently the yacht changed owners a few times in the recent months," says Paul, with no hesitation.

"Oh, okay. Could you show it to us?" asks the other Hispanic.

"Sorry, we already gave the keys back. We were just on our way out, but it was nice meeting you both. Maybe we'll see you around then," says Linda with a pleasant smile, trying to hide her fear as best as she can.

Sergio, Paul and Linda slowly and nonchalantly walk out of the coffee shop, get on the rented Honda that Sergio picked up at the airport, and start driving. The two Hispanics quickly board a pickup truck and closely tail the Honda. Sergio immediately notices the truck in his rear-view mirror and asks Paul to call Phil, who is sitting with Bianca in the backyard of Maria's parents' house.

"Phil, Sergio picked us up as planned but two Hispanic men approached us with questions about Freedom and are now tailing us on the road," explains Paul in a distressed voice.

"Try to find a safe way to get Freedom back into the open water. And Sergio has to get back in the air. Put Sergio on the phone," commands Phil as Paul places the call on speaker phone.

"I'm here Phil," says Sergio.

"Sergio, fly the jet to a low-key location in the U.S. Somewhere safe outside of the big markets like Florida, New York and California. A place where criminals may have less operatives looking for us," requests Phil.

"Okay. We'll do our best," replies Sergio.

"Keep me posted. And don't let anyone into the yacht or the jet. Each of you call me with updates, no later than 30 minutes from now," concludes Phil before hanging up.

Sergio drives in circles around Nassau, staying close to crowded areas and police presence. The pickup truck is still right behind them. Paul suggests that they enter the Atlantis resort, and figure out a way to discreetly get back onto Freedom without directly driving to the Marina. The resort sits on Paradise Island, which is right across from the Marina. Perhaps they could even swim across to the Marina. Paul feels confident about his swimming skills but is concerned that Linda would be at risk.

Sergio drives the car to the valet parking of the resort and the three of them walk as nonchalantly as possible into the lobby. A hotel attendant approaches them.

"Welcome to Atlantis Resort. Are you checking-in?" says the attendant.

"No, we're just looking around. Can we have lunch at one of your restaurants?" asks Paul.

"Of course, but you have to purchase a daily resort pass for a $50 fee per person," replies the attendant.

"Sure," says Paul. He pulls out his wallet and looks towards the entrance. The pickup truck pulls up. "Hey, you might want to look into the guys getting off this truck. We saw them bully a couple of kids at the Marina this morning. They might scare off your clients."

"Oh…" says the attendant while looking towards the truck. "Euh, no problem, sir. We will look into this," continues the attendant as he quickly takes Paul's money and hands plastic bracelets to each one of them.

As they walk towards the pools, Sergio turns towards the entrance and witnesses security guards getting into an argument with the Hispanic thugs. Hopefully they will be held long enough to allow time to figure a way back to Freedom. Once on the yacht, they'll have to find a place to drop Sergio off for him to reach the jet.

Paul looks in the direction of the beach and sees a tent where jet skis are available for rent. The three of them casually walk around the pools and onto the beach.

"Hey, can we rent out two of your jet skis?" asks Paul.

"Sorry, only one is available. The other ones are reserved," says the attendant.

"That's ok, we'll squeeze in to fit the three of us," says Linda.

"Uh, ok… but don't you want to change into your bathing suits first?" asks the attendant, sporting a puzzled look while looking at Linda's long dress, Paul's dress shirt and shorts, and Sergio's long black pants and black leather shoes.

"Ah that's ok… just a few drops of water won't ruin our clothes," says Sergio.

"Alright. You'll have to remove your shoes though; we have to put the jet ski in the water before you get on. It'll be $75 for 30 minutes, I will need to keep one of your driver's license," says the attendant. Paul looks at Sergio, not knowing what to do about the driver's license.

"I'm afraid we left most of our things in the room. Could we leave you with a cash deposit instead of a driver's license? Say

$1,000? And a $100 tip for you, my friend? We're in room 1204 if you need to find us later," asks Sergio, seemingly comfortable with handing out a bribe.

"Well..." replies the attendant as he looks around to see if his boss is watching. "Alright, just make sure to bring it back in 30 minutes."

Paul, Linda and Sergio remove their shoes, roll up their clothes and get on the jet ski, which is sitting in a foot of water. The attendant gives them a push in between the waves crashing on the beach. When Paul looks back towards the resort, he notices that one of the thugs seemed to have broken free from the resort's security and is running towards the beach. Paul squeezes the throttle, almost ejecting Linda into the water. But everyone holds on and they are off to the open water.

They need to loop around the small island to reach the marina on the other side. Sergio keeps looking behind to see if anyone is following. Since only one jet ski was available, Paul hopes that the thugs will have a hard time catching up.

Paul slows down as they approach the marina and hides the jet ski behind a large yacht. They observe the surroundings of the marina for several minutes to see if there is any unusual activity near Freedom and determine whether it's safe to jump on the docks. Unfortunately, a few men in leather jackets emerge at the entrance of the marina, yell some obscenities in the direction of the marina manager and make their way down the docks. Sergio takes a few pictures and sends them to Phil, who calls right away.

"Are you guys safe?" asks Phil.

"For the moment. We're on a jet ski, watching from a distance. It might be a while before we can access Freedom," says Sergio.

"Forget the yacht, it's compromised for now. Call the police and get out of there. The three of you get back to the plane as soon as possible. We'll deal with the yacht later," orders Phil.

"Ok," replies Sergio.

"I'll talk to Claudio and text you some instructions," says Phil before hanging up.

Phil calls Claudio and asks him to prepare the jet for departure but to remain locked inside until Sergio, Paul and Linda are back. Phil then looks carefully at the satellite image of Nassau on his phone and finds a place near the airport, where his friends could beach the jet ski and be picked up to go to the airport. A one-mile street links the spot on the beach to the airport. They could even walk to the airport from there.

Paul has the throttle of the jet ski at maximum RPM as Sergio barely holds onto Linda with one hand, and continues to text with Phil. When they reach the area on the map where Phil wants them to beach the jet ski, Sergio extends his left arm and points to let Paul know that they've reached their re-entry point into the island. Paul takes a sharp turn towards the land, again almost ejecting his passengers.

"Hold on tight!" he yells, still riding at maximum speedThey're getting bounced by the waves and they all hold on for dear life until they finally hit the sand hard. The sudden braking, when the jet ski reaches the dry sand, yanks everyone's head forward. Paul hits his forehead on the steering control. A cut is visible on his head, near his hair line.

"Paul, are you ok?" asks Sergio as Linda looks at the cut.

"I think you'll be ok," says Linda to comfort Paul, but she's worried that he may need some stitches.

"There is a first aid kit on the plane. Hopefully, that will be enough. Waiting for medics could be a problem. Let's start walking towards the airport," says Sergio.

Paul looks over his shoulder toward the water, waiting to see if anyone has followed as they started walking. Once clear, they hurry forward, wanting to get out of there as soon as possible.

They reach the airport terminal twenty minutes later, sweaty and tired from their fast-paced walk. They spot a vending machine to buy water. Linda looks around and realizes that they are definitely drawing lots of attention: wet clothes, no luggage and blood all over Paul's face and shirt. Moments later, a security agent approaches them.

"Can I help you with something?" asks the agent.

"Oh no, we're ok… our car broke down and we had to walk the rest of the way to the airport. Twenty minutes under this hot sun is not easy," explains Sergio.

"I see. What happened to you?" asks the agent, looking at Paul's forehead.

"This little cut? It's nothing. I just lost a step, fell down and hit my head on a rock," says Paul with a smile, but starting to look a bit pale.

"No worries, I'm a nurse and I'll take care of my husband as soon as we're back onto our jet," says Linda.

"Your jet, hey?" asks the agent looking at their clothes, skeptical that three ordinary looking people would be about to board a private jet.

"Yes sir, and we have a landing spot at Miami airport that we cannot afford to miss. So, we need to be on our way. Thank you for checking on us sir," says Sergio with a confident tone as they walk away. The agent is not convinced though and radios his colleagues, alerting all security personnel of the airport that potential drifters are heading toward the private jets area of the airport.

Sergio knows exactly where to go, so he leads Paul and Linda through security lines and other airport procedures. Once they reach passport control, Sergio is easily let through with his flight crew documentation and looks back as he waits for his friends. Paul smiles nervously as he reaches into his fanny pack and pulls out wet passports.

The immigration agent is in no mood to laugh. He slowly turns the pages with a disgusted face, not knowing in what liquid the documents were soaked in. After a few minutes, the agent waves in a colleague and starts a long discussion, pointing intermittently at Paul and Linda. The volume of their voices is too low to be perceptible. Suddenly, Sergio sees the Hispanic thugs accompanied by police officers, presumably bribed by the criminals, making their way through the security and immigration lines. Sergio decides to approach the immigration agents dealing with Paul and Linda.

"Hey officers? These are the passengers traveling on my jet. Due to their celebrity status, would you mind taking us to a separate room to resolve the matter that you're looking into? I just wouldn't want that people recognize them, start posting pictures and stories on social media that they are in trouble in the Bahamas. You have private rooms, correct?" asks Sergio.

"Of course, sir," says one of the agents, also concerned about how any negative publicity on social media could spin out of control and reflect poorly on their unit, or worse, make any other celebrities find other places to vacation.

"Right this way," says the other agent.

Paul, Linda and Sergio are escorted to an interrogation room. Through a small window, Sergio continues to monitor the thugs and police officers as they make their way through the lines, and pass by the interrogation room without stopping. Sergio breathes a sigh of relief.

After ten long minutes, the immigration agents come back to the room, hand over the passports, and tell Paul and Linda that they can head over to their flight. Everything seems to be in order.

Chapter 8

After a thankfully uneventful flight back to Columbia, Paul and Linda disembark from the jet, somewhat apprehensive about being in an unknown foreign land. With Claudio guarding the jet at the Bogota airport, Sergio, Paul and Linda get on a rental car to meet the rest of the group at Maria's parents' house. As soon as they arrive, Bianca runs to the car to give a warm hug to her friend Linda. Phil, Tiago and Maria are right behind, and smile as they reconnect with the rest of the group.

"Sorry about the yacht Phil. I wish we could have pulled it out of there in time," says Paul.

"What are you talking about? It's just a boat... I'm glad you guys made it out of there safely. And I'm the one who needs to apologize to have put you guys in harm's way. The Bahamas was not a good idea," whispers Phil in Paul's ear, as he wraps his arm around his shoulders, trying to keep his voice to a minimum to avoid stressing Maria more than she already is.

"Paul, are you alright? What happened to your forehead?" asks Bianca.

"Ah, I came a little too hot onto shore with the jet ski. My fault. I should've been more careful. No worries about the cut though, I have my private nurse," replies Paul as he looks lovingly towards Linda.

"Well, I'm glad you're all ok. Don't worry about the yacht, we'll find a way to get it back," says Phil, who is much more worried that he cares to let on in front of his friends. Not for the yacht. But for the stark evidence that thugs are still watching and just waiting for one of the team members to show up at some strategic places, like the Bahamas. They will need to be more careful from here on out. Which means, of course, that they will have to keep moving again, which Bianca probably wouldn't like all that much. Phil will do anything to keep her safe, though.

They make their way inside the house, chatting loudly about the beautiful and rustic look of the area. Once inside the house and after the newcomers' introduction to Maria's family, Tiago pulls Phil, Paul and Sergio aside for a conversation.

"Hey fellows, let's have a beer in the backyard," says Tiago, as they walk to the back of the house.

"How are the wedding preparations coming along?" asks Paul.

"Good. The celebration is tomorrow, we probably need to get you and Linda some clothes this afternoon," says Phil.

"Any of your family flying in from Brazil for the occasion, Tiago?" asks Paul, genuinely interested in Tiago's relationship with his relatives.

"No. We're trying to keep the guest list to a manageable number, so I didn't invite anyone from my family," replies Tiago, clearly uninterested with talking about his relatives. "Listen guys, this episode in the Bahamas is evidence that we have thugs after us. They are watching closely, even after more than a year since the last time we were in Nassau. For heaven's sake, they were after you guys within minutes after you docked," says Tiago, looking at Paul and immediately getting into business after Paul's attempt for a light conversation.

"I know. Let's not worry the girls with this today," says Phil as he watches Bianca in the distance pour some cold drinks for Linda and Maria.

"I watched the surveillance tapes from the yacht and I recognize these guys, they used to work for Norrid. They may be part of a new organization or just re-formed Norrid, months after it came apart. To be watching us so closely, they probably have significant resources at their disposal," says Tiago.

"Once we're through with the wedding, we need to be on the move again. Immediately. You guys might have to wait a few weeks before your honeymoon. Do you think Maria will understand that?" asks Phil.

"I'll smooth her over as best as I can," replies Tiago.

"Ok, keep me posted. Perhaps Bianca can help. Sergio, please head back to the jet and think of a flight plan that would reduce the risk of being tracked or followed. And be ready to depart at any time," commands Phil.

"Yes sir. You guys be safe," says Sergio as he embraces his friends, waves goodbye to the ladies and heads back around the house to get on his rental car.

At night, Phil takes advantage of a light pillow talk to whisper to Bianca that they will have to leave hours after the reception. She is not happy. Bianca had hoped to relax in Bogota for a few days and explore the dining scene of the city with Linda and Maria. Bianca tells Phil that he is being paranoid and that he needs to give more consideration to the fact that they now have a pregnant woman as part of their crew that cannot necessarily be traveling all the time. She turns her back to Phil with a quick and dry 'good night'. Phil rolls his eyes and hopes that Bianca will get her head back in the game before it's too late. Perhaps Linda will relate more details of the chase in Nassau to Bianca, which could persuade her that the safety of the group is being threatened.

The following morning, the house is bustling with all the last-minute preparations. Tiago and Maria are kept in separate rooms, not permitted to see each other, per the traditions of Catholic weddings. Tiago is already wearing his tuxedo, ready to head to the Church, while Maria is still in her night gown, receiving the treatments of a make-up artist, a hairdresser and a manicurist. Various other people who work for the wedding planner are also buzzing around the house. Tiago starts feeling dizzy from the activity in the house, so after studying and scrutinizing every stranger, and becoming satisfied that the threat level was low, he suggests to Phil and Paul to head over to the church.

Hours later, Tiago is standing alone near the altar, looking closely at every single person coming into the doorway of the church. Despite being packed with more than 200 people, the church continues to fill up as the Priest stands by the entrance and welcomes every guest warmly. Tiago gives a look of desperation to Phil, who is sitting with Bianca, Paul and Linda in the sixth row, behind Maria's close family members. Tiago and Phil are both extremely worried about the large crowd. Tiago, eyes wide opened, shakes his heads as he looks at how tightly people are getting packed in the back of the Church. He has absolutely no idea how he could get Maria to safety if a threat manifested itself during the ceremony. Phil regrets that he did not sufficiently insist that Maria restricts the guest list. Trying to manage down the crowd would create a significant drama with Maria's family at this point, which Phil finds as too big of a price to pay. He figures that he'll just have to remain alert and improvise if need be.

Finally, the room becomes completely silent when the two large doors of the church open and Maria begins a slow walk down the aisle with her father. Everyone is in awe at Maria's magical beauty. She is truly the most beautiful women that all guests have ever seen. For a minute, Tiago forgets all the risks that they are facing and just stares intently at Maria. He quietly thanks God for the unbelievable chance to have met her in Grand Turk. He reaches for her hand, pats her father gently on the shoulder and nods politely to her other family members.

"Take good care of my princess," commands Maria's father in a slow and broken English. Tiago smiles, nods again and genuinely believes that he would take a bullet to protect her.

Bianca carefully watches every move of the bridal couple, and squeezes Phil's hand. They turn to each other and smile softly. Tears are running down Bianca's cheeks, ruining her makeup. Phil knows that Bianca's bridal expectations are growing. He desperately wants a life with Bianca. He'd love to stand with her on an alter, and promise to love her for better, or for worse, until death do they part. However, Phil is increasingly worried about the security of their group. He feels that every tender moment, like the one he is currently experiencing with Bianca, could be exploited by his enemies. Phil puts his arm around Bianca's shoulders and holds her tightly against his body, as they continue to watch the ceremony closely.

Linda turns to look at her friend Bianca, still closely held by Phil. "You guys are such love birds, I can't wait to see you on the altar," says Linda with a wide smile. Phil would like to fully embrace the moment but can't help to think that they've overexposed themselves with this wedding. He just cannot give in to the emotions in fear of letting his guards down. It's almost like he can sense that something is just not quite right.

Chapter 9

The reception in the courtyard of the beautiful castle Castillo Marroquin, in a suburban area of Bogota, is sumptuous to say the least. Phil worries that Maria's parents might have spent their retirement savings to host hundreds of people in this romantic outdoor setting. Wine and spirits are flowing for the guests as the bride and groom smile for countless pictures throughout the cocktail. Phil and Bianca stand on the edge of the bar, offering a slightly elevated view over most guests, thereby allowing Phil to scan for any brewing trouble. Per Phil instructions, Paul is also keeping close watch for any sight of the thugs from the Bahamas, or any similarly tattooed thick neck.

Suddenly, Phil senses a large and strong hand grabbing his shoulder from behind. With his nerves already on the edge, Phil turns and steps away in one movement, knocking over Bianca's glass of champagne from her hand. "Hey watch out," reacts Bianca, unhappy about wasting the precious liquid. A few guests give a dirty look to Phil as a waiter hurriedly picks up the pieces. Phil looks up at the man: Agent Turner from the FBI, who, over the past few years, had tracked Phil and Bianca throughout Asia while they were laundering money for Norrid.

"Phil, so good to see you!" says Agent Turner as he grabs Phil for a tight hug.

"I don't quite remember seeing you on the guest list," says Phil quietly, with his body still against the agent, offering much less of an embrace to the surprise guest.

"Ah, it's much more fun to crash a wedding than getting invited... And I wouldn't miss this gathering of criminals for anything in the world," says Agent Turner.

"We are completely clean. You are so out of line on this one, my friend, and you know it." says Phil before being interrupted.

"Phil, I'm not talking about you guys. Look around you, there are dozens of guys here that used to work for Norrid or their closest competitors. I'm actually surprised that you let this happen, especially here in Columbia. You're usually such a careful guy," explains Agent Turner, as Phil pushes him away with a hard shove, breaking the hug.

"If there are ex-Norrid guys here, you're out of your mind to make it look like we're old buddies," says Phil angrily.

Tiago gets up from the table of honor when he notices the shoving and looks in the direction of Phil and Bianca. Tiago recognizes Agent Turner and frowns. But Phil raises his glass and shakes his head in a way to let Tiago know that he does not need to bother.

"Listen, if myself and a couple of agents weren't here today, these thugs would've already skinned you alive," says Agent Turner in a stern and threatening voice.

"Why didn't you contact me before?" asks Phil.

"And then what? Would you have asked Maria's parents to cancel the wedding? Or make a big scene to attract even more attention? I don't think so... Look, we have a proposal for you. Are you willing to listen?" asks Agent Turner.

Of course he had a proposal. Phil should not have expected anything less. He closes his eyes, shaking his head. They'd been home free for so long, he'd hoped his days of working for both he FBI and the criminal elements of the world were over.

"You're a real schemer, you know?" Phil says, looking around, wondering who might, or might not, be former Norrid employees. "The celebrity cop status that I provided to you wasn't enough, right? Do you actually ever conduct any real police or investigative work? Or do you just spend all your time coming up with evil plans and then forcing other people to carry them out?" asks Phil, in his best condescending voice, wanting to take the opportunity to openly insult the agent for showing up at this celebration.

Agent Turner laughs and places his hand around Phil's shoulder. "Very funny. Jokes aside, I have a proposal that's approved by the highest levels of the FBI. Do you want to hear it or not?" asks Agent Turner, adopting an annoyed and impatient attitude that Phil knows is fake and only designed to exert pressure.

"Here you go again. I'm not here to listen to any idea that will get me or my friends into more trouble. This is a wedding and we are trying to celebrate here," replies Phil. "And let me put it as clear as I can; you're not welcomed here."

"Come on. Have I ever disappointed you?" asks Agent Turner.

Boy, is that a loaded question. Phil takes a deep breath, quelling the need to punch the agent in the face for all he'd put the team through.

"Well, you didn't have any choice last time because your case was going nowhere without my help, and we made sure to have a bullet proof written agreement with you." Not that these facts would change any of his current situation, but he feels better pointing it out. "Anyway, go ahead with your so-called proposal. But if it involves one of my close friends or myself, I'm telling you in advance..." says Phil but gets interrupted again.

Agent Turner tightens his grip on Phil's shoulder, forcing him to walk out of earshot of the other guests. "Just listen for a minute. We want to hire you as a special agent contractor," says Agent Turner with a wide smile.

A contractor? What is this guy talking about. Red sirens go off in Phil's mind, screaming at him to run in the other direction. Still, he's intrigued. "A contractor? What do you mean?"

"Yes, you heard me. We want you to come in and help us dry all the money laundering pipelines," explains Agent Turner.

"Dry? What are you even talking about?" asks Phil, knowing full well that the agent cannot possibly have enough intellectual capabilities to understand how complicated money channels actually work.

"Infiltrate their laundering operations, block the flows, divert the money and cutoff the supplies of cash from these criminals. We want you to reverse the schemes that they use, some of them you've setup yourself, and dry them out of all their resources." The agent releases Phil, turning to him with a smile. "According to our calculations, this will force them to commit stupid mistakes and make them come out of their bunkers so that we can pick them up at the appropriate time," explains Agent Turner.

Phil narrows his eyes, wondering if the agent is stupid, or just plain crazy.

"You make it sound so scientific. But in fact, you have no idea what you're even talking about. I would even venture to say that you're desperate, and that's why you're standing in front of me right now. Last time, it became very obvious to me that you had absolutely no idea of what was going on. You barely knew where to start," says Phil with a wise smile, knowing that he just caught Agent Turner at his game.

The agent sighs and drags his fingers through his scalp. "Alright... we're desperate. We want to catch Li and the top guys of some of these criminal organizations, and we're running out of ideas," says Agent Turner.

"I think you're running out of cells in your brain. All these guys know Bianca, Tiago and me. We can't infiltrate anything," says Phil.

"We'll provide a few agents to you, under your supervision. You can use them for covert operations," explains Agent Turner.

Phil's eyes widen. Maybe the agent has actually lost his mind. "Covert... you think you're military now?" says Phil with a laugh and looks away for a few seconds to display his annoyance with the conversation.

"Phil, work with us. You have as much if not more to gain to put Li and others behind bars. They're going to be after you for the rest of your life if we don't properly handle them. And being with us will afford you some extra protection."

Extra protection? Who's protected who so far? Wonders Phil. He shakes his head and starts walking away.

"Hold on!" The agent grabs Phils's shoulder. "Also, you'll earn decent wages. You must be running low on funds without your Norrid salary for more than a year now. I'll tell you what, we'll even get your yacht back for you," says Agent Turner.

Phil cringes beneath the agent's grip. How had the FBI found out about that already?

Phil looks toward the table of honor. Maria smiles, accepting a flower from a young man with a wide smile on his face. She introduces him to Tiago who smiles, greets the child, and then he looks back to Phil with a concerned furrow in his brow.

Phil grits his teeth. This isn't fair. Tiago should be enjoying his special day, not worrying about Phil and their unexpected guest.

The good news is that Agent Turner thinks that Phil needs money, so he must have no idea that Phil has a fortune stashed away all over the world. But from a security standpoint, would this proposal make Phil's team safer, or at a higher risk of being targeted by criminals? And how does Agent Turner know Li and others are after Phil? Was the FBI tailing Paul in the Bahamas? They must have been, or how would they know that the yacht had been compromised? Phil decides to leave these questions for another day. Police protection to safely get out of Columbia might not be such a bad thing.

He turns to Agent Turner. "I need time to think about it, but I'll tell you what, how about you bring my yacht to Aruba within a week as a gesture of good will? Once we are safely onboard, we can meet there to finalize this discussion." Phil bites his lower lip, hoping the agent takes him up on his offer. This would give Phil a chance to reflect on this and ensure that he has support from his team.

Agent Turner politely declines the Aruba invitation: "Phil, you have to be on the U.S. mainland to learn the basics of handling service weapons, how to make an arrest and be sworn as an officer. We'll meet in Miami. I'll have your yacht moved there over the next few days," says Agent Turner with an unusual authority and confidence in his voice. Phil is uncomfortable with losing control of the team's movements, especially that a trust relationship with Agent Turner was never properly established. Still, at the bare minimum, this will get him his yacht back. He'd said it was only a boat, but over the course of their travels, it has become more like home, and he has to admit, if only to himself, that he really wants it back.

He nods. "Okay. We'll meet at the FBI office in Miami in a week."

"Perfect, I'll text you the details," says Agent Turner.

"Ya, and I'll text you my conditions," replies Phil with a smirk. "I'm not a cheap date, you know."

Agent Turner chuckles, backing away from the party and into the bushes. "I wouldn't expect anything less."

During dinner, when Maria and Tiago walk around the room to thank everyone for their attendance, Tiago asks Phil how on earth was Agent Turner able to crash the wedding reception. Phil tells Tiago that they'll have to discuss that later, but for the moment, the agent's presence is helping the team's security from ex-Norrids' operatives in the attendance. Tiago gives a puzzled look to Phil and says that he has not seen any familiar faces from Norrid at the reception thus far. Phil immediately wonders whether the notion of former Norrid operatives in attendance was just an FBI scare tactic to help secure Phil's cooperation. Phil turns around nervously to scan the room again, trying to locate Agent Turner, to no avail.

"Don't worry, I think we're fine for tonight. Relax and enjoy the company of your beautiful bride," says Phil to Tiago, with a warm pat on the shoulder.

"You know I can't turn off my radar. But anyway, it's great to be here. Thank you for everything," says Tiago, as Bianca and Maria join them for a hug.

"I'm so excited about our future adventures," says Maria.

Phil smiles and is truly happy for Tiago and Maria. There is a lot of happiness ahead of them, especially with a child to be born in the near future. However, Phil wishes that Maria had been given a real choice given the challenging times ahead. In fact, it seems to Phil that given the turn of event of the last few years, both Bianca and Maria, each for different reasons, unknowingly signed up for risky endeavors.

When they sit back down at the dinner table, Phil looks sternly into the distance. Bianca sees the nervousness in Phil's eyes. She knows that Agent Turner's presence and his conversation with Phil cannot be good news. She places her hand on Phil's thigh and squeezes lightly to get his attention. "We're going to be fine, honey. We always figure things out, right?" Asks Bianca, gazing into Phil's eyes in search of his usual calm and confident demeanor. Phil nods positively, smiles, gives a kiss to Bianca on the cheek, and whispers to her that he loves her very much.

Chapter 10

Phil allows the team just a few short days of rest after the wedding before announcing that everyone needs to pack up for a long trip. Maria is excited for a few seconds about the prospects of what seems like a partial honeymoon, and an opportunity for her to be away from her family for the initial months of the pregnancy. However, with everyone else staring seriously at Phil, and realizing that trouble might be brewing, Maria's smile dies down because she knows that some risky adventures are coming. No one asks the destination. They know that, in any case, Phil wouldn't reveal it for sake of the team's safety.

Goodbyes with Maria's family are emotional but rather orderly. Tiago smiles when Maria's mother mentions to the newlyweds that, next time, they have to come back with grandkids for her to spoil them. "Mamá, por favor…" replies Maria with a smile and emotions in her voice. She holds back the tears though and gets in the now overcrowded vehicle. Maria sits on Tiago's lap and waves goodbye to her family and the neighborhood kids with her head sticking out the window.

When they reach the jet, Phil orders Sergio to prepare a flight plan to Mexico City. Bianca rolls her eyes and Sergio takes off his shiny aviator glasses to look closer at Phil's eyes. He knows that this is not the destination but plays along.

After take-off, Phil picks up the intercom phone and reveals to Sergio that the destination is the Boca Raton airport.

"Boca what? Where the heck is that? We can't be stuck out of nowhere with a pregnant woman. Where on earth are you taking us?" asks Bianca, with a strong Australian accent that Phil can barely understand.

"Relax girl, that's near Miami in the good old U.S. of A. It's the airport that executives use to go to South Florida. We're going to have a blast," says Linda.

"Yep. And our yacht will be delivered at the Miami Beach Marina, which is just a few blocks away from South Beach, ladies. Shopping, outdoor dining, Latin dancers and beautiful beaches," says Phil with a smile, trying to put people in a good mood before explaining the tough parts of the upcoming months' mission.

"Oh, I love South Beach," says Bianca, still processing what Phil just said. "But wait, what do you mean by *delivered*? I thought you said the yacht was compromised in the Bahamas. And you're being unusually permissive about walking around in a busy city. Why is all that?" asks Bianca with a suspicious look.

"Well, the FBI will take the yacht from the Bahamas to Miami for us. It's part of a deal that I just made with them," explains Phil.

"A deal with the FBI? Haven't you got enough of these guys?" asks Bianca, uncharacteristically raising her voice.

"Phil, we really don't need the FBI for protection," says Tiago, with disappointment in his eyes, wondering if Phil lost confidence in his abilities to protect the team.

Phil holds up his hands. The last thing he wants is for Tiago to believe that he wasn't the prime muscle for this little clandestine operation, because the guy definitely still fits that bill. "It's much more than that. I have just agreed that Tiago and I would join the FBI as special agents to dry out the money laundering operations of criminal organizations, including Li's, so that the FBI can arrest them," says Phil, then pauses to let this sink in with the team.

"Dry out operations? What does that even mean?" asks Paul while looking at Phil and Tiago but doesn't receive an acknowledgment.

Tiago shakes his head. "I really wish you would have asked me first, my friend." He glances at Maria, and Phil nods at him.

Tiago was not part of the original deal, but Phil *made* him part of it. Phil wasn't going anywhere without someone to have his back. FBI be damned, he wanted Tiago there to keep him safe. There was no FBI deal without his friend. Of course, he would not force Tiago to do anything. But hopefully he would see things like Phil once he has the facts.

"Normally I would have. You know that. The FBI really didn't give me a choice, though." Of course, it was entirely possible that the agent was lying, and there really were no criminals at the wedding, but in cases like this, you never really know the facts, and it is always what you don't know that might kill you.

Tiago stands. "Phil, You know that usually I'm ready for any type of mission, but I'm uncomfortable about agreeing to something potentially dangerous, now that I'm married and a soon-to-be father." He looks at Maria for an approval. She smiles lightly and rubs his back.

"To be honest," says Maria, "I like the idea of Tiago having a stable job and perhaps working for a U.S. Federal agency. For me, I think this would help erase the memories of crimes with Norrid." She takes Tiago's hand and smiles at him. "This might set us on a more normal course to start our family life." Maria gives Tiago a look of approval, obviously without the knowledge of the kind of danger that Li or similar criminals could present for Tiago.

Phil rubs his hands together. "I really think this is the best thing to do for all of us."

"How's that?" Bianca asks, twisting her hands nervously.

Phil takes a deep breath. "We are all lying to ourselves if we think we are not in any danger.

Despite your concerns about getting closer or even infiltrating criminal organizations, the truth is that as long as Li and others continue to operate, we will constantly be in danger and spend the rest of our lives looking over our shoulders. This is an opportunity to cooperate with the FBI in order to make a real difference." He looks at each of them, making sure that sinks in. "This could be it for us. If we pull this off, we might actually be free again. *Really* free."

Paul nods. "Yeah, I'm in." He takes his wife's hand. "This will be good."

Tiago pounds his fist on his chest. "For my baby, I will do this."

The others nod, although somewhat hesitantly.

Phil looks at Bianca. Despite giving her support to Phil to avoid creating discord amongst the team members, she sits arms crossed and looks through the window. Phil knows what this means. He sits beside her.

She turns to him and grabs both of his hands. She looks into his eyes for a moment, and he can feel the love, but there are tears there as well. She tightens her grip on his hands. "Honey, I know you're trying your best to protect everyone. I'm just worried that you will put yourself in arms way by collaborating with the FBI. They won't necessarily be as careful and thoughtful as you, and might take advantage of you," says Bianca, with her eyes tearing up.

"Baby, you know what these criminals are capable of... if we don't deal with the situation, we will have to run for the remainder of our lives. We need to resolve this and we need help from experienced field officers," says Phil, trying to sound as convincing as possible. In the back of his mind, however, he is unsure whether Agent Turner really knows what he is doing. Phil has a feeling that resolving issues during missions with the FBI will fall squarely on his own shoulders. But working with the FBI might be a good way to operate on the right side of the law instead of being under the grip of a criminal organization.

"I understand. I wonder though if our odds would just be better if we just continued to run away or sail until these thugs just forget about us," says Bianca.

"With Maria's baby on the way, I think that's not sustainable anymore. I think it's better if Linda, Maria and you stay put in the U.S. while Tiago and I handle this mission," says Phil.

"Absolutely no way. We're coming with you. I'm not going to wait and worry about you 10,000 miles away. We're doing this together or not at all," says Bianca firmly, her eyes locked with Phil's for a few seconds, clearly putting her foot down to set the boundaries of what's going to be acceptable for this mission.

Phil really appreciates Bianca's support and does not want to disappoint her. He also agrees that given their experience with the volatile environment that they lived through when they were laundering money for Norrid, being away for long periods of time would drive Bianca crazy. Phil will have to find a way to keep the team together and safe.

Upon landing at the Boca Raton airport, immigration agents board the jet, closely followed by Agent Turner. Phil is surprised that the FBI was able to track his jet so quickly. Agent Turner comes on board all smiley. However, his excitement to celebrate the onboarding of Phil and Tiago into the FBI is short-lived. The passengers give an indignant look to the agent, who immediately stops smiling. Then, everyone silently deplanes, except Phil and Agent Turner, who sit for a quick chat, at Phil's request.

"How did you track us down?" asks Phil.

"The air traffic control system has your aircraft's tail number. We've had a tracker on your plane for a while and received notification as soon as you entered the United States' airspace," explains Agent Turner.

"Yeah? Well, we signed agreements last year that made you a celebrity cop, remember? That paperwork also says that you can't come after us for anything of the past. So, you better take the tracker off if you want me to save your butt again, or I'll get a restraining order for invading my privacy. And by the way, we were doing perfectly fine before you showed up at Tiago's wedding," lies Phil, in an attempt to exert a position of power over Agent Turner. Phil believes that the FBI is abusing the rights of a US citizen with its surveillance and will not shy away from expressing his view. Especially at this point of the mission, when Phil believes that the FBI needs him more than he needs them.

"Phil, we were tracking you for your protection," says, Agent Turner, starting to mellow down, not wanting to lose Phil's cooperation.

"I'll let you know if we need your protection. For the time being, just back off." He points at the agent's face. "And you're going to need to be more careful and discreet. We can't be seen near you again in public. If these thugs know that we're collaborating, our security will be at risk. So, don't take initiatives like this anymore unless we agree in advance and leave limited room for your poor improvisation skills. Anyway, it makes you look desperate and puts on display the insecurity that you're dying to hide from everyone," says Phil angrily with a few insulting words, taking advantage of the situation to impose himself as an efficient informal leader, even before putting one step into the FBI academy.

The agent holds up his hands in surrender. "No problem, we're on the same team now. We're here to support each other and collaborate to achieve common goals," says Agent Turner with a smile, which Phil sees as similar to a used car salesman.

"Well, you and your fellow agents at the FBI have got some work to do to impress my team members. I gotta be honest with you; so far we're not exactly sure that you've got the brain power to manage an operation like this," says Phil, in a condescending tone, as he turns away, pretending to look through his luggage in order to ignore Agent Turner.

"I'm up for the challenge," says Agent Turner, trying his best to avoid taking offense. "On our side though, we're not convinced that enrolling Tiago into the FBI is such a great idea. He has a history…" says Agent Turner, clearly trying to push a difficult agenda, but gets interrupted by Phil.

"I was very clear in my texts to you after we met in Columbia. You don't get me without him. Do you remember that I told you back at the wedding reception that I'm not a cheap date? Well, that's part of the price you have to pay. I trust Tiago, and only Tiago, to keep us alive," says Phil, as he stands up and heads towards the jet's exit door, clearly expressing his desire to avoid any reconsideration of their deal. "And I know that I'll be stating the obvious, but I assume that you've arranged a discreet security detail for the rest of my team that will be stationed in the yacht and around South Beach while Tiago and I get onboarded and trained at your facility," concludes Phil before turning his back on Agent Turner. Phil shakes his head as he walks away and says under his breath "can you believe this guy? I already can't stand him."

The team gets into a minivan and drives off leaving Agent Turner by himself on the tarmac, trying to wave goodbye. Phil doesn't even look in his direction. "What a loser," says Linda as she watches the tall agent wave like if he were a kindergarten teacher.

Sergio closes the aircraft's door to make sure that Agent Turner does not come back into the jet to sniff around Phil's possessions.

Chapter 11

On the first day of training at the FBI's Miami office, Phil and Tiago are taken to a completely white and windowless room. Six agents, including Agent Turner, are huddled in the corner shouting at each other. Phil looks at Tiago, who nods as the group discontinues their rather heated conversation and jeer at their new trainees. Phil takes a deep breath and Tiago taps his back for support. This is exactly why Phil wanted his own contingency plan, in the form of a six foot tall ex Navy SEAL. He knew that he wouldn't be welcomed, despite being invited to meet them here at the FBI.

Agent Fuller quickly approaches and squeezes Phil's hand with heavy force. He pulls him closer, and whispers into his ear, "I want to make one thing perfectly clear. Criminals are never welcomed into the FBI."

Phil forces a smile. "I guess that's good that I'm not a criminal, because I've been exonerated, as I'm sure you know." He lifts his chin, keeping the agent's gaze. "I was an integral part of taking down a major celebrity criminal, as I'm also sure you already know."

"Oh, I know full and well what you've done." Agent Fuller leans even closer and whispers, "Once a criminal, always a criminal."

Phil keeps his composure, but winces slightly when Agent Fuller starts applying even more force to the handshake. Less than a fraction of a second and a few martial art moves later, Tiago appears and boxes Fuller's ears. As the agent stumbles back, Tiago uses only his left hand to spin him around to easily subdue the agent. Stuck in a painful armlock, his face against the wall, Agent Fuller grimaces from the hyper-extension of his wrist, elbow and shoulder joints.

There was a silence of three heartbeats while the other agents gaped, before they jumped into action. But an FBI agent is no match for a trained Navy SEAL. Especially one that had been deep in the world of criminal security for so many years.

Phil steps back as Tiago uses his right arm to keep the other agents at bay, easily shoving them to the ground one after the other without losing his grip on Agent Fuller. When one of the officers draws his service weapon, Agent Turner and Phil both step in to cool everyone off.

"Hold on. Don't shoot!" Phil yells.

"Stand down!" Agent Turner says. "For goodness sakes, Phil. Call off your muscle!"

Tiago slowly releases the armlock and simultaneously pushes Agent Fuller, who falls awkwardly on his shoulder. The agent gets up slowly, holding his arm and rubbing his shoulder. He narrows his eyes at Tiago, his expression dark and foreboding. Good. It would be a cold day in Hell before any one of these guys would be able to pull anything over on Tiago.

Phil enjoys the position of power that Tiago's physical abilities can afford him. Nevertheless, Phil turns his palms up and gives a disapproving look to Tiago to try to make amends with the agents.

Tiago's nose flares, and Phil gets it. He doesn't trust these guys any more than he can throw them, but the simple fact is this: at the moment they are in this together. For better of for worse, they are all partners until this all plays out. Whether they like it, or not.

Agent Turner steps between Tiago and the other agents. "We're working as a team now. There are people out there who we need to dry out, find and arrest. Let's focus our energy on them, not hurting each other." He spins and points at the man still holding his gun at the ready. "And nobody can draw a weapon inside a Federal building. Are we all clear on this?" commands Agent Turner, his loud voice echoing in the empty room.

"This behavior was completely unwarranted," says Agent Fuller, pointing to Tiago, who raises his eyebrows.

"We all saw what you did to Phil," Agent Turner says. "Don't try to deny that you were the one who started all this." He looks toward Phil. "I see now why you brought your own guy, and frankly after what I just saw, I can't blame you." He looks to the ground, shaking his head before he returns his gaze to the other FBI agents. "It's now clear to everybody that Phil is under the close protection of Tiago. I highly suggest you all behave yourselves like the trained agents you are supposed to be. All right?" His gaze lances each of them. "If we all calm down, we're going to get through this together," says Agent Turner, lowering his voice, trying to effect reconciliation like a football coach in the middle of a locker room full of teenagers loaded with testosterone.

Everyone nods in agreement except Agent Fuller, who is busy rotating and stretching his arm, as if he were trying put his bones and joints back into place. *Excellent,* thinks Phil. He deserves no less, and he'll probably think twice about giving Phil lip again.

The agent gives a dirty look to Tiago, who replies with a half-smile and moves his head from left to right, to communicate to Agent Fuller that he made a big mistake that could not go unpunished, and would not go unpunished next time, either, should he try to lift a finger against Phil.

"Well, I'm glad that we got this out of the way on our first day together. I guess improvements from here will be easy," says Phil, with a smile, his arms open, trying to be inclusive of everybody while extending an olive branch. That olive branch is mostly received with looks of disdain, contempt, or completely turning away, which is fine, as long as no one is planning to threaten each other anymore.

The training consists of a mix of classroom teaching, various combat and immobilization techniques when dealing with suspects, the handling of common firearms used by the FBI, and a review of basic money laundering operations and facilities used by various organizations that operate businesses similar to what was once part of Norrid. The FBI has limited information about Li's operations, but have built an extensive profile of his residences, yachts, airplanes and the women that he has been seen with in the recent months. This information is supplemented by loads of pictures. Some of the photographs include Phil, Bianca and Ernesto and many other people from Norrid, Goang and Equit's organizations that Tiago and Phil have met over the last few years. It's a little unnerving to Phil, seeing himself in FBI profiles. So many pictures of him had been taken. Worse than that, there were a plethora of pictures of Bianca. He needed to be more careful to keep her out of the public eye and safe. He doesn't want her on any police of FBI radar anywhere.

Phil narrows his eyes, taking in a picture of him beside Ernesto in his tapers, five thousand dollar suit. Ernesto had been at Phil's side for so long, but now he is behind bars, like so many other people they'd worked with at Norrid.

Agent Turner taps his keyboard, and a picture of Li appears on the screen. The old man is smiling at a woman Phil doesn't know. His gray hair gleams in the sunlight of what looks like a tropical island, or maybe a luxury beach vacation oasis.

"Li is believed to have retreated to his hometown in Vietnam," Agent Turner begins. "He has bribed enough officials to be impossible for us to reach." He advances to another picture. "CIA agents on the ground have gathered intelligence about his whereabouts, but short of a commando style operation of the type that was used by the Navy SEALs to reach Osama bin Laden, Li would be difficult to catch."

Tiago smiles for a few seconds at the excitement of participating in this kind of operation to find Li and his men, but he quickly reminds himself that he will soon be a father and Maria needs him. He cannot afford these kinds of risks anymore.

Given the difficulties associated with any attempt to extract Li, the possibilities of drying out Li's operations are discussed at length.

"It's going to be the only way to make Li come out," Phil says. "I've seen this guy in action. He stays on top of everything, and is not the hands off kind of boss. If there are transactions going on, he won't be too far away. We just need to find out where his base of operation is."

"How do we do that?" Agent Fuller asks.

"We stake out one of his places and make notes on the transactions. We see who comes, and who goes." Phil paces the room. "Once we see their patterns, we can start messing with them slowly, and before they know what hit them, we will have dried them up."

Agent Fuller folds his arms. "That will dry that one location, but we still need to get Li or he will just open up another one."

Phil nods. "Did you catch the part about messing with them? We are not just going to dry them up. We are going to do it fast, furious, and infuriatingly." A smile bursts across his face. "Li will make a mistake out of frustration, and then we can arrest him in the open without having to fire a single shot."

The FBI agents exchange glances, some nodding, others frowning. It is good that the FBI is uncomfortable, though. It will make them depend on Phil more, which will hopefully make them start treating him like part of their team, and not the enemy. With this context in mind, Phil warms up to the idea of disrupting the flows that allow Li's organization to launder money.

When it comes the time to discuss the legality of the group's operations to engage with Li's money laundering operations in Asia, Agent Turner admits to the group that only Singapore will allow the FBI to truly operate as a law enforcement agency. Any other country in Asia would not officially recognize the help from the FBI, thereby risking that any agent could be arrested and spend months in prison before the U.S. would be able to negotiate an exit. Therefore, Agent Turner stresses that the team must only focus on Singapore to operate its drying operation.

As far as exactly what needs to be done to dry out Li's money laundering operations, everyone turns to Phil for a plan.

"You expect me to have a drying plan without even knowing the nature of the operations?" asks Phil, trying to make the FBI agents feel like amateurs.

"Well, Li is operating currency booths throughout Asia. Some of the outlets are actually the ones that you setup for Norrid, which Li just bought out of receivership when Norrid went under. We believe that he is also using a money management firm that poached some employees from Equit. So quite literally, a copycat of what you were doing," explains Agent Turner.

"Very original." Phil grits his teeth. It is a bit annoying that Li has been profiting from all of Phil's hard work, while Phil and his new found family had been on the run. Still, with Phil's insider information, this might be a boon to bringing Li down faster. He looks up. "Well, we're going to have to do some surveillance to find gaps that we can leverage. But, before we try new things, what have you tried in the past year to get Li to come out of hiding?" asks Phil.

"In partnership with the DEA, we disrupted the flow of narcotics and intercepted cash transfers between the production groups and the dealers," says Agent Turner.

Phil smirks. Every time FBI agents open their mouths, they seem like more and more of amateurs. "So, nothing new in the past year. Just same old police work. Sounds like you didn't try anything for the money laundering part. Did you even try to arrest Li?" asks Phil.

"It's not as easy as you think..." says Agent Turner before being interrupted by Tiago.

"No really, you didn't do anything to find and arrest Li and others." Tiago folds his massive arms over his chest, making himself look even more imposing. "You just stayed here, comfortably seated in the leather chair of your office while these thugs were chasing us," says Tiago.

"That's not completely fair. But the good news is that you guys are here now and we're going to do this together," concludes Agent Turner as he closes his files and places them in his briefcase.

Phil and Tiago look at each other, and now understand that they will have to carry these intellectually limited agents. After obtaining Phil's collaboration last year, the FBI only performed the painless part of the job: arrest the Norrid operatives that could easily be found based on the information that Phil had provided. Now, it seems like they have been sitting tight, probably waiting for Phil to resurface so they could use him again to get Li. The wedding had been a perfect opportunity, so they'd swooped in and sealed the deal. Seemingly no attempt to chase after Li was made since they last spoke with Phil. Now, once again, they'd use him to do all the work, and then the FBI would take all the credit. Annoying, yes, but freedom was still a pretty big carrot to dangle over a guy who'd been on the run so long.

After hours of debate on the first steps of the mission, Phil finally agrees that setting up in Singapore makes sense to initiate some surveillance on the ground and get cooperation from local authorities. However, before heading out to Asia, Phil insists to review all interrogation notes of Ernesto and Henry to see if any clues about Li could be found. Since there was some level of cooperation, at least in Macau, between Norrid and Li, Phil even suggests further interrogation of both men by an expert, with Phil and Tiago discreetly watching.

Agent Turner raises his eyebrows to communicate that he does not seem to agree. "We'll see if that can be arranged," says Agent Turner, unconvincingly. Phil doesn't get the impression that the agent will even try to arrange what he is asking for.

While farfetched, Phil thinks that some level cooperation or communication could still exist between Li and former Norrid executives, even perhaps directly with Henry, Phil's former boss at KexCorp who was simultaneously managing Norrid. So, Phil sees value in interrogating Henry.

"I really think that Henry could be a valuable source of information for us. He might even reveal names of people that we could tail in Singapore," says Phil in the direction of Agent Turner.

"Phil, Henry continues to claim absolute innocence and being the victim of a setup. Also, he is in the middle of being moved from his house arrest location to a prison. Nobody could show up and start asking questions without his army of lawyers scrutinizing every detail of our motives," says Agent Turner categorically.

"Unfortunate," says Phil, tightening his lips and shaking his head. Maybe that was the good thing about working on the wrong side of the law. Phil didn't used to have to worry about bureaucracy.

"Yeah, welcome to the FBI, we can't always do the things that make the most sense," concludes Agent Turner while turning his back to Phil.

No, they couldn't but Phil has seen deals cut before. There was a heck of a lot that they could do, and maybe this was the time to use the cards Phil had been played to not only help his current mission, but to get a friend of his out of a bad place he didn't deserve to be in.

Phil waits for the meeting to end to ask for one last request, as he is wrapping up his paperwork and standing up, trying to give a non-negotiable impression.

"I want Dr. Debo's sentence commuted. I need him to participate in the mission," says Phil categorically while starting to make his way towards the door. "You can't deny all my requests."

"NO WAY," says Agent Fuller loudly. "There are already enough criminals on this team." Agent Fuller is especially sensitive about the Norrid operatives that were subject to prosecution because he spent countless hours building the cases against them and testifying in court.

"Do you want to put all the odds in our favor for this mission? Dr. Debo has many connections in political circles and intricate knowledge of all previous money laundering setups from his experience in forging all the paperwork needed. He is invaluable to this mission," says Phil, as he walks towards the door of the room.

"You're not listening. Police work is going to be done by FBI agents. And anyway, who's calling the shots here? Is Phil going to be our new team leader?" asks Agent Fuller in disgust, turning to Agent Turner for a reaction but he remains stoic, moving his eyes between the two men.

"Guys, remember that this time around, I have no obligation to help you. I can leave you out in the cold at any time. So, think twice before contradicting me. And yeah, to answer your question about leading the team, I need some kind of authority for this mission to work well. I already sense that leadership is lacking here," says Phil in a condescending tone. And he exits the room closely followed by Tiago, before even hearing an answer from Agent Turner. Phil wants to be dramatic to ensure that everyone understands that he is not here to compromise.

Chapter 12

Bianca and Linda absolutely love Miami Beach. Under the loose tracking of a few FBI agents, they shop on Lincoln Road every day, and take long walks by the ocean. Most importantly, they sip tropical alcoholic drinks while under the watchful eye of people tasked with making sure they are safe. Maria comes along most of the time, but her pregnancy is tiring her down, so she ends up just sitting on public benches and enjoying the humid Florida air as she waits for her friends who go in and out of shops. Maria attracts a lot of men attention everywhere in Miami as Latino men revere her beauty. She usually plays along with their flirting by offering nice smiles for a few minutes, and then rubs her belly with her left hand, showing her sparkly engagement ring and wedding band. Or she speaks about her pregnancy, which makes men run away in seconds.

Paul, who was initially thinking of a way to make his case to also join the FBI team, is now very happy with his yacht-guarding duties, and his newfound exercise passion. He joined a local gym near the marina, and escapes for a workout whenever another member of the team can watch the boat. All the swimming of the past year has really developed his desire to remain in good physical condition. Paul also very much enjoys his time as part of Phil's crew and believes that staying healthy as long as possible will keep him onboard, and useful, for at least a few more years. Despite his experience with the criminal thugs in the Bahamas a few weeks ago, and not knowing the extent of the risks that Linda and he are facing, Paul would not want to go back to the boredom that he felt in Bali, before meeting Phil and Bianca. Paul sees himself as a soldier-sailor, ready to take on whatever mission the team requires him to accomplish.

Phil cracks a few jokes every night when he comes back to the yacht with Tiago, when he finds boxes and shopping bags from the day's expeditions. He is slightly concerned about the space available onboard but mostly encourages Bianca in her shopping sprees because he knows that the team will soon be in tough conditions. If shopping can make everyone happy, stable and ready for a few months of misery, Phil sees nothing wrong with it. Therefore, he leaves a few thousand dollars by the bed every morning for Bianca to freely spend. Phil also has no complaints about the newly acquired pieces of light lingerie that Bianca proudly displays in their cabin. She jokes to Phil that the FBI agents that follow her all day help her make some of the difficult choices of undergarment colors. As they wind down in their cabin after dinner with a glass of wine, Phil enjoys sitting with Bianca for a light conversation. He rubs her feet, looks into her beautiful blue eyes and listens to how she recounts her adventures of the day, especially her pleasures of outsmarting and making fun of the FBI agents.

"I guess you guys were on break yesterday afternoon because Agent Fuller joined my fan club of FBI operatives. You should have seen his face," Bianca calls from the bathroom. "I made him sit in the lingerie shop while I tried things on." She busts out laughing. "I tried on an Italian one in three different colors, and he blushed more and more each time I came out." She opens the door and steps out in a pale lavender, nearly see through ensemble.

Phil frowns. "That one was Fuller's favorite?" He grips the chair, wanting the throw it at the agent.

"Heavens no!" She smiles, crawling over the bed. "The ones I showed them were outfits that covered a lot more. This one, my love, is only for you." She kisses his nose and forehead, before righting herself. "Do you like it?"

He smiles. "I like it a lot." Phil resists her as long as possible, before carefully giving in to the temptation of slowly removing the delicate pieces of lingerie.

***

Once the decision is made about getting stationed in Singapore, Phil opens up about the loose plan during dinner on the yacht.

"I want everyone to be comfortable with our plan and make sure that nobody feels like they have to come along. We will leave the yacht right here, so if you feel safer in Miami, I will completely understand," says Phil, making contact with every member of the team, one-by-one.

"We need to stay together. I feel like Singapore is very safe and we can take care of Maria over there," says Bianca with assurance while grabbing both Linda and Maria's hands.

"Will we be able to stay together in some sort of a 3-bedroom apartment?" asks Linda, wanting to help Maria, but also be close to Bianca and have some privacy with her husband.

"Yes," replies Phil quickly to avoid that any concerns grow in people's minds.

"Oh, that's a vacation then!" shouts Linda.

"Well, here's the thing. We're going to setup a surveillance location in a large top floor loft that will have enough space for everyone who wants to join. We will have a balcony and some amenities; however, our movements will be extremely limited. I wouldn't be surprised if we end up staying in the apartment for weeks without stepping outside. I'm sure we'll be able to have stuff, including alcoholic beverages ladies, delivered to the apartment," says Phil, looking at everyone with a smile. But he notices that Maria and Tiago look at each other rather puzzled.

"If we can easily sneak out to a hospital and the health system can accommodate all of your pregnancy needs, I would prefer to have you close to me," says Tiago, looking at Maria, who nods in agreement. Tiago clearly wants to closely control the security arrangements for everyone, especially Maria's and the baby's.

Phil cringes. He'd actually forgotten that Maria might need to see doctors before the birth of her baby. This is inconvenient, but not insurmountable. "I'm sure we'll figure something out for emergencies," says Phil but in fact, he has no idea.

On the day prior to departure, Phil and Tiago have a final meeting with the FBI agents. Phil explains that the first step of the mission will be to setup in front of one of the currency booths operated by Li's organization in Singapore. The objective will be to track the ins and outs of the people that come to the booth with cash to potentially exchange at unfavorable rates. Phil presumes that Li is using the same strategy that he had setup for Norrid, which involves running dirty cash through the currency exchange booth at rates that leave wide profit margins for the laundering operation.

"Agent Turner, can we count on you to find an apartment large enough for my whole team, and strategically located in front of one of the currency booths? Large enough for three couples to co-exist. Preferably with a balcony, please, so that we can get some fresh air in case we get stuck in there for long periods of time," asks Phil.

"Sure, we'll find a three-bedroom apartment. And Agent Fuller will be just fine on the couch," says Agent Turner, as he turns to Agent Fuller with a smile.

"Excuse-me? No disrespect to you all, but you're not cut out for this. We'll handle this without you," says Tiago, raising his voice, and alternating his gaze between agents Turner and Fuller. But Phil gives Tiago a quick dirty look to make sure he remains calm. Tiago closes his eyes and shakes his head, thinking of the additional security measures that will be needed with having a stranger in their apartment.

"Well, Phil himself didn't think that any of you could safely infiltrate any criminal organizations. So, we decided that you need a babysitter to stay with you at all times, and maybe serve undercover if we decide to infiltrate," says Agent Turner, rather firmly, while Agent Fuller smiles at Tiago.

"And we just assumed that you guys would stay in another place. It sounds unnecessary to be roommates," says Phil.

"The rest of us will also be in Singapore, but not as close to the action as you guys. We'll run a mission control operation and serve as backup, if needed. You guys need an experienced agent with you, who will liaise back with us, at least once a day," explains Agent Turner.

"Ya, more like someone to spy on us. You don't trust us, do you?" asks Tiago, still in disbelief that he will have to tolerate Agent Fuller 24 hours per day. "Why do you even want us over there? It sounds like you think that you can do this job without us," continues Tiago, but Phil turns towards him again and raises one hand to make Tiago take a deep breath.

"Look, it's fine, but at the first sign of trouble or provocation of any member of my team, Agent Fuller leaves our apartment," says Phil. Tiago would like to add some more conditions for Agent Fuller's cohabitation, but he respects Phil's authority and keeps his mouth shut.

"Fine," concludes Agent Turner, while giving an intense look at Agent Fuller to ensure his cooperation.

Phil and Tiago leave the Miami FBI facility with each a badge and a service weapon. Four weeks of various types of police training has not made Phil any more comfortable with carrying a firearm. In fact, he is quite sure that he will never use it. Perhaps he can procure a gun safe in Singapore so that nobody walks around the apartment with a loaded weapon. This could prove especially wise given Tiago and Agent Fuller's reciprocal acrimonious feelings.

That same night, Agent Fuller meets the whole team to board Phil's jet at Boca Raton's airport. Despite Phil's request to his friends to treat the agent as part of the team, nobody acknowledges him, except Paul who is always nice to everyone, and wants to show to Phil that he closely follows instructions. As the aircraft is taxiing and ready to depart, Phil is happy that everybody quietly gets setup for the night, which he believes will avoid awkward silences or even confrontations with the agent.

Bianca cuddles near Phil and whispers to him, "Phil, I know you don't want to hear this, but I do not trust Agent Fuller." She sighs. "I think that there is just something odd with him."

Phil Nods. "I don't disagree with you, but you know that the FBI is well-intentioned, if not actually skilled for the type of work they are trying to do." He kisses her forehead. "Give the agent and the team a chance to acclimate to each other. I think we'll be okay."

Bianca rolls her eyes and lays her head on Phil's shoulder. She thinks that Phil has become too naïve, and not sufficiently on his guard. She hopes to be proven wrong, but she just has a feeling that collaborating with the FBI will not serve the team well.

Chapter 13

The team immediately moves into the Singapore-furnished apartment upon their arrival; however, the first few days are quite rocky. The surveillance equipment brought in by the FBI takes a large part of the living and dining rooms, leaving limited space to maneuver around the computers, screens, cameras and hundreds of wires. After Bianca and Linda complain to Phil that they cannot cohabitate in such tiny quarters with a stranger, referring to Agent Fuller, Phil calls Agent Turner to have him check with the landlord if perhaps an adjacent apartment was available to make the living conditions acceptable to everyone. "It would have been better to leave the family at home. But okay, I'll look into it," says Agent Turner, followed by a sigh to express his deep annoyance with having to deal with household dramas.

With everyone jet lagged and grumpy on their first morning in Singapore, Agent Fuller does not help his cause with the rest of the team by walking around the kitchen in his boxers, trying to show off his muscular body.

"You're disgusting, go put a shirt on! You're making me nauseous; I don't want any of your chest hair in my cereal," says Bianca with a look of disdain, pointing at the bathroom for him to leave the kitchen and cover himself.

"Sorry honey, I know that my ripped body has a strong effect on women," replies Agent Fuller with a flirtatious smile.

"Look, we all know that Tiago neutralized you with just two fingers, so stop your act, little man." She narrows her eyes. "Oh, and if you dare call me honey again, I'm gonna find a very nice nickname for you. Something really short. It will fit you very well," says Bianca, waiving her hand up and down his body to highlight his small stature.

"Well, as they say, the best things come in small packages," says agent Fuller, while flexing his biceps.

"You know, you've got sophisticated women in this apartment, so you're gonna need more than muscles to impress us," says Bianca as she looks at Agent Fuller's boxers as if she were judging his male parts. She tightens her lips, shakes her head left and right, looks at him in the eyes, raises one eyebrow, turns around and walks away.

Agent Fuller stays in the kitchen by himself, petrified and speechless. He looks down and observes his boxers from various angles to find out what Bianca was able to see. "It's obvious you were kidding, you know?" he says loudly with limited conviction. Phil enters the kitchen at the same time.

"Seems like we're all starting to get along," says Phil with a smile, while grabbing the bottle of orange juice from Agent

Fuller's hand, as Bianca and Linda can be heard laughing in the living room.

"Oh ya, ya, no problem. Funny girl you've got, there. She really likes to make people laugh," says Agent Fuller, raising his voice to make sure that everyone hears him trying to downplay Bianca's comments.

"Actually, she's usually quite authentic and likes to speak her mind. Anyway, you should really put some pants on, because ladies usually don't like to see guys' junk through their boxers," says Phil with a smile. One problem solved, he thinks, as he walks away.

The chemistry of the team worries Phil more than he cares to let on. He knows that a sense of cabin fever could quickly develop, especially if they're unable to step outside of the apartment. Keeping everyone busy and entertained is probably the key to avoid dramas, thinks Phil. He doesn't want to have to separate Tiago and Bianca from Agent Fuller every few hours. Giving specific tasks to each one of them may help ensure that they don't get on each other's nerves for mindless matters.

The team initiates heavy surveillance on their first full day in Singapore, each armed with a high-resolution camera, recording the heavy traffic of people in and out of the currency booth across the street, and photographing every client from different angles. The FBI's equipment allows to quickly measure the height, estimate the weight and recognize hair color. All this information, along with Phil's observations, as he is watching live from the screens and through binoculars, is recorded in an attempt to identify any pattern used by Li's team.

On the first day alone, they are able to pinpoint eight suspects that visited the booth at least twice. One of them actually went a total of five times in a span of just a few hours. Phil is not surprised by Li's sloppiness. Sending the same people multiple times per day is like asking for trouble.

Under the skeptical look of Agent Fuller, Tiago uses the joint FBI/Interpol database to search for the identity of the eight suspects. "How do you know how to operate this system?" asks the agent. Tiago just shakes his head, not wanting to engage with him, or revealing too much of his experience as a Navy SEAL. Tiago quickly retrieves the profiles of the suspects. Only one of them is known to be working for Li and has been arrested for petty crimes and questioned a few times by various authorities in Asia. The other seven suspects appear to be Singaporean citizens with no criminal records.

After dinner, Phil, Tiago and Agent Fuller debrief their first day with Agent Turner over a video call. Phil resists the Agents' overeager action plan, which would involve tailing the suspects as soon as possible. Phil is not convinced that all of the suspects are collaborating with Li. Instead of going after random people, he suggests installing a few mirrors on posts and street signs that will allow them to see, from their surveillance station, the exchange rates posted in the booth at the moment that transactions are made. The true suspects will be the people that come to exchange money immediately after the currency rates fluctuate widely to operate the money laundering operations – assuming of course that Li is running the same scheme that Phil had designed for Norrid. This initiative is approved by Agent Turner, and necessary parts are ordered to install the mirrors that Phil requested.

At the end of their video call, Agent Turner takes the opportunity to announce that the only additional living space that he was able to secure for the team is an exclusive rooftop balcony access, just one floor above the apartment, which is accessible through a small staircase at the end of the hallway. Phil briefly looks at Bianca for her concurrence. She nods an approval. Bianca then turns to Linda and Maria, and whispers that the balcony will be a ladies-only drinking getaway.

Later that night, FBI agents disguised as city workers install the mirrors that Phil requested. After the setup is complete, Phil uses a laser pointer on the mirrors to see if it properly reflects into the currency booth. Everything is in place for their second day of surveillance. Phil continues to watch for several minutes when suddenly, a small Asian man appears in front of the booth, unlocks the door and enters. Phil snaps his fingers and waves nervously for Agent Fuller and Tiago to come and watch what is unfolding in the booth. The agent is sound asleep, but Tiago comes by the window to witness what is going on.

"Do you think that could be Li?" whispers Phil.

"I would find it unlikely… and it's hard to tell from here. We would need to go down to the ground floor," says Tiago.

Phil looks back towards the living room. Agent Fuller is snoring and everyone else has gone to their bedrooms. "Let's go," says Phil. Tiago looks at him for a second, unsure if this is really safe, but nods his approval and grabs a gun.

"Agent Turner is going to be pissed, especially that you just turned down his plan to tail people," whispers Tiago.

"If this is Li himself, it's completely different. Let's get down there," replies Phil swiftly.

They quietly leave the apartment and walk down the staircase on the tips of their toes. Once on the ground level, they continue to watch the man inside the booth, who seems to be packing things in large bags. Most likely money from the day's activities, thinks Phil. A few minutes later, an armored vehicle pulls up. Three men get off, unload some boxes from the back of the vehicle and enter the back of the booth. "Let's have a closer look", says Phil. Tiago shakes his head 'no', but before he can stop Phil in his tracks, he's already opening the door and crossing the street.

Phil and Tiago crawl under the truck and lie on their stomach, elbows on the curb, in order to more closely monitor the activity inside the booth. It's hard to determine what the men are doing but they're shuffling things around, presumably extracting some cash and restocking the booth for the following day. All of a sudden, the face of the first men that Phil observed entering the booth a few minutes earlier comes into light. It's Li. Phil is shocked. His mind goes into overdrive: why would Li handle the pickup or drop off operations himself? And what is he doing here in Singapore. Agent Turner's intelligence report had Li hiding in Vietnam.

When the booth's door opens again, Tiago grabs Phil to move to the other side of the truck, still underneath, in order to be less visible from the sidewalk. The four men come out with seemingly heavy boxes in their hands and load them in the back of the truck. One of the men comes around to the other side of the truck to get on, so Phil and Tiago now have to move to the center. Once three of the men are in the truck, the engine starts. When it becomes clear that someone is still standing on the curb, presumably Li who arrived independently from the truck, Phil and Tiago realize that they will soon be out of cover, just lying on the street, when the truck starts rolling. So, they hang onto the undercarriage of the truck with their hands, their feet dragging on the asphalt as the truck starts rolling.

Fortunately, the truck is moving slowly. Less than a hundred feet later, the truck stops at a red light, so Tiago and Phil slowly rest back to the ground. Phil wants to roll to the curb, but Tiago stops him. "They'll see you from the side mirror. Wait for the truck to move, they don't have rear view mirrors in armored trucks," whispers Tiago as he's looking behind the truck to make sure no other vehicle is following, which could roll over them once the light turns green. Thankfully, there is no traffic in sight.

After the truck departs, Phil and Tiago quickly hide behind a car parked on the side of the street. They observe Li for several minutes as he smokes a cigarette, eventually gets into a Mercedes G Class and drives off.

"That wasn't the safest move that I've seen you do," says Tiago looking at Phil and quirking his eyebrows.

"I know. I'm sorry. I needed to get up close to validate whether it was Li. I wanted to be 100% sure that it was him. What could he possibly be doing here at this hour?" asks Phil.

"Maybe he doesn't trust his guys with the handling of large amounts of cash," suggests Tiago.

"But he can't be doing this by himself for all the booths. He has dozens around the city," says Phil.

"Yeah, well, we'll have to think this over tomorrow. For the moment, we need to get back inside before we're seen. But let's take a small detour, in case Li has security cameras in or around the booth," suggests Tiago.

Phil knows that his desire to uncover Li's whereabouts, and perhaps even help to arrest him, has made him a bit reckless. He realizes that he might have become overeager in his quest. As he lies down in bed beside Bianca, she wakes up and places her head on Phil's chest and feels his rapid heart rate and sweat from the Singapore humidity. He couldn't be sweating that much inside their air-conditioned apartment. Bianca raises her head to look into Phil's eyes.

"Where were you? Seems like you just ran the marathon," whispers Bianca with concern.

"Tiago and I went downstairs to check on some activity in the booth. We saw Li, right there in the booth, less than five feet in front of us," says Phil, looking at Bianca straight in the eyes. She sits down beside Phil, a hand on his chest and the other hand over her mouth.

"This is incredible. He's right here in Singapore? Did you see where he went? You guys should just go and arrest him and get this thing over with, so we can go home," says Bianca.

"Yeah, let's chat with Agent Turner tomorrow," says Phil, as he takes a deep long breath. "I'm guessing he won't be too happy that we did this without Agent Fuller.

Phil looks at the ceiling in the quasi-obscurity of their bedroom, with one hand under his head and the other one tightly hugging Bianca, who has fallen back asleep. He can see light at the end of the tunnel. While there are still a number of ex-Norrid thugs out there, putting Li behind bars would be a major break for the team, and would probably allow them to go home, as Bianca wishes. Phil smiles as he wonders whether they could even leave in short order and just rely on Agent Turner to arrest Li during his next visit to the booth. In the end, making Li come out of hiding wasn't as hard as the FBI made it sound, thinks Phil.

Chapter 14

"You did what?" asks Agent Turner sitting by himself and watching Phil, Tiago and Agent Fuller on the video screen.

"I saw a suspect enter the booth late last night, went down, and was able to visually confirm that it was Li," says Phil with calm.

"Yeah, I understood that part the first time. For someone lecturing me over tailing people, undercover plans, and the ease at which you or Tiago could be recognized by these criminals, I must say that wasn't exactly your smartest move," says Agent Turner.

"Alright, I agree. It was risky. But I had a hunch that it was him and wanted to confirm. And now we know. You can arrest him right there, in front of this booth. Perhaps as early as tonight, or whenever he shows up again," says Phil, wanting to move to immediately end this whole adventure and go home.

"Phil, the mission is: drying. We hired you to dry them out of their cash and resources. We're not doing any arrest at this point," says Agent Turner, raising his voice.

"What? The drying was to make him come out of hiding. He's out now and you don't want to arrest him. What is your problem? The worst criminal of a generation is going to be standing a few feet in front of us maybe as early as tonight and you're not going to arrest him? What kind of police work is this?" asks Phil, in complete disbelief, as he stands and bangs his fist on the desk. Tiago watches, expressionless, arms crossed, from the back of the room.

"That's right. We're not making arrests in this case yet. Remember: dry them out. I'll call you guys tomorrow morning, you better show me some drying plans," concludes Agent Turner and hangs up.

Phil places both his hands on his face, then looks away towards the kitchen. Bianca is standing there and overheard the conversation with Agent Turner. She shakes her head and walks away. She's disappointed. Bianca had hoped to leave within a few days if Li could be arrested. There isn't any dry-out plan laid out yet, and whatever that plan ends up being, Bianca knows that it will take weeks maybe months to take enough resources away from a criminal cartel to make a meaningful difference. Bianca grabs Linda and Maria and walks up to the rooftop balcony to enjoy a peaceful coffee.

An hour later, the ladies are suffocating from the Singapore humidity and re-enter the air-conditioned apartment. Phil takes advantage of everyone's presence in the living room to lay out a plan for the day, to try to identify the patterns used in Li's currency booth. He proposes to send Agent Fuller, Linda and Maria, the three members of the team that are unknown to Li, to exchange currencies at various times. When Phil mentions Maria's name, Tiago looks at him sternly. But Phil explains that the booth is so busy, especially during lunch time, that there is virtually no safety risk.

Phil pulls a stack of ten thousand U.S. dollars, hands it to Agent Fuller, and directs him to exchange it at the booth for a set of Singapore dollars, Euros, Pounds, Australian dollars, Yens and Malaysian Ringgits. Phil plans to then watch the rates posted by the booth throughout the day using the mirrors, and instruct Maria and Linda to exchange certain pairs of currencies back at the booth.

When Agent Fuller comes back with the first set of monies, Phil is surprised that he brought back more of every currency than Phil had anticipated. He looks up the exchange rates on the internet, only to find out that the booth just suffered a loss in exchanging Phil's U.S. dollars. "These guys have no idea what they're doing," says Phil, as he gives a puzzled look to Tiago.

The booth is again subjected to heavy traffic, with at least three or four people queueing up at any point in time. "Were the Norrid Singapore booths as popular as this?" says Phil, while looking through his binoculars, but nobody answers. He keeps capturing the exchange rates posted and feeding them to Bianca to look up the real time rates of the market on the internet. Throughout the whole morning, she constantly observes that the booth is giving favorable rates to all clients. Phil looks at her with a perplexed look every time.

Suddenly, the suspect who was identified as working for Li on the previous day, appears in the queue at the booth. Phil sends Linda to the booth. He tells her to queue behind the suspect and to keep looking at her phone as he will text her which currency to exchange. Like clockwork, a few seconds before the suspect places a briefcase on the counter, the rate to exchange of U.S.

dollars for Singapore dollars changes significantly giving this fake customer a rate that is extremely unfavorable. Phil now sees the replica of the strategy that he had designed for Norrid. He then texts Linda to do the opposite of that trade, i.e., exchanging Singapore dollars for U.S. dollars. The attendant looks at the bills that Linda put on the counter, examines them with a special light and pulls out a magnifier. After a few minutes, he completes the transaction with Linda, and she runs back to the apartment.

"Did he say anything special?" asks Phil, when Linda comes back.

"No. He didn't say anything. I think he just verified that the bills were authentic, that's all," answers Linda, with absolutely no worries in her mind.

"The attendant hadn't spent that much time scrutinizing the bills with other customers since we started the surveillance," says Phil while scratching his scalp.

"Was he looking at you weird?" asks Tiago in Linda's direction.

"A little bit. I thought maybe he was trying to see if I was nervous when he was evaluating the bills," replies Linda.

Phil piles all the currencies bills and hand the stack to Agent Fuller. "Get this evaluated to determine if it's counterfeit money. Our friend Li might be doing much more than we thought."

Later at night, Phil and Tiago observe Li and his guys perform the exact same operation as the previous night. Tiago photographs the license plates of Li's Mercedes and the armored vehicle as they pull up.

This time, Li spends much more time in the booth, cross checking some information between the desktop register of the booth and the boxes of money. After the armored vehicle leaves, Li stays in his car for several minutes, seemingly yelling at someone over the phone.

"I wish I could hear this conversation. I bet you that we threw off his sequence when we sent Linda down there immediately after Li's accomplice. We gotta do more of this stuff tomorrow and see what happens," concludes Phil while yawning.

"Ya, let's see what tomorrow brings but for tonight, you need to rest. No hanging from under a truck for you tonight," says, Tiago with a hand on Phil's shoulder before heading towards his room.

When Tiago opens his bedroom doors, Phil can hear some seemingly unhappy words in Spanish from Maria in Tiago's direction. "It seems like Tiago is going to have to learn some Spanish after all. And go to bed earlier," Phil mumbles under his breath.

Chapter 15

The following morning, Agent Fuller receives, via a secure email, a report from the Singapore police showing that all the currency bills sent by Phil were counterfeit, except the U.S. dollars that Linda received when she exchanged the Singapore dollars. Phil calls Agent Turner.

"Li has outdone himself one more time. He attracts loads of customers by offering rates better than the market, only to give them fake bills in exchange. The attendant presumably gave Linda real currency because he became nervous when he realized that she handed in the fake Singapore dollars that actually came from the booth, just a few hours earlier," explains Phil.

"What if those were the only U.S. dollars that the attendant had in the booth? Or maybe he just grabbed U.S. dollars from the wrong pile. He had just received a stack of U.S. dollars from the suspect a minute before," says Tiago.

"So, is Li laundering money? Or just integrating counterfeit money into the system?" asks Agent Turner, with a deep sigh and raising his voice, clearly disliking the counterfeiting twist to the story.

"Both. We caught them running the Norrid scheme yesterday, but only once. Perhaps it was a large amount though. We can't see the transaction amounts from here. But it seems like the main scheme here is distribution of fake money," says Phil.

"Well, that won't last for long. The Singapore police wants to know how we obtained those bills. They're going to shut the booths down before we even have a chance to do any kind of drying," says Agent Turner in frustration. "Get to it gentlemen, we need some drying. Intercepting counterfeit bills won't do it. We need drying of real money, not toilet paper."

That was the trick, though, wasn't it, because toilet paper was all they had to work with.

"You have to stall the Singapore police for a few days. We need more time to figure out a solution," says Phil. A few days might not even be enough. This was far more complicated than Phil had anticipated. He needs to figure out a way to come at this from a whole new direction.

"I'll try," says Agent Turner before hanging up.

Phil sighs, hanging up his own phone. He wished he could trust the agent at his word, but chances were, the man was not going to try at all.

As the sun is setting, Phil joins Bianca on the rooftop terrace for a glass of wine. Bianca offers a fake smile as Phil sits down beside her. He knows that she is not enjoying her time in this crowded Singapore apartment, so he needs to somewhat walk on eggshells with her. Phil is also seeing fear coming back into Bianca's eyes, which he hadn't seen since her last encounter with Li in Macau.

She takes a sip of her wine and seems to savor it for a moment. "Will we ever set our own course?" asks Bianca.

"I'm sure we will, baby. At least now, we don't have to worry about getting caught by the authorities. We're on their side and we're helping to catch the bad guys," says Phil with confidence.

"I know, but I feel like unless all the criminals that we've interacted with are sent to jail, which I'm not sure anymore whether the FBI really wants that, we'll always have to look over our shoulders." She sets down her glass and turns to Phil. "And I get the impression that these cops don't even care about us. They're just using you for your ingenuity, but in the end, we'll probably be left to fend for ourselves," says Bianca in a low voice almost whispering, her eyes slightly tearing up.

Phil knows that she's right. Her intuition continues to impress him, but he needs to cheer her up to keep her head into the game.

"You're probably right," says Phil, looking into Singapore's pink sky in the distance. "But for the moment, helping the FBI is our best chance to make a difference. And I could really use your help," says Phil as he turns towards Bianca.

She looks at him from the corner of her eyes, her head still pointing to the horizon.

"What do you mean? I helped you today to look up the exchange rates," says Bianca with hesitation, trying to avoid getting drawn into too much of the police work.

"I know and that was great, thank you. But I need more of your brain power to figure out ways to dry them out. Remember how motivated you were when we setup Equit? I think getting more involved with the masterminding would get your intellect juices flowing and keep you happier," says Phil.

She seems to ponder this before nodding. "Alright, I can help. But you know my boundaries, I won't get involved in schemes and deceptions. And if this little piece of crap agent gets me started, you're gonna have to deal with him," replies Bianca as she grabs Phil's hand and reaches for a kiss. She then sits on his lap, leaning her body over his, and continues to watch the sunset in the distance. "I just wish we could relax and lie naked next to an open fire on a bear rug."

"Me too baby. We will, I promise," replies Phil.

Phil keeps his emotions to a minimum to avoid alerting Bianca or any other team member. He believes that if he showed any kind of insecurity about the outcome of this mission, the team's spirit could fall apart very quickly. They are counting on Phil to be strong and in control of any situation that may arise.

Deep inside, however, Phil is worried. He wonders why the FBI wouldn't go for Li's quick arrest. Phil is no longer sure what the FBI really hopes to gain by drying out Li. Back in Columbia, Agent Fuller claimed that the drying out was going to be used to make the criminals come out of hiding, then they would make a mistake and authorities could arrest them. But with Li coming into plain sight every night, Phil doesn't understand why more time and opportunities need to be wasted, especially with all the international arrest warrants already out in Li's name – perhaps even the Singapore police would love to pick him up based on his loaded history of crimes. Phil finds it completely unnecessary to wait for Li to make a mistake.

Phil is also worried about Bianca. While he is certain that their love and commitment to each other is rock solid, he wonders whether the slow progress of the mission, if it continues, would lead Bianca to reach a point of depression or anxiety, which would prevent her from staying with the rest of the group. Phil knows that Bianca is a strong woman, but everyone has their limits. He remains confident that keeping Bianca busy will help the stability of the group.

***

The following morning, Phil announces a new tactic for the day to further disrupt Li and attempt some drying.

"Tiago, as soon as we spot one of Li's guys coming in for an exchange, you're going to walk out, bump into him hard enough to knock him to the ground and make him drop his briefcase. And while you help him back up, Agent Fuller will empty the content of the briefcase in a garbage bag. All of this, of course while attracting the attention of passers-by to the man on the ground and not the briefcase being emptied," explains Phil.

"This is not just an accidental shoulder-to-shoulder brushing. I'm going to need to give him a heck of a blow to send him far enough from the briefcase that he wouldn't see what we're doing," warns Tiago with his hands on his hips.

"I don't like this plan. What if he cracks his skull opened on the sidewalk?" says Bianca in disgust while Phil looks at her apologetically. She really hates when Phil's mind turns diabolical.

"She's right. You gotta make him fall forwards. That way, he will break his fall with his hands, avoid the skull fracture and let go of the briefcase. While you discreetly walk away from the scene, Agent Fuller will handle the briefcase," says Phil turning back to Tiago.

"Sounds like a plan," concludes Tiago, leaving the three ladies in astonishment that fighting financial crimes has turned into attempted assaults.

"You're certainly not securing my support to help with this rather violent part of the mission," says Bianca rolling her eyes at Phil and walking away with the other ladies.

An hour later, Phil spots one of Li's guys carrying a briefcase a block away from the booth and gives the signal to Tiago and Agent Fuller to go down to the street to execute the plan. The move is carried out as Phil had designed it, except that the briefcase goes flying much further than anticipated, rolls onto the street and a heavy truck drives over it. Bianca bursts out laughing, looking at the scene with the binoculars, but places her hand over her mouth, ashamed of her reaction. "Oh no, I hope this doesn't attract too much attention," says Phil, worried about someone calling law enforcement.

Fairly certain that nobody noticed him tripping the man, Tiago walks away casually around the block. Meanwhile, Agent Fuller retrieves the briefcase on the pavement, brings it to the other side of the street in-between two parked vans, quickly empties the content into his garbage bag and leaves the briefcase on the sidewalk. After a few minutes of being attended by passers-by, Li's operative gets back on his feet with a minor bloody nose and looks around for his briefcase. When he finds it on the opposite side of the street, he immediately realizes that he had fallen victim of scammers. He dreads having to explain this to Li.

Chapter 16

The team is busy picking through an odd selection of take-out when the doorbell rings. Maria stands to answer, and Tiago stops her.

She pushes him away. "I will not have you treating me like an invalid. I am only pregnant."

Tiago gulps, glancing at Phil. None of them were worried about her pregnancy at the moment. The small woman knew what they were doing in Singapore, but she was lucky enough not to see anything too seedy yet, so she still has no understanding that someone might hurt her simply for being friends with Phil and Tiago.

Still, Tiago lets her go to the door, but stands behind her like a lion ready to pounce.

Maria opens the door and smiles.

An older voice greets her. "Oh, hello young lady. My apologies. I was told to come here for an explanation of my newfound good fortune."

Phil knows that voice, and he leaps from his chair and swings the door the rest of the way open. "Dr. Debo!" The old man looks extremely frail but freshly pardoned and out of jail with his sentence commuted.

His eyes widen. "My goodness. Phil!" They embrace. "Do I have you to owe my freedom?"

Phil nods and fills Dr. Debo in on their current situation. "We could really use your help."

Dr. Debo shrugs. "Well, it certainly sounds like more fun than basket weaving and good-citizenship seminars." He looks around the room. "But will this just land me back in jail again?"

Phil shakes his head. "Nope. You are working for the good guys now." At least, Phil hopes this is true. He needs to believe this or he might go insane.

Bianca and Tiago also embrace Dr. Debo warmly, overjoyed from finally reconnecting with such a nice gentleman. Dr. Debo will have to share the living room with Agent Fuller, however, for sleeping arrangements, which as he says, is so much better than prison. "Yeah, and we need to feed you properly. You look like you lost fifteen kilos since last time we saw you," says Bianca, gently patting Dr. Debo's arms.

Phil explains, at a high level, the FBI's objective of drying criminal organizations out of the resources they use in money laundering schemes. Dr. Debo listens intently to Phil's explanation, raising his eyebrows a few times, skeptical that the approach would lead to anything useful given the large amounts of money that those organizations have access to, but he does not want to express any disagreement in front of Agent Fuller. And after all, if this mission is the reason that he got out of jail, Dr. Debo is not about to complain about the frivolity of the stated objectives.

Phil also describes the counterfeit money scheme that Li is operating, seemingly printing illegal bills and offering them at favorable rates to any client visiting the booth.

"But he's not laundering any money with that scheme. Li ends up with legal bills in his hands, but it's still dirty money that is yet to be integrated in the system," remarks Dr. Debo.

"Correct, but he also operates the same scheme that we had designed for Norrid, by having some of his operatives come to the booth to exchange money at unfavorable rates," says Phil.

"I guess Li's everyday goal is to push all of his available counterfeit money to clients and retain all the legal bills, which he then launders using the booth on the following days, correct?" asks Bianca.

"You're right. Which is probably why Li was unhappy when he ended up with fake Singapore dollars that Linda handed in for valid US dollars over the past two days. We disrupted part of his sequence," says Phil.

"Not as unhappy as yesterday when he lost nearly $200,000 when we sent that briefcase flying to the street," says Tiago with a wide smile. Dr. Debo looks at him with a perplex look.

"An act of unnecessary violence concocted by men with a surplus of testosterone. But don't worry Doctor, I won't let that happen again," says Bianca while giving a dirty look at both Phil and Tiago. "But let's get back to business." She places her hands on the table. "In order to ensure that Li pushes out all the counterfeit money on any given day, he probably modifies the rates of the currencies for which he has the most fake money in his hands. In other words, he is leading the clients towards the fake money that he has available." She rubs her chin, staring across the room. "Therefore, if we want to dry him out of his valid money, we need to determine which currency pair's exchange rate is most popular over the day, and show up at the booth with fake money, and do the reverse trades of what other clients have done. And we keep doing this until the booth runs out of the real money. This way, we will dry them out of all real money and Li is going to go back home with the fake," says Bianca with a wide smile. Phil looks at her and nods an approval. He is proud that Bianca is bringing her smarts and expertise back to the execution of the mission.

"It's worth a try. We need some fake currencies," says Phil looking at Agent Fuller. "Make yourself useful and call your buddies at the FBI to get us some fake money."

***

Overnight, Agent Turner is able to secure counterfeit money of various currencies for the team to start the scheme on the next morning. By closely monitoring the booth and cross-checking the rates against the market, Phil identifies that the most likely currencies being counterfeited today are the Australian and New Zealand dollars, which customers are exchanging for Singapore dollars. Half an hour before the booth closes for the day, Phil asks Agent Fuller to walk across the street and exchange AU$75,000 and NZ$50,000 for Singapore dollars.

When Agent Fuller comes back with the presumed real Singapore dollars, Phil calls Agent Turner to have someone pick up the money for analysis.

Later at night, Li shows up at the booth at his usual time and starts shuffling things around. Suddenly he starts being visibly angry and throwing things around inside the booth. He just realized the Singapore dollars that he was hoping to collect are not there.

Li steps outside, paces on the sidewalk for a few minutes, then crosses the street. He starts looking closely at street signs, benches and inside the street level shops.

"It seems like he's trying to determine if someone is recording him from the street level," says Tiago closely following Li's every step with night vision binoculars.

"I hope he doesn't find our set of mirrors," says Phil, watching how closely Li gets to the mirror installed on a street sign.

"He's going to increase security around the booth," says Dr. Debo, cautioning the team about the possible next step in this chess match.

"Guys, duck down, he's looking this way," says Phil as he hopes that the light from the computer monitors in the back of the room is dim enough to avoid revealing their silhouettes through the window.

Phil raises his head slightly and looks at Li through his binoculars. Phil watches Li's arrogant face intently and whispers "I'm going to get you, Li. Your days on the street are numbered." Dr. Debo turns towards Phil, surprised to hear even the slightest aggressive words coming out of Phil's mouth.

"Be careful, Phil. You don't want your eagerness to turn into overconfidence," cautions Dr. Debo.

"You're right, doctor. Please keep us in check so that we continue to evaluate our risks properly. I'm really glad that I brought you here," says Phil with a hand on Dr. Debo's forearm.

After a few minutes, Li, presumably frustrated with the lack of any clue to resolve this mystery, looks up to the sky, moves his arms up in disbelief, walks back to his Mercedes, and drives off.

***

The following morning, Phil is up early to see if Li's operatives will change something around the booth. As Dr. Debo expected, a van pulls up in front of the booth at eight o'clock. Two men step out, and quickly install high quality surveillance cameras on each corner of the booth, providing Li real time visibility of who comes into the booth to disrupt his business.

"We need a way to neutralize these cameras, otherwise we won't be able to come near that booth again," Phil says. He turns to the others. "Any ideas?"

"Can't we blind out the cameras with a laser pointer?" asks Bianca.

"Yes, but it will need to be mounted on something like a camera tripod to avoid the imprecision of a human hand. And I believe that we would need to be closer, like no more than twenty feet away," explains Dr. Debo.

"So, we're going to need to park a car on the booth's side of the street and operate the laser from inside the car without being detected," says Phil.

"The window will have to be rolled down with the laser pointing directly at the camera. Otherwise, there will be reflections through the windshield or windows, and as a result, a loss of intensity of the laser beam," continues Dr. Debo, as if he were lecturing a physics class.

"Yep, we'll roll down the window for a few minutes when we send someone to exchange money. Agent Fuller, make yourself useful again, please find us four high power laser beams, four tripods and a small van with heavily tinted windows," commands Phil as he continues to look outside, purposely not making eye contact with the agent to affirm his power. "We need all of this early afternoon. And we'll send you to the booth again to exchange money", adds Phil, generating a long sigh from Agent Fuller. "Come on, chop chop, we're in a rush. And I don't need your attitude. Get off your butt and do as I say," commands Phil with authority.

Late morning, Phil receives a call from Agent Turner with the news that the equipment requested isn't available until the next day. Phil is frustrated with having to waste a whole day making no progress in Li's arrest. He wonders whether something else could be accomplished today, so he asks Agent Fuller to continue the monitoring of the booth's activities while he gets some fresh air with Tiago on the roof top terrace.

"I want to do something useful today while we're waiting for the lasers," says Phil, looking at Tiago with an evil smile and rubbing his hands.

"You and me both, but I can tell that you have some diabolical plan in mind, so go ahead, tell me," replies Tiago slowly, arms crossed over his chest, looking at the horizon, and taking a deep breath. He knows that whatever Phil wants to do will not be a walk in the park, otherwise they would be having this conversation in the apartment. It is clear that Phil intends to keep his project secret from everyone else.

"I think we shouldn't bother the operation of the booth today. Let's give Li a false sense of security when he comes tonight to check on his cash. But then, let's tail him to see where he's hiding," says Phil with a smile. At the suggestion of starting a discreet pursue through the heart of Singapore, Tiago stops smiling and turns towards Phil.

"Are you out of your mind? We all keep telling you to take plans a notch lower on the risk spectrum. Yet, you're suggesting a very perilous mission that the FBI would never allow us to do," says Tiago firmly.

"They'll never know. Look, we need a break in this case. We need to know what Li is up to around Singapore, so that we can intercept larger amounts of money. If we just continue with the pace that the FBI has set for us, we'll still be here in a year, grabbing a few dollars from Li left and right every couple of days. Here's the plan, let's watch some television with the team tonight, chat in the living room and wait until everyone's asleep. Then, we sneak out," says Phil, with the simplicity of a teenager that wants to escape his parents' house to attend an unapproved party.

"Did you forget that Agent Fuller and Dr. Debo are sleeping in the living room?" asks Tiago.

"We can count on Dr. Debo's discretion. Heck, if he were a couple of years younger, I'd bring him along. For Agent Fuller, we just need to crush one of Bianca's sleeping pills and slip it into his beer tonight," replies Phil, intentionally using a style to reduce the appearance of the risks involved. Tiago is very aware of the risks associated with Phil's proposal, but he doesn't want to argue with him. And frankly, Tiago also wants to get moving with this mission and put Li behind bars once and for all.

"Alright, let me put a plan together this afternoon," concludes Tiago as he turns back towards the stairs to indicate to Phil that he wants to end this conversation and come up with the tactical plan without Phil's influence.

Given the relative ease of convincing Tiago, Phil smiles at the thought of making progress in the quest of getting Li into police custody. He is confident that this mission is sufficiently low risk, else Tiago wouldn't have agreed.

Chapter 17

Phil and Tiago head out of the apartment an hour before Li usually arrives at the booth. They sit, parked a block away, in a Toyota Corolla that Tiago rented a few hours earlier while running errands for the team despite Maria's disapproval because she worries that his face would now potentially appear on Li's cameras.

Tiago explains the details of his plan for the night to Phil, emphasizing multiple times that he reserves the right to pull the plug on this exercise at any time for any reason whatsoever. Phil agrees and is glad that their safety will be the utmost priority.

Phil looks into the binoculars and as he predicted, soon after Li's gang perform their usual cash collection exercise, Li sports a wide smile when he realizes that his cameras have deterred whoever was trying to mess with him. Today, he is collecting all of his money, so, confident as ever, he high-fives his employees and feels emboldened by his ability to run his two schemes simultaneously without anyone trying to take his resources.

As soon as Li's vehicle starts moving, Tiago turns the ignition and follows Li's Mercedes from a distance. The traffic is light but sufficient to blend in. Using a Corolla is also perfect because it is a very popular car in Singapore, and therefore, Li would need a trained eye to notice that someone is following him. Li's Mercedes G Class, however, is higher than most cars, so he is quite easy to tail. "I can never decide whether Li is brilliant or stupid. Only he, would be extravagant enough to drive such an easily recognizable car," says Phil while shaking his head left and right.

Li stops at a night club, leaves his keys with the valet parking attendant and enters the establishment. As Tiago and Phil drive up in Li's tail, music of growing intensity emanates from inside the club and blinding strobing nights illuminate and blanket the neighborhood. Phil quickly unbuckles, jumps to the back seat, and unlatches the seat leading to the trunk.

"Leave the car with the valet attendant and go in. I'll quickly search Li's car and meet you inside," says Phil as Tiago is pulling up near the night club.

"What are you doing? You're being reckless," says Tiago, raising his voice, his meticulously prepared plan dissolving with Phil's improvisations.

"Stay close to your phone and come get me if I'm not inside in twenty minutes. And try to keep an eye on Li," orders Phil as he gets into the trunk and closes the back seat without latching it, so that he is able to come out again at the opportune time.

Tiago approaches the entrance of the night club. He looks down at his clothes to see if his attire is plausible enough for a single man on a night out. Not quite, as he'd dressed for stealth, not the kind of attire to attract the ladies. He looks more like one of the club's security agent with his dark jeans and tight black t-shirt, stretching the fabric to its maximum with his muscular shoulders and biceps. He turns around to watch the valet attendant drive off with the Corolla and sees that a group of six girls, probably warmed up from an earlier drinking session, walking in the direction of the club's entrance, so he slows down to try to blend in with them for a less noticeable entry.

"Hey girls, how is your night?" asks Tiago.

"Getting better by the second. You're cute," replies one of the girls as she grabs and squeeze Tiago's left bicep to enter the club. "Where are you from?"

"Originally from Brazil," replies Tiago lowering his heads towards her, trying to reduce any chance of being seen by Li. Once inside, he gently escapes from the girl's grip and says "okay girls, I'll see you in a bit. Let's have a drink later."

The darkness of the club offers some cover for Tiago but his size, compared to the other patrons, may pose a risk. So, he casually moves along the edges of the establishment, constantly scanning to make sure that he doesn't come across Li. When he sees a group of men, probably foreigners, hanging around a table filled with champagne bottles, he stops by and taps the tallest of them on the shoulder, making it look like he knows him.

"Hey man, how have you been?" asks Tiago, as the man looks at him oddly.

"Sorry, do I know you?" replies the man.

"Dude, we met here before, and we drank some tequila shots with your buddies. Don't you remember?" bluffs Tiago in order to hang out with that group for a few minutes while continuing to survey every corner of the club. When he looks up to the second-floor area, he sees Li being led into a room by two security guards, whom he recognizes from their bloody encounter in Macau, more than a year ago.

"I don't. But I've been messed up so many times recently that I probably just blanked out the night that we hung out together. Hey, help yourself to some drinks from our table, and help us attracts some ladies over here," says the man, his breath reeking from alcohol and tobacco. Tiago slowly moves to the man's other side to keep as much cover as possible from Li and his security guards, in case they look in Tiago's direction. They could potentially recognize him.

Meanwhile, Phil quietly comes out of the car's trunk after the valet attendant walks away. He sees Li's Mercedes thirty feet away, so he lays low and walks over to the driver's door. As Phil expected, the door is unlocked and the window is rolled down. The keys are even loosely left on the dash. Clearly, valet attendants see no risks with leaving cars exposed to thieves.

Phil enters Li's car and starts looking through the content of the glove compartment, inside the arm rest and every other storage area of the car. Nothing special. So, he quietly makes his way to the back and lifts the floor panel in the trunk. Phil finds a black nylon bag, similar to the ones that he is now accustomed to see with Li and his guys, presumably filled with cash. He grabs the heavy bag and discreetly takes it back to his car. "How is that for drying a criminal from his resources," whispers Phil under his breath with a smile.

As he weaves through cars trying to exit undetected to meet Tiago back at the club, Phil has to stop and hide a few times when valet attendants pass by. When Li realizes that he doesn't have his cash anymore, Phil doesn't want Li to be able to extract information from the attendants about who they may have seen roaming around the parking garage.

When he emerges on the ground floor, Phil's mobile phone returns to service, and he receives a series of text messages from Tiago, providing his location inside the club. Phil promptly enters and painfully makes his way across the floor, wondering what he ever found attractive in these places when he used to frequent some twenty years ago.

"I was starting to wonder if you fell asleep in the trunk of the car," says Tiago with a smile when Phil joins him and the group of drunk foreigners. They offer a drink to Phil but he politely declines.

"Yah... I searched his car but didn't find anything useful. Just did a little drying," says Phil with a laugh, his words barely audible due to the loud music.

"Drying?" replies Tiago. "You mean you took his cash? Oh lord, the man is going to be pissed."

"That's the mission, right? We need to have him commit mistakes. Getting him angry about losing a big bag of cash should get the job done," says Phil while tapping Tiago's back.

Tiago explains to Phil that Li entered a guarded room on the second level when suddenly, someone grabs both Phil and Tiago from the back and yells loudly.

"NO WAY!" says Alex, Equit's head of currency trading, with whom Phil worked a year ago when Equit was in its infancy. "What are you guys doing here?"

"Wow, good to see you. You're still in Singapore, good for you," says Phil, unhappy to have run into someone that he knows.

"Yeah man, Singapore is great, and Equit is thriving. We're now owned by a private equity firm that lets us manage the place however we want, as long as we produce good enough returns. But most importantly, we got to keep the exotic cars and Li lets us drink here for free. What else could anybody possibly wish for? Pretty much all the firm's analysts come here," says Alex, like a teenager who's drinking in a club for the first time.

"Li lets you drink here? Is this place owned by Li?" asks Phil.

"Sure is. And it's the best club in town. Let me get him, he'll be so excited to see you guys," says Alex.

"Oh no, you know what, we have to go. And do me a favor, please don't tell Li that we were here", requests Phil.

"Really why?" asks Alex.

"We're throwing a surprise party for him in a few days, and he doesn't know that a bunch of his old buddies are flying in," says Phil with a wide smile. "And wait, did you mean that Li is still involved with Equit?"

"Well, I still see him in the office once in a while, but I don't know what he does. He's certainly not as involved as he used to be. Some people say that he's starting his own fund, and maybe leveraging our resources," replies Alex.

"Alright, we'll see you around," concludes Tiago, while gently grabbing Phil's arm to head for the exits. The last thing that Tiago needs is having to deal with Li and his thugs while Maria and the rest of the team are sleeping.

"Hey, don't leave, I'll introduce you to the guys," says Alex but Phil and Tiago have already left and the loud music easily overcomes Alex's voice.

Phil is flabbergasted. Arrest warrants for Li are supposedly widely distributed to authorities all over the world, yet he is roaming around Singapore, handling his currency booths, showing up at Equit's office and operating one the most popular clubs in town. How on earth? That man obviously operates above the law. And how long will it take for Li to become aware that Phil and Tiago paid a visit to his club? Alex is the last person that Phil would trust with a secret.

Chapter 18

When early morning sunshine partially illuminates the bedroom, Bianca becomes conscious and can't remember hearing Phil coming to bed the night before. She wonders if she again abused alcohol with Linda. But wait, she didn't even drink last night, so she quickly turns towards Phil's side of the bed. He's there, sound asleep, so she breathes a sigh of relief.

Bianca sits up and puts her feet on the floor. She slowly stands, her eyes still partially shut. She takes a few steps towards the bathroom and hits her right foot against the black nylon bag that Phil brought back. She looks at it and immediately recognizes the type of cash carrying bag used by Li.

"Phil, what the heck is this?" asks Bianca, loud enough for all the roommates to hear. Phil wakes up and knows exactly what she's talking about. Tiago, sleeping in the adjacent room, with Maria tightly tucked against him, also wakes up at the sound of Bianca's voice and hopes that Maria doesn't wake up to whatever drama Bianca is creating about the bag of cash.

"We did some drying last night," says Phil in a calm and soft voice.

"What? Where did you go? And what did you do?" asks Bianca as she jumps back on the bed, her knees on either side of Phil's body, shoving his chest until he blinks, rubbing his eyes.

"Relax honey… We just followed Li, then ran into Alex. It turns out that Li is operating a night club and is still at least tangentially involved with Equit. There seems to be a lot more going on than what the FBI knows," says Phil, slowly opening his eyes and rubbing Bianca's thighs to calm her down.

"Baby, you're taking too many risks," whispers Bianca, now trying to avoid alerting Maria, who will probably be kept in the dark about last night's escapade.

"Don't worry, I'm staying close to Tiago." Phil rubs the back of his neck. "Most of the time," recalling that he was searching Li's car by himself last night, which in hindsight, he finds to be a pretty significant risk.

"Yeah well, you're probably not telling me the whole story. You need to involve me in these things going forward. I think you'll take less risks if I'm with you. And anyway, I'd rather take those risks with you, than sitting here, wondering where you are and whether you're getting tortured by these thugs," says Bianca, tightly hugging Phil as if they hadn't seen each other for weeks. "You said you wanted me more involved. We're a team now, I want to be involved." Bianca keeps her head against Phil's chest, grateful that she didn't lose him in whatever adventure he took part of the night before. Phil takes a deep breath. He knows full well that going forward, Bianca will not let him go out on surveying missions with Tiago.

An hour later, right before the morning debrief with Agent Turner is about to start, Bianca asks Linda to take Maria to the rooftop so she won't overhear what her new husband had been up to the night before. When Phil starts to explain last night's events, Agent Turner immediately interrupts and becomes angry and doesn't approve that Phil and Tiago planned this and tailed Li without his approval – and again didn't involve Agent Fuller. But as Phil continues to recount the night, Agent Turner turns ecstatic when he learns that they were able to take a bag of cash containing more than $4 million from Li's Mercedes.

"Now that's some serious drying. Are you sure it's not counterfeit?" Asks Agent Turner with his hands behind his head.

"We haven't looked at every bill but it all seems legit. His scheme is to bring back real cash from the booths. I don't know why he didn't have his armored car last night though. And why he thought it was a good idea to leave all that in a public parking. I honestly can't figure out this man," replies Phil.

"That is some very good news gentlemen. I'll send someone to pick this up later today, and we'll look into the night club that you mentioned," says Agent Turner with a wide smile. Bianca shakes her head in disbelief as she listens to these congratulating words from the man who was unhappy about Phil and Tiago's risky behavior just a minute ago.

"Alright, but if you're going to get close to Li's operations, do it discreetly. Don't start sending a bunch of agents to interrogate people at that night club. Be smart!" cautions Phil before receiving a puzzled look from Agent Turner looking directly at Phil on the video screen. "You know what I mean, you guys could be such happy triggers sometimes. Anyway, I think we should tail him again tonight, and see where else he goes. That might give us more drying opportunities than just watching the currency booth all day," says Phil.

"If you're able to do more drying of that magnitude, I'm okay with that – but you're taking Agent Fuller with you," says Agent Turner followed by a silence. Phil, Tiago, Bianca and Dr. Debo turn to Agent Fuller, who is slouching on the couch, sipping his coffee and eating a doughnut, watching the debrief from a distance and listening quietly. He produces a fake victory smile when the four of them look at him. Phil raises one eyebrow, takes a deep breath, turns back to the screen and nods in agreement.

Wanting to prove his usefulness to the team, Dr. Debo takes charge of the surveillance operations while the rest of the team plans their upcoming night of covert operations. He even volunteers to sit in the newly FBI provided van with Paul to jam the cameras with lasers at strategic times of the drying operations.

On three separate instances during the day, they turn on the lasers and have Maria, Linda and Agent Fuller go down to the booth to exchange money, extracting precise amounts of valid bills that Li's guys laundered minutes before. As the women appear near the booth for the first two exchanges, Tiago's voice come on the radio to request that Paul physically intervenes if they somehow get harassed by anyone in any way whatsoever and hold for the fifteen seconds that Tiago would need to come down to the rescue. "Agent Fuller, on the other hand, does not need protection and will have to handle his own safety," says Tiago with a smile, generating laughs, both in the van and the apartment.

The attendant of the booth seems completely unperturbed by what's going on. Dr. Debo suggests to Phil that it probably means that the attendant has no idea of the crimes that are being committed in that booth – both the laundering and the passing of fake bills to customers. "Just like we had setup for Norrid, a central team is probably setting the rates for the laundering acts. The same team likely steers customers towards certain currencies for which they have fake bills by tweaking the rates throughout the day. The attendants just literally process the transactions," says Dr. Debo, as if he were reading from a textbook. He also tells Phil that the lack of reaction during or after the jamming of the cameras suggests that the cameras are not actively being monitored. But he also cautions that Li will probably review the footage later and realize that parts of the recording are missing.

At dusk, Phil, Tiago, Bianca and Agent Fuller, tightly packed in the FBI van, finalize the preparations for their upcoming night together. They have with them loads of recording equipment and various weapons. Phil hopes that they don't have to use any of the ammunition but, nevertheless, is counting on Tiago to make that decision, especially if Bianca were placed in any kind of risky situation.

Phil is not entirely convinced that bringing Bianca along is such a great idea. Keeping her eagerness to help with the mission is important, but she could be a liability, and used against Phil if she got caught. Phil would prefer that Bianca's careful senses of observation and deduction were used behind the scenes, away from all the threats. Little does he know, however, she would prove much more valuable than expected.

Chapter 19

After less than ten minutes sitting in the van, just as Phil is starting to doze off, sitting on the front passenger seat, Tiago gives him an elbow nudge when Li shows up in his Mercedes. The booth is not even closed for the day. Li is at least one hour earlier than his usual time, visibly angry. He storms into the booth.

"He must have realized that part of the security footage is missing," says Dr. Debo over the radio.

Phil uses the binoculars to closely observe as Li scans through the drawers of currencies, shouts at the attendant, shoves all the currencies in two boxes and heads towards the back of his car. He pops the trunk open and raises the panel that was hiding the money that Phil took last night, realizing for the first time that the nylon bag had gone missing. Li freezes for five seconds, removes his glasses, looks back at the booth and places a hand over his eyes. He shakes his head left and right in disbelief. Then, he slams his trunk shut and gets back into his car.

"Yep, we took that precious bag from you, my dear," mumbles Phil, watching Li's every movement.

"The man is going to be livid, dangerous and unpredictable. It's not a good idea to tail him tonight," says Tiago, expressing his disagreement with this mission in no uncertain terms.

"No doubt he's going to be livid. But tonight is the perfect time to see what's going to happen," replies Phil. "Let's see if the FBI's theory about upcoming reckless acts is going to prove itself."

"Li is plenty reckless already, I don't know what other proof you need. I could have explained that supposed theory to the FBI a year ago and saved them the hassle of finding out," says Bianca with a smart attitude, offering a fake smile to Agent Fuller with her arms crossed over her chest.

Although Li's Mercedes' windows are slightly tinted, Phil can see him sitting behind the wheel, yelling at someone on his cell phone and hitting the dash with his fist. All of a sudden, he steps on the accelerator and drives off. Tiago quickly turns the van's ignition and attempts to follow Li but gets blocked off by a delivery truck that is slowing down to make a turn at the next traffic light. When the lane finally clears, Li has disappeared. Tiago starts driving in the same direction as last night, guessing that Li is heading back to his club.

They approach the night club at a much earlier time than the night before. The place is very quiet. Tiago drives slowly and keeps a distance. Everyone in the van is scanning the surroundings to try to spot Li.

"Here's Li's Mercedes," says Bianca pointing at the entrance of the valet parking, more than 500 feet away.

"Ah, and Li is by the garage's entrance. What is he doing?" asks Tiago looking at Li. "It seems like he is holding a knife at the throat of the valet attendant."

"Oh no, he's accusing that poor kid of stealing the money that we took yesterday," says Phil as he quickly retrieves his mobile phone, tightly tucked in his jeans pocket. He dials up Agent Turner, who picks up immediately. "Agent Turner, we need permission to move in to arrest Li, he is about to hurt an innocent man because of the money that we took from him last night."

"Nice try but negative, Phil. Let it unfold and let the Singapore police deal with this," says Agent Turner in a cold, almost military tone.

"WHAT? This poor kid is going to get killed because of your stupid mission. We have to do something," says Phil loudly, with deep concerns in his voice.

"We cannot make arrests in Singapore for aggravated assaults. We're here for financial crime investigations. That's it! Plus, Li may have a bunch of operatives right around where you are. You're not equipped for this," answers Agent Turner, but Phil already hung up.

"Agent Fuller, pretend that you're some sort of security guard and intervene to save this man," orders Phil as he turns his head towards the back of the van.

"This is a volatile situation that we shouldn't get in the middle of," says Agent Fuller, prompting sterns looks from everyone else in the van, followed by a silence. Phil sighs and shakes his head left and right, as he looks in desperation at the boy. "And... why me?" asks Agent Fuller.

"Because Li doesn't know you. Come on you little piece of crap, make yourself useful, for once. Be a man," says Bianca as she opens Agent Fuller's door, places her hand on his face and pushes him outside.

Although not offering much physical resistance, but a bit insulted by Bianca's manner, Agent Fuller awkwardly gets off from the van and straightens his clothes. With a hand on his holstered gun inside his jacket, he jogs towards Li, who still has a knife against the throat of the valet attendant. When he reaches a safe distance of approximately fifty feet, Agent Fuller stops and yells, "Hey, what's going on here?", ready to pull out his gun. Li releases his grip, runs to his car and drives off.

"Are you okay kid?" asks Agent Fuller.

"This guy's a maniac," replies the attendant, running inside the garage for safety.

Tiago immediately follows Li's car and leaves Agent Fuller standing in the middle of the street, his arms raised in the air. He starts running after the van and yells, "STOP, COME BACK", as if he had been left in the middle of a dangerous slum.

When Agent Fuller's caller id comes onto the screen of Phil's phone, Bianca grabs it.

"Are you guys coming back to get me?" asks Agent Fuller.

"Oh ya, ya. We'll be there in a minute. Or not. What do you think? We're in pursuit of Li, and not turning around for you. Take a taxi and get back to the apartment right away," orders Bianca and hangs up. She smiles from the satisfaction of not having to deal with this annoying person for the rest of the night.

Agent Fuller dials up Agent Turner, who promises to send a driver to pick him up.

Li drives fast and recklessly through the streets and dense traffic of Singapore for 45 minutes. Given his military experience with vehicles of all types, Tiago is able to follow Li from a safe distance until Li goes off road to discreetly enter the shipping terminal by the Singapore port, an area that houses hundreds of thousands of containers. Li parks his car behind a large tree, gets off and crawls under a fence.

"Tiago, stop here and let's see what he does," orders Phil. Bianca, please pass me the night vision binoculars," asks Phil as he continues to closely watch Li's movements in the darkness.

"What is he doing here?" asks Bianca while passing the binoculars to Phil.

"We're going to find out," replies Phil calmly.

Phil sees Li enter a container near the fence that he crawled under, and he closes the door quickly behind him. Five minutes later, Li comes out, climbs a ladder and enters another nearby container.

"Seems like he's hiding stuff in these containers," says Phil, handing the binoculars back to Bianca, and looking sternly at Tiago. "I'm going to go in to check out the container that he just came out of. You guys stay here. Ring my phone if and when he comes out of the other container. I should have time to quietly exit and hide on the side."

"What? Are you crazy?" Asks Bianca, but Phil is already out of the van, running towards the fence.

As Phil approaches the container, he looks around for any sign of security or other personnel from Li's organization. No one is in sight. He slowly moves the sliding lock and opens the door. It's completely dark, so he uses his mobile phone's flashlight to illuminate the inside of the container. Phil is stunned to find out that this is actually an air-conditioned living quarter with three, maybe four containers attached together with side openings to move from one to the other. A noticeable chemical smell fills the air as Phil walks to his right and finds a room filled with cash of various currency denominations, a large color printer and cutting boards, presumably being used to produce all of Li's counterfeit money.

Phil smiles as Li, yet again, is full of surprises with a money printing operation hidden inside shipping containers. This will hopefully be more than enough to justify a quick arrest.

As Phil quietly moves to the other side of Li's makeshift apartment, which looks like a bedroom, he hears squeaky sounds as if someone is moving on a mattress. So, he turns off his phone's flashlight and hides behind a desk.

"What are you doing honey?" says a woman voice in the dark. Phil presumes that she believes that Li was moving around the apartment.

"Are you coming to bed? You know we can't sleep until you're here with us," says another woman. Phil shakes his head, thinking about Li's kinky lifestyle with two women in his bed.

Phil's phone starts vibrating. Bianca is calling. Phil can't pick up but he knows what this means; Li is coming back, and Phil also knows that he doesn't have enough time to quickly come out without making noises walking on the metal floor of the container, which the women would hear.

Bianca is looking at the container through the night vision binoculars and sees no movements from Phil. She starts to panic and sweat forms on her palms. Her hands start nervously shaking, and she drops the binoculars. She grabs her phone, ready to call Phil again, but she sees a text from him that he's hiding inside, unable to move at the risk of being detected.

When the door opens, some light shines through the opening and Li's shadow reflects on a wall. Phil's stomach tenses up as the memories of his interactions, or rather confrontations, with Li come rushing back to his mind.

"Li, is that you?" asks one of the women loudly.

"Of course, it's me, who else could it be," says Li nonchalantly.

"Someone was in here a minute ago with a flashlight," says the lady voice coming from the bedroom. Phil sighs, shakes his head, and he hears Li run across to the room that houses the printer. Phil knows that Li is trying to grab a weapon. If he waits, there will be even more of a chance he'll end up dead. His best course of action is to do the unthinkable, and play Li's bluff, so he comes out of hiding with his phone's flashlight turned on and his gun pointed at Li.

"Don't move Li, you're under arrest," says Phil firmly.

Li busts out laughing. "Phil? What are you doing here and what did you say I was? Arrested? You are either dummer than I thought, or you have completely lost your mind." says Li with a smile as he continues to move around.

"Li, STOP! I'm with the FBI and I came here to arrest you," repeats Phil.

Li laughs again, slapping his hand on his thigh. "You're as much a criminal as the rest of us. Actually, more than us. You're the mastermind behind so many illegal businesses that we still operate." His face twists into a snarl. "As if it wasn't enough for you to snitch, now you want to arrest me? You're a joke, I bet you don't even know how to remove the gun's safety," says Li as he crouches beside a gun safe and spins the dial.

Phil may be stupid, but he knows that Li is a seasoned criminal and will not hesitate to use whatever weapon he has hidden in that safe, so he sees no choice but fire a warning shot towards the ground.

Taking a deep breath, he pulls the trigger.

The boom echoes through the room, the sound bouncing off the metal walls over and over, making Phil cringe and tighten his shoulders. Given the wide angle of the gunshot, the bullet ricochets off the metal floor of the container and lodges in the metal wall near Li, who simultaneously steps aside, closely avoiding contact.

The criminal mastermind's sneer turns to a full-on grimace as he holds his hands to the side. Li is surprised and angry that Phil actually fired a shot and stops moving with his hands halfway in the air. "Maybe you do have some cajones after all, my friend. You know how to remove the safety, but do you have the bolts to actually shoot a man?" He snickers. "We are white collar criminals, you and me. We don't need to get our hands dirty like this."

Phil tightens his grip on the gun. He is certain that Li has gotten his hands dirty on many occasions. Phil would be another notch in his belt, and Li wouldn't think twice about plowing through Phil to get what he wanted… dirt or no dirt.

But that means that now they are in a standoff, and Phil isn't sure who would call who's bluff first.

***

When Tiago and Bianca hear the gunshot from the van, Bianca gasps.

"Phil!" she whispers. No! This isn't happening. She didn't want to come. She wanted to lay low for a while, stay safe. Why had he gone in there on his own!

She and Tiago both get out of the car and start running towards the fence.

Is Phil inside there, bleeding, gasping for air? Bianca needs to get to him. She ignores her burning lungs and runs with all her might, until they are cut off by a large black Chevy Suburban that comes just a few feet from hitting Bianca. "What the…," she says as she moves away from the dangerous moving vehicle and turns in time to notice Agent Turner behind the wheel.

She grits her teeth. Turner. He sure as blazes better be here to help!

***

Phil slowly moves towards Li.

"Steady Li. We've got you trapped," orders Phil.

"Trapped? We? Ahh… you've been following me, haven't you? You and your friends? Is that turncoat Tiago with you?" He shakes his head. "Now I understand. Have you been messing around with my business over the last few days? My booths? My cash?" asks Li.

Phil closely follows his every move. He could have a weapon stashed in any one of a hundred places within reach of a few quick paces. The question is, what will Phil do when Li makes his move. Will he pull the trigger? His itchy finger says yes. The only real question is, where will the bullet land?

Bright headlights light up the edges of the container's entrance. Li hadn't completely closed the door when he arrived, now allowing a stream of the container to me illuminated, offering Li a timely distraction from his standoff with Phil.

During the fraction of second that Phil moves his eyes towards the entrance, he gets violently hit on the head with a frying pan by one of the women from Li's bedroom. Phil falls hard on the ground. The world spins, and Li leans over, holding his stomach, laughing.

"Stupid boy," Li shouts. "Never forget to look over your shoulder."

Phil struggles to get up. He needs to move. He needs to save himself. Painted toe nails walk past him, and a metal frying pan hits the floor.

Li gives the woman a long, deep kiss, then smiles at Phil. Pushing the girl to the side, Li walks toward Phil, his shiny shoes glinting in the headlights before all goes dark.

***

Bianca hears the thumping of someone's body hitting the floor of the container. She's frightened by the thought that one of Phil or Li was presumably shot a few seconds ago and has now fallen flat on the ground.

She slams her palms down on the hood of the sedan. "Phil!" He has to be okay! He just has to!

Agent Turner gets out of the car. "Bianca, you need to calm down."

"Calm down?" She points to the container. "Did you just hear that?"

Agent Turner holds up his hands. "Yes, and we're here, now. Let us handle it."

Her eyes turn to fire. "Handle it? HANDLE IT? You could have handled it days ago!" And now Phil is in that tiny metal box with gunshots going off!

***

Inside the container, Li again kisses the girl who'd hit Phil, and then the other on. Amelia…Amanda… Amalie? He could never remember their names. Not that it mattered all that much. He taps the first one on her bare bottom. "You better go get dressed. Things are about to get ugly." Their eyes widen and grab the clothes strewn across the furniture, and quickly dress up.

Li knows that anyone driving so noisily and erratically has to be the American police. Their dumb foolery is notorious and the stuff of jokes to international white collar crime extraordinaires. Right now, Phil is the only bargaining chip he has, and he needs to make sure to keep his cool to slip through their fingers as he always does. So he drags Phil's body behind the printer in order to use him as a shield or some kind of negotiating advantage. Meanwhile, the two women grab the rest of their belongings, head for the exit and come face-to-face with agents Turner and Fuller.

"Who are you?" ask Agent Turner loudly to the women.

They skid to a stop and hold up their hands. "We have no idea what's going on here, we're just going home," says one of the women as they start running barefoot with their high heel shoes in their hands. Agent Fuller grabs them, and they struggle for a few seconds.

"Let them go. We can't make any arrests here," orders Agent Turner loudly. Agent Fuller releases his grip and watches as the girls run to the nearest road and jump into a taxi that speeds away.

With her ears still ringing from the gunshot that presumably killed either of Phil or Li, Bianca stares at Agent Turner in shock. Why is he letting witnesses run away?

Tiago grabs four bullet proof vests and some automatic weapons from the Suburban and heads towards the fence with Bianca.

"Guys, put these on. Bullets could come right through the metal container," says Tiago as he hands over the vests.

"Thank you. What's the situation here?" asks Agent Turner.

"We saw Li come in and out of this container, so Phil went in for some surveying, but Li came back in too fast. Then, we heard a gunshot and you guys barged in like the cavalry," explains Tiago, concerned about his friend's safety. Agent Turner gives Tiago a dirty look when he alludes to the way that they arrived at the scene.

"Yeah well, Phil might have taken one too many risks. Now, let's just take care of Li," says Agent Fuller while pointing an automatic weapon through the door of the container, still angry that Tiago left him out to dry in front of Li's night club earlier in the night. Agent Turner gives him a disapproving look.

"Get that thing out of there, you pea-brain," says Bianca firmly while putting on her vest. "We're not going to start assuming that Phil is dead and start a shooting match with Li."

"You really want to let Li escape again?" asks Agent Fuller.

"You guys should have thought about this when Li was in the currency booth right across the street from us, and not endangering anyone. I'm not going to let you shoot in that direction without knowing if Phil is alive. You better point your gun in a different direction, else I'm going to shove it so far up your behind, that it's going to bother you when you brush your teeth," says Bianca, now with fire in her eyes. Tiago also gives

Agent Fuller a stern look. The agent complies and retracts his weapon.

Meanwhile, Li shuts the door of the container section where he is located with Phil and calls his team for help. Seconds later, a shipyard crane extends its telescopic arm, grabs the container and swiftly moves it to another area. Tiago runs around the piles of containers to retrieve Phil, but by the time he reaches the approximate area where the container was taken to, the crane has moved a series of other containers around, making it impossible to figure out which one houses Phil. Tightly piled up, the containers all have similar colors and formats. This confusing movement of containers gives Li several minutes to escape undetected, painfully dragging his unconscious prisoner through the dirt alleys.

Tiago, Bianca and the two Agents test the doors of dozens of containers, but to no avail. The opening of the container that they are looking for was on its side, so pressed against other containers, finding the correct one amongst these hundreds of containers of similar color, is like a needle in a haystack. Moreover, the crane is still moving containers dangerously near where they are standing, in an attempt to slow them down as Li completes his escape.

Suddenly, they see a BMW 7-Series drive off from another aisle of containers. Phil is under Li's grip. Once again.

Chapter 20

With an emotional vertigo, sitting on the front passenger seat with her hands covering her face, Bianca is sobbing like a child during the drive back to the apartment. Agent Fuller reaches from the back seat and places his hand on Bianca's shoulder.

"Don't you dare touch me, pea brain... Leave me alone!" shouts Bianca, her voice carrying such authority that Agent Fuller retreats back to his seat, not knowing what to say. Even Tiago is afraid of her tone and he doesn't know what to say to sooth her concerns.

"There is a good chance that Phil is still alive," says Agent Fuller, trying to break the silence to find encouraging words.

"Yeah, good thing I stopped you from trying to shoot through that container," says Bianca as she turns back to look at Agent Fuller, exposing her eyes full of tears, swelled and red from the agony of losing the man she loves. "And can you explain to me, why on earth would you guys barge in like you were doing some drug bust in a crack house? What were you thinking?"

"Well, you guys left me stranded, and then when I was picked up by Agent Turner, we thought you needed help," replies Agent Fuller softly, looking away as if he did something that he regrets.

Bianca turns to Tiago, palms up and shaking her head, wondering how the agents were able to figure out that they needed help. Through the rear-view mirror, Tiago stares at Agent Fuller and finds him fidgety and suspicious, so he abruptly stops on the side of the road, grabs Agent Fuller by the back of the collar and squeeze his head tightly against the front seat.

"How did you find out where we were and what was going on in the containers?" asks Tiago, with his face inches apart from Agent Fuller's.

"Hey, I don't call the shots here," replies Agent Fuller, pushing forcefully against the front seat with his hands to try to relieve that pain in his neck.

"That's not what I asked you. You're going to stay like this until you tell me," threatens Tiago. Bianca watches anxiously, not approving such use of force. She taps Tiago's thigh gently to try to de-escalate the situation.

"Alright, alright, I'll tell you. Let go of me," pleads Agent Fuller.

Bianca affirmatively nods to Tiago for him to let the agent go, which he does.

"This van has a tracking device and surveillance cameras in the front and back," continues Agent Fuller.

"I guess that's probably standard for police cars. What else? What was so important for Agent Turner and yourself to arrive at the scene all guns blazing? And you almost swiped me with your vehicle in the process, by the way," says Bianca, still very emotional, her voice cracking. Tiago follows with a murderous look towards Agent Fuller.

"Well…" starts Agent Fuller but stops mid-sentence, sighs loudly and looks away as if he changed his mind about sharing more information. Tiago grabs him by the neck again and squeezes hard. "Okay, okay… we bugged Phil. I slipped a recording device in his pocket earlier today. Agent Turner was concerned because you guys followed Li last night without involving me. Then, when Li entered the container and Phil confronted him, attempted to arrest Li and, we believe, fired a warning shot at Li, Agent Turner said we couldn't let that happen," continues Agent Fuller as Tiago releases his neck.

Bianca looks at Agent Fuller for another few seconds and quietly turns back to face forward. Tiago does the same, engages the van's transmission and starts driving again. They both feel completely blindsided by the FBI. Controlling the details of the mission is one thing. Keeping track of them with GPS and recording devices is annoying but understandable. But trying to stop Phil from arresting one of the worst criminals on this earth is completely unexplainable. Phil might have put himself in grave danger by breaking into the container, but if he fired a warning shot, he might have actually had the upper hand over Li.

For the first time in his life, Tiago is ravaged by sorrow. He might have lost his best friend – the only real friend he has ever had. And even worse, he feels awful that Bianca lost her lover. Tiago knows that it was his job to protect both of them. Had he been with Phil in Li's container, things might have turned out differently, so he thinks. Tiago feels the desire for vengeance. More than ever before, he wants to catch Li and give him a taste of his own medicine. Punish him for daring to hurt the people that he loves.

As Tiago's heart rate and adrenaline normalizes during the remaining fifteen minutes of their ride back to the apartment, his thoughts move to Maria and their unborn child. He loves her very much and wonders whether he can continue with the same desire to put everything on the line to go after Li. Bianca certainly wouldn't expect him to risk his family for a simple vengeance. But Tiago doesn't see how he could live the rest of his life not knowing whether he did everything he could to save Phil.

Past midnight, when they open the door of the apartment, Maria, Paul, Linda and Dr. Debo are still awake, stressed out about their friends who have been out for more than six hours. Maria hugs Tiago, but she senses that something is wrong and looks closely at his saddened eyes.

"Where is Phil?" says Dr. Debo. No one answers.

Linda grabs and hugs Bianca as her body becomes numb and they slowly come to rest on the sofa, tightly embracing each other. Bianca starts sobbing loudly. "I can't believe we've lost him. I'm not even sure if he's still alive… or worse, being tortured by Li," she says, weeping extensively for ten minutes until she is completely exhausted.

Chapter 21

Bianca was raised in a hard-working blue-collar family in the Sydney suburbs. She had gone through school with straight A's by studying hard and never compromising on her schoolwork. More often than not, she turned down her friends who wanted to party too much or didn't give enough considerations to the work that had to be done for school.

But Bianca always had an adventurous side. She regularly embarked on new or unusual adventures that she kept secret from her parents, especially her dad, whom she never wanted to disappoint. A man who would never get angry or raise his voice around the house, he would sometimes figure out what his dear Bianca was up to, give her a little hint that he knew what was going on, and she would admit everything. The support and the authentic bond with her father persisted over the years and allowed Bianca to become a strong and determined woman, unwilling to let other people dictate what she ought to do or think.

Bianca had a few lovers before Phil, who had admired her beauty and stood ready to promise her the moon, but turned out to be egotistic, came short of really supporting her, and weren't reliable when it mattered the most. One had even been slightly abusive, which had made Bianca guarded and skeptical of successful men that sometimes seemed too confident. When she met Phil, Bianca immediately liked his unassuming ways, his commitment, and realized that Phil would go to great lengths to protect her and make decisions that made sense for the both of them.

The morning following the container incident, when Bianca wakes up to the warmth and heartbeat of another human sleeping beside her. She believes, for a second, that all this was a nightmare and Phil is right there with his arms around her. But Bianca's eyes open to reveal Linda's perfectly manicured hands wrapping her body in a spooning position. She feels the sad emotions rushing back through her heart but holds back the tears, twists out from under Linda's hold and sits on the edge of the bed, her feet firmly planted on the ground.

For a moment, Bianca wonders how she was even able to sleep given last night's fiasco. As she turns to look at the clock on the night table, she sees her bottle of sleeping pills and remembers that Linda had her take a few to calm her down and put her to sleep, which probably explain her groggy state of mind. She leans forward, places both hands on her head and elbows on her knees, thinking about the days, weeks, maybe months to come of pain and sorrow. She starts shaking in her head in disgust of the pills and whatever else will be needed to control her emotions. Her thoughts shift to her dad, always encouraging her through life's challenges and hurdles.

"That's not how it's going to be," says Bianca loudly, hitting the night table with her fist, knocking the bottle of pills to the floor, and waking up Linda in a jolt.

"What is it honey? Come back here," says Linda in a comforting voice.

"No. I'm not going to let it happen this way," says Bianca as she stands up, and starts dressing. "I'm going to put up a fight." Bianca storms out of the bedroom.

She quickly moves through the living room and turns on all the equipment, awaking Dr. Debo, who quietly sits on the couch and puts on his thick glasses. Bianca dials up Agent Turner with a video call and turns up the volume to make sure that everyone in the apartment hears her determination.

"Good morning," says Agent Turner.

"Yeah whatever, same to you," replies Bianca in a very dry tone.

"I've been in communications with our U.S. office overnight to evaluate…" starts Agent Turner but gets interrupted.

"I don't care. We're going to find Phil on our own. With or without your help," says Bianca, knowing that she will have the full support of Tiago, Maria, Paul, Linda and Dr. Debo, without even asking. "Are you going to help us or stand in our way?" asks Bianca, as Tiago comes out of his bedroom and into the living room to support her.

"The FBI, umm, I mean we, are going to investigate Phil's disappearance just like we would do for any American citizen," replies Agent Turner with limited conviction.

"Yeah, that's what I thought. I'd like to remind you that he's also an FBI agent, and you trained him for a mission that got him captured. But you know what, never mind. We won't need you,

you'd just slow us down," says Bianca with fire in her eyes. "And you've got another agent right here," says Bianca with a hand on Tiago's shoulder, "so now you're going to hand over the recording that you illegally made last night. I want to hear what happened in the container when Phil was captured by Li. And whatever else happened after."

"Bianca, I know you're sad," says Agent Turner but Bianca interrupts again.

"NO! Enough! Stop your bull crap right there," shouts Bianca and pauses for five seconds to regain her composure. She takes a few deep breaths while the agent stays silent. "You're going to do as I say. You've messed up enough in this mission. Your judgment about the timing of Li's arrest was completely off. We could be sipping pina coladas on our yacht in Miami as we speak, with Li safely behind bars. So from now on, I'm calling the shots, and if you don't listen, I'm going to call the New York Times immediately to reveal the massive mess that you've created. I have nothing to lose. You can kiss whatever fame and celebrity cop status you've earned from taking down KexCorp goodbye. I'm going to make sure it all goes down the drain. Americans are going to love to see my face on all the talk shows, taking pleasure in exposing your incompetence. I'M going to be the celebrity now."

After pointing furiously at the screen, Bianca rests both hands on the desk and stares at Agent Turner, who is sitting comfortably with his arms crossed over his chest. They look at each other in silence for at least fifteen seconds, which makes Agent Turner increasingly uncomfortable. Bianca feels in control and wants him to blink first by torturing his weak mind.

"Alright, we'll send the recording to Tiago and help in any way we can," says Agent Turner. "Please continue the surveillance in case Li comes back."

"Thank you but Li is not going to come back here. He knows better. Once again, you are showing the limits of your intellectual capabilities," says Bianca as she hangs up the call.

Bianca turns to Tiago and asks him to be ready for another night of tailing whoever is going to show up at the booth today. Then, she orders Agent Fuller to search through the FBI database for all known acquaintances of Li in Singapore, Malaysia and Vietnam. Agent Fuller, who heard the shouting match with Agent Turner has no intention of contradicting Bianca, so he just nods an approval. In fact, everyone remains completely silent and would not dare to rebut any of Bianca's wishes after seeing the fury in her eyes.

Dr. Debo, who quietly watched the whole exchange between Bianca and Agent Turner from just a few feet away as he was waking up, mutters under his breath: "this was certainly The Rise of Bianca". Li certainly underestimated Bianca's resolve when he kidnapped Phil, thinks Dr. Debo. After a few moments, he joins Bianca by the window, watching the early morning foot traffic in front of the currency booth.

"My old body may not be of very good use to you, but I would be happy to contribute any intellect that you need to support the search. I owe my freedom to Phil and you. Would you like me to join you in the search of the city? I know Singapore quite well," whispers Dr. Debo, unsure whether Bianca wants the conversation to be heard by Agent Fuller.

"We might have a long drive, so I'd rather go alone with Tiago. Please stay here with the rest of the team, and keep tabs on Agent Fuller," says Bianca in a low voice, imperceptible to everyone else. Dr. Debo looks at her with a puzzling look at the mention of a long drive. Bianca stares at Dr. Debo in the eyes with an unusual intensity. Then, she pulls out her mobile phone and turns the screen towards Dr. Debo. It shows Phil's last recorded location as Kuala Lumpur: at the exact location where Norrid had offices. Dr. Debo keeps a poker face but is in total shock that Li took Phil to Malaysia.

"Why don't we just fly there and stay together?" suggests Dr. Debo, knowing that Phil's jet is stationed here in Singapore.

"I want you guys to have an easy exit route, with the jet, to the other side of the world in case anything worse happens. And I want you to keep a very close eye on Agent Fuller. I don't trust him. Please keep the team safely locked up in this apartment," concludes Bianca, still whispering.

Chapter 22

An hour later, Tiago receives the audio recording of Phil's encounter with Li in the shipping container. He plays it on a small speaker so that Bianca can hear. The stomp that knocked Phil out frightens her and she places her hands on her face, covering her eyes that are starting to tear up. But she quickly regains her composure and stands up while simultaneously hitting the table full of equipment with her palms.

"He's alive. Li spoke to Phil after the gunshot. And they just knocked him out with some metal object," says Bianca confidently, sporting an encouraging facial expression.

"Indeed. And knowing Li, he's going to want to bargain for something or make some threats, so most likely, he will keep Phil alive," says Dr. Debo.

"Let's hope so. Tiago, you and I will drive around the city using the FBI van to see what we can find. The rest of you, please monitor the booth and call me if you see Li," requests Bianca with an authority that no one dares to question. Maria stays quiet in the corner of the room, worried about more encounters between Li's thugs and her beloved Tiago.

A few minutes after they start driving, Bianca points to the side of the road. "There, Tiago. Stop in front of that rental car shop." Tiago parks the van near the curb and turns off the engine.

"What are we doing here?" he asks.

Bianca takes a deep breath. "Phil's phone is inside Norrid's former office in Kuala Lumpur, and that's where we're heading to."

Tiago nods. "I'm with you, so why are we stopping?"

She points to the shop again. "We need to use a rental car to avoid the FBI tracking us down. I'm done with them, to be honest. And I don't want them to know where we're going." Tiago looks at Bianca for a few seconds with mixed emotions.

"I know this is a lot to take in," Bianca says. "But it's the only way, and you know it." She points down the street. "There is a multi-level parking garage a block away. I'll leave the van there." She turns to Tiago. "Meanwhile, you rent a nice, nondescript sedan, and meet me there in, say, half and hour?"

He takes a deep breath, looking through the window of the shop. He's happy that Phil's potential location is narrowed down but driving across to Malaysia to rescue him means that he won't be protecting Maria for an extended period of time. He is her husband, and he should be there with her, especially in her tender condition. Things had been so much simpler before, when he was his own man. Responsibility is hard, but he needs to figure out a way to fulfill all of his duties. Not only to his wife and baby, but to his friends.

Without giving any sign of concurrence or acknowledgment to Bianca's plan, Tiago gets off the van and enters the shop, his mind wandering through a series of what ifs and the fear of potential regrets, were something going to happen to Maria and their unborn child. As he enters the shop, Bianca takes the driver's seat and drives the van away.

Tiago wonders whether there would be a way to bring his wife along or keep her closer to him. Perhaps he could contact some old acquaintances of Norrid to help with Maria's security while he's following Phil's trail. However, having been branded as a snitch probably eliminated any kind of goodwill that Tiago might have had with his former teammates from Norrid's enforcement division. So, Tiago's thoughts shift to Agent Fuller. Perhaps Paul and Dr. Debo can make sure that Agent Fuller stays on his game to protect Maria.

Bianca drives the van a few blocks away and leaves it in an underground parking garage, multiple levels below ground to prevent the FBI from easily tracking it. That way, it will take more time for the FBI to figure out that Bianca and Tiago are driving across the border to Malaysia. Bianca really doesn't trust that the FBI can help to rescue Phil. She thinks that they may actually do something that could again jeopardize a critical situation and drive Li to further hurt or even kill Phil.

Tiago picks up Bianca in front of the parking garage per their previous agreement.

"Let's go," orders Bianca after closing her door and wondering why Tiago is not driving off immediately.

He turns off the engine and looks at her. "We can't leave our friends without protection. I would suffer so much if something were to happen to my Maria," says Tiago in an unusually soft voice.

"I know but bringing them along will put them at an even greater risk. I think it's better if they stay locked up in the apartment and take off with the jet at a moment's notice," explains Bianca.

"You're right and I agree that the apartment is probably safe enough from criminals, but do you really trust the FBI?" asks Tiago.

"No but I trust that Dr. Debo would flag irregularities quick enough to make the whole team pack up and head to the airport precipitately," replies Bianca with a calm voice that surprises Tiago given the circumstances.

"Yeah, I guess," starts Tiago and pauses for a few seconds. "But only Agent Fuller would have sufficient training and abilities to physically defend the team. Obviously, Dr. Debo could only be leveraged for his intellectual capabilities. Maybe we should call Paul and Dr. Debo and make them scare the living hell out of Agent Fuller to make sure he truly protects our team from physical threats."

"Alright, start driving and I'll talk to Dr. Debo," commands Bianca.

***

Following Bianca's instructions, Paul and Dr. Debo sit with Agent Fuller on the roof top terrace of the apartment building and pass along the threats of physical harm by Tiago if Agent

Fuller were to fail to protect the team against any kind of danger that they would face. The agent remains relatively silent because he fully understands the perils potentially associated with contradicting Tiago, so he just nods in agreement. He anyway can't think of a situation where he wouldn't do his best to protect innocent civilians and feels confident that Agent Turner or anyone else at the FBI would think along the same lines. However, Agent Fuller is puzzled by the intensity of the warnings that he is receiving because he was under the impression that Tiago would be back relatively quickly.

"Hey, are Tiago and Bianca going to be back soon?" asks Agent Fuller as they are walking back down to the apartment.

"I'm not sure, why?" whispers Dr. Debo, not wanting to expose their conversation to Maria as they approach the front door of the apartment.

"Well, you guys are making it sound like I need to step in to defend the team because Tiago will be away for an extended period of time," says Agent Fuller innocently, then gets unexpectedly pushed and held against the wall by Paul.

"Listen, can't you see that we're trying to keep this conversation quiet from the ladies? If you can't step up to be a man and defend the team, tell us now and we're going to find someone else," whispers Paul with fire in his eyes.

"No, I get it. I'll take care of you guys," says Agent Fuller, still confused about the pushing and sudden intensity of the conversations.

Once inside the apartment, Agent Fuller pulls out his phone to alert Agent Turner of the situation. But Dr. Debo turns around just in time to see him and puts a hand over the phone's screen. "This is part of what we mean by protecting the team against any threats," says Dr. Debo, while gently taking Agent Fuller's phone from his hands and placing it on the table.

Agent Fuller stares at the back of his phone. He has to admit to himself that Agent Turner has made a lot of mistakes on this mission. Heck. Agent Fuller has made a lot of mistakes too, mostly at the request of Agent Turner. The truth is, though, that the FBI is supposed to protect people. Yes, American citizens, so it does not apply to everyone in this group. But still, these are people helping the cause. And he has to also admit, they would not be anywhere near as close to nailing Li without them. He nods to himself. Turner might not agree, but Fuller would do his duty. These people deserve the FBI's protection.

***

Meanwhile, Bianca and Tiago drive to Kuala Lumpur in a record time. Tiago's detailed knowledge of the roads separating these two populated areas allows him to keep them moving at optimal speed without the risk of an unfortunate encounter with the police. Unlike during his time with Norrid, Tiago now has an FBI badge that he could potentially use to get out of trouble, but actually flashing that badge may come at the cost of a police authority contacting the FBI for verification. Since they need to remain under the radar of the FBI for as long as possible, the badge will need to be used as a last resort.

As they approach the core downtown area of Kuala Lumpur, Bianca loses the location tracking of Phil's mobile phone. She presumes that the battery has died, its last charge having taken place approximately twenty-four hours prior.

They park the car in the garage of the KLCC shopping mall, located at the base of the Petronas Towers, less than five hundred feet from the office building where they believe Phil is being held. As they come up through the mall, they stop at a few stores to pick up their disguises: a maintenance crew looking overall for Tiago to make him look like an elevator repair man, some sexy clothes for Bianca to seduce and soften up the security guards, and other equipment that Tiago will need for the rescue efforts.

Walking as normally as possible, with Bianca a few steps behind Tiago, they quickly scan the lobby to determine if their plan has some legs. They need to get access to a service door that Tiago had used a few years ago to install surveillance equipment for Norrid. If all the wires are still in place, Tiago is confident that he can get a visual into Norrid's former offices. Out of all the possible places they were aware of, that was the most likely place where Phil might be held.

"Good afternoon Ahmad, long time no see. I love how you brushed your hair today," says Bianca with a flirtatious smile as she approaches the front desk and places a hand on Ahmad's shoulder and gives him a kiss on the cheek. "Ah, this is so heavy," says Bianca as she winces a little to appear like she is struggling to roll her carry-on size luggage, which contains two small tanks of sleeping gas that can be released remotely. And the shell of the luggage is equipped with hidden cameras and audio transmitters.

"Oh mam, it is so good to see you again," says Ahmad, blushing, fumbling his words and visibly becoming uncomfortable in front of Bianca. "Let me help you with your luggage. It's been a long time since we've seen you here, I was starting to worry."

"You're so sweet Ahmad. I've been working mostly from Singapore the past few months. You know, we were just talking about you the other day," lies Bianca. "So diligent in everything you do. Anyway, could you take my luggage to the 42nd floor and leave it by the reception. I'll be there in a minute. I just need to let this technician into the service area to make sure that all the safety equipment is in place before the fire department comes in for the inspection," says Bianca, holding Ahmad's arm for a few seconds, as if they were going on a date, then slowly letting go.

Ahmad is confused for a second as he had not heard about an inspection. But he is not about to contradict the beautiful Bianca, who has been the talk amongst the security guards since the first day she walked into the building with Phil, almost two years ago. Ahmad feels like he's now going to be the hero amongst his peers for being the first to befriend Bianca.

Bianca and Tiago enter the service area behind the main desk of the lobby. While Bianca stays by the door to slow down any potential visitor, Tiago walks confidently towards a control box and punches in a four-digit sequence that unlocks a panel. "Too easy," he mumbles under his breath. "They didn't even bother to change the passcodes." Then he hooks up a small screen and obtains visual on the 42nd floor, and quickly flips through a dozen of images to get a sense of the security detail that they will be up against.

"Here's Li," says Tiago loud enough for Bianca to hear. So, she leaves her post to get a close look at the screen that Tiago hooked up.

"Do you see Phil anywhere?" asks Bianca anxiously. "This office has in-office suites, right? Look into the bedrooms."

"We didn't install cameras in the bedrooms, we're not that creepy," says Tiago with a half-smile as he keeps flipping the images.

"Wait, go back," says Bianca pointing at the screen. "Is that…?" Her gut clenches, staring at the screen. "Oh my god, this can't be right." Her head swivels as she stares at a ghost from their past. A man that is supposed to be in jail.

Chapter 23

Bianca is sitting on the ground with her hands on her face while Tiago is carefully scanning the rest of the 42nd floor and using the surveillance equipment mounted on the luggage, now in the waiting area of the floor's reception, to assess the number of people that he is going to have to deal with. He is waiting for a good moment to release the gas and put everyone to sleep.

"I don't know why you're so surprised. These men have powerful connections," says Tiago as he continues to work through the video feeds.

"I'm sure they do, but if we can't even rely on the authorities to keep people like Ernesto long enough behind bars, how are we ever going to be in peace? And how was he able to make his way from the US to here?" asks Bianca. After witnessing Phil's misery, and her own, from having to launder money for Norrid under the direction of Ernesto, Bianca had been happy to see Ernesto convicted of enough white collar crimes to ensure that his sentence would be longer that his life expectancy. Who in their right mind would let such criminal walk out of prison. Or, could he have escaped? Thinks Bianca with her hands still covering her face.

"My only instrument of peace is the 9mm pistol that I carry with me at all times. I highly recommend that you do the same. You could easily conceal it in your purse or in a thigh holster under your dress or skirt. It'd be quite sexy actually," says Tiago while raising his eyebrows and nodding in Bianca's direction.

"Tiago, I liked you better when we were sailing quietly in the Caribbean Sea. You didn't carry a pistol while we were sailing. Actually, you weren't focused on weapons at all at that time. Anyway, as for myself, I'd rather rely on my charm," says Bianca, earning a look a disapproval from Tiago. "Are we ready to roll?"

"Yes mam. To make sure that nobody sees us roaming around the floor, I'll discontinue the video feed for 30 minutes. And I'll initiate the gas. There you go. Now let's get up there," says Tiago.

On the ride up the elevator, Tiago hands a gas mask to Bianca and a stack of tie-wraps. "Put the mask on immediately. And we'll have to tie everybody that we encounter to neutralize them in case they wake up too quickly. Hopefully they'll be asleep throughout the extraction process, but stay on your guard, these guys might be equipped with masks too – or guns. Or both, which could make this quite volatile," says Tiago with a stern military-like voice.

When they arrive on the 42nd floor, a thick white smoke already fills the air. The receptionist is asleep, hands on her desk. So, Bianca proceeds to tie her wrists and ankles while Tiago opens the luggage slightly and pushes it to the middle of the floor to help the dispersion of the gas.

They walk low and head straight to the office in which Tiago saw Li on the video screen. He wants to confront his security guards before they potentially have a chance to reach for a gas mask. Suddenly a man in a suit, who is lying on the ground, affected by the gas, grabs Bianca's ankle and she emits a muffled yell for help. Tiago quickly turns around and swings a violent hook punch to the man's temple, which knocks him unconscious.

Bianca's hands are shaking nervously, her fine motor skills not allowing her to handle the tie-wrap job on the man.

"Go back to the reception and hide under the desk, I've got this," orders Tiago as he ties up the man.

"No, I'm okay. I'll hide if I need to. For now, I want to keep going," pleads Bianca, hoping to find Phil somewhere in the office. And they start moving again.

The smoke is so thick that they see less than two feet in front of them. Tiago keeps Bianca behind him as they hug a long wall and move slowly, limiting the directions from which someone could attack them from. Tiago stops in a flash when he sees the hand of a security guard appear in front of him. The hand is out in front, moving left and right while the man is covering his whole face with a thick sweater using his other hand. Tiago grabs the guard's hand to perform an arm's lock, swiftly getting him to the ground with his elbow and shoulder overextended. The sweater doesn't remain into place, so the man's body goes numb when the gas fully enters his respiratory system. Seconds after he hits the floor. Tiago grabs the man's gun from his belt and hands it over to Bianca. "Keep this, for now. Finger off the trigger at all times unless you really intend to fire."

When they finally reach the office where Li is located, they look through the floor-to-ceiling glass wall and find Li in his underwear, with tissues over his nose and mouth. He is trying to isolate himself from the gas and used most of his clothes to block the fumes that are seeping through the gap below the door.

Li's eyes lock with Tiago's. Li hasn't seen Tiago for more than a year, but he is not surprised to see that he's attempting to rescue Phil. Fidgety and in panic mode, Li stops for one second to look at Bianca. He smiles nervously while attempting to cover his old-men underwear. Li has always been weak for Bianca, so exposing his skinny and lightly covered body to her makes him feel somewhat uncomfortable. When Li suddenly moves to retrieve his gun from the closet, Tiago, in a single move, drives his elbow to shatter the glass and extend his arm to point his gun at Li's head.

"Stop right there, it'd be unfortunate to stain this beautiful rug with blood pouring from a hole in your head," says Tiago, cold blooded. "I only need some information from you. Then, I won't hesitate to put an end to your miserable existence. In the meantime though, I'd be happy to help with those knee issues that have been bothering you for years. A well-placed bullet could solve all kinds of arthritis or other tightness in your joints, you know," continues Tiago with a smile, his voice muffled by his mask, now pointing his gun towards Li's legs.

"It's so funny how your brain has always been in a permanent malfunction, floating through all the swelling from all the beatings my men gave to you. And there's more suffering coming for you and Phil. I'd cut my losses if I were you because you have no idea what you've gotten yourself into. In fact, you're even missing the big picture here..." says Li as he falls to the ground, no longer able to block the smoke from entering his lungs.

"Tie him up and stay here while I look for Ernesto," orders Tiago.

"But wait, what did he mean by big picture?" asks Bianca.

"I don't know but we don't have time to solve a riddle right now. Wait for me here," replies Tiago as he quickly leaves the room.

Bianca moves Li's numb body with difficulty to tie up his wrists and ankles. She is still wondering what he meant by 'big picture'. There must be some grand plan going on, which Li is part of. After seeing Ernesto on the video feed, Bianca feels like nothing would surprise her anymore. Are there more sinister people from the defunct Norrid still roaming around that would have incentives to hurt Phil, she wonders. She feels sick to her stomach that Phil might have possibly walked into a trap set by Li. Or even worse, what if the FBI set the trap or, Agent Turner fell into a trap set by Li? These thoughts are like a whirlwind in Bianca's mind.

Chapter 24

Tiago continues to move around the office, searching every room and suite. But nobody else is on the floor, so he makes his way back to Bianca.

"No sign of Phil. And Ernesto must have escaped when we released the gas," says Tiago.

"You GOTTA be kidding," shouts Bianca while shaking her head, with emotions creeping back up and tears filling her eyes. Ernesto ends up being more slippery than all the hair product he's used in the past. Her hopes to easily find the man that haunted Phil and her for so long, just lying on the floor from the gas' intoxication, were crushed.

"No time for this, let's go," says Tiago sharply as he grabs Li's numb body by his tied wrists and lifts him up over his shoulder.

The smoke is starting to dissipate and it's now possible to see across the floor. Tiago worries that anyone could now come onto the floor without being affected by the remaining gas. One of Li's thugs, who might have escaped with Ernesto to another floor, could come back to try to save Li, thinks Tiago. So, they run towards the staircase.

"Walk down two floors, then take the elevator to the lobby and execute the rest of the plan," Tiago tells Bianca. He grabs her mask and the gun that she had been nervously holding for the last twenty minutes.

Bianca starts walking down the stairs, looking back at Tiago with a distressed look. She had hoped that this part of the plan would involve walking out of the building with Phil. All they have now is Li as a possible bargaining chip. Tiago looks back at her and pauses for a few seconds. "Don't worry, we'll get him back. Now hurry back to the car," says Tiago as he places Li's body on the floor to seal his mouth shut with heavy duty tape to avoid that he starts screaming when he wakes up. Tiago is trying to keep Bianca's spirits up, but he knows that escaping with Li, and probably torturing him, is absolutely crucial to be able to recover Phil, and will not be as easy of a task as he makes it sound to Bianca.

Tiago places Li's body back onto his shoulder and starts walking up the stairs. When he reaches the 46th floor, he hears the clicking sound of the metal door being opened on the floor below. He freezes for a moment to avoid making any noise that would reveal his presence and grabs the ramp to hold his balance. He hears the heavy footsteps of overweight men that he presumes are Li's security guards. When they start chatting about the smoke that engulfed the 42nd floor, Tiago confirms his suspicions but sees limited danger as they seem to be walking back down.

Tiago keeps his balance to wait for the men to be far enough before continuing his climb. When the last man seems to have started his descent, Tiago peeks over the ramp to check that the thugs have all dissipated, but unfortunately, his eyes lock with Ernesto, who is a few steps behind Li's security guards, dressed in his trademark Italian fitted expensive suit and tie.

Tiago pulls out his gun and starts running up the stairs. Ernesto moves to a side and is able to catch a quick glimpse. He sees that Tiago is carrying a body over his shoulder. "Tiago, wait! Come back. I'm sure we can resolve this together," pleads Ernesto, using a friendly appeal to Tiago, reminiscent of their years of working together at Norrid.

Racing to the roof carrying an additional 150 pounds on his shoulder, Tiago can hear the footsteps and heavy breathing of at least four to five men behind him. Although Tiago has to carry the extra weight, the security detail's lack of conditioning slows down the pursuit and makes everyone move at similar speeds. Therefore, Tiago is able to keep a little more than a floor of distance, reducing the risk that they can shoot at him. They would also risk hitting Li if a random gunshot were fired.

The 53rd floor provides roof access, but Tiago is met by a locked metal door. Wasting no time, he kicks the door open in a violent movement, and once outside, he forcefully swings the door back onto the first thug in pursuit, knocking him unconscious, and slowing down the rest of them.

Tiago quickly runs over to the building's window cleaning platform, which is suspended off the building with a small crane unit attached to the roof. Tiago throws Li's body into the platform's cage a few feet below, which wakes him up and he starts panicking when he suddenly finds himself perched at 600 feet above the ground. His cries for help, however, are muffled by the heavy tape rolled around his mouth and the back of his head.

Still on the roof, Tiago hides behind a metal structure and starts exchanging fire with the thugs. He is able to injure most of them with precise aiming to shoulders and arms to neutralize their ability to shoot at him, so that he can start making his way back to the ground onto the window cleaning platform. He also doesn't want to kill them, to avoid that the Malaysia police brings the whole city to a lockdown. A few non-life-threatening well-placed bullets may not even be a cause for a concern at a local hospital.

"Hold you fire," shouts Ernesto as he steps onto the roof. He thought he would be saving Tiago from being killed but he quickly realizes that all of the men that were supporting his security are no longer able to hold firearms. Instead, they are all on the floor in agony, holding their bloodied arms close to their chest.

"Hands in the air Ernesto, and step forward," orders Tiago. "I will not hesitate to use deadly force at the first sight of a sudden move," continues Tiago as if he were a military commander in a nuclear submarine.

"Tiago, we're on the same side, why are you doing this?" whispers Ernesto, trying to avoid that Li's thugs hear their conversation. And he slowly raises his hands above his head.

"Not anymore. Turn around, get on your knees and place your hands on your head," says Tiago firmly.

Ernesto complies with the instructions but keeps murmuring vague insinuations of dangers to Tiago as he ties up his wrists and ankles, and tapes his mouth shut. Ernesto is still trying to communicate with Tiago while he quickly searches him for weapons, phone, panic buttons or anything else that could spell trouble down the road. Ernesto's voice is so muffled that Tiago only hears something about the FBI. He figures that they'll have time to debrief all of that later, so he grabs Ernesto and drops him into the window cleaning platform, on top of Li.

Tiago then swiftly moves the platform on the side of the building which he believes is less exposed to the street and jumps into the platform. Both Li and Ernesto move their bodies around the platform, like bacon in a frying pan, in an effort to resist their capture, and testing the efficiency of the tie wraps used by Tiago. "Gentlemen, don't waste your energy just yet, you won't have an escape route until we get to the ground," says Tiago with a smile as he lowers the platform by operating the control switch that is attached to the metal cage.

Sitting in the car a block away, Bianca watches as the platform descends and awaits the perfect moment to place the car underneath it. Tiago gives her the signal by raising his arm in the air and she starts driving. At the exact moment that the platform reaches its lowest possible level, Bianca rolls in and opens the car's sunroof. Tiago unloads and lowers each of his two prisoners onto the back seat, one lying on the ground and the other across the full back seat. Bianca is surprised to see that Tiago also brought Ernesto along. "Good to see you Ernesto," she says with a wide smile in testament to the increased chances of recovering Phil.

Tiago jumps to the ground and takes the driver's seat as Bianca quickly moves to the front passenger seat. "Seatbelt gentlemen," jokes Tiago, looking at his prisoners through the rear-view mirror. "This is going to be a long ride." With their uncomfortable ties, the two captured passengers protest Tiago's attempted humor with a muffled senseless grumble.

Chapter 25

Well sedated and tied up for the night in separate but connecting rooms of a cheap hotel on the side of the highway connecting Kuala Lumpur to Singapore, Li and Ernesto's limbs are tied to the four corners of the beds.

After a few hours of sleeping in alternating shifts, Tiago and Bianca agree to play a 'good cop, bad cop' routine on Li, starting with a short and awakening waterboarding. They leave Ernesto asleep in the other room for the time being.

"Pfffss... what do you want?" asks Li, still in his underwear, as he coughs out the water that Tiago poured down his throat for five seconds.

"You know, it's pretty amazing what one can learn in the U.S. military," says Tiago with a wide smile, looking at Li directly in his eyes. They then both turn to Bianca who sports a disapproving look, her arms crossed over her chest.

"Yeah, no wonder you're such a dummy," says Li but gets rewarded with a painful strangulation that Tiago easily performs with just his index and thumb tightly wrapped around Li's slim neck. His face turns blue in just a few seconds.

"Enough, stop that!" yells Bianca and swiftly places a hand on Tiago's shoulder, who releases the tension and moves a few feet off the bed.

"You know that I'm not in favor of violence. Just tell us Phil's location and we'll let you go," pleads Bianca with a flirtatious voice, while passing her fingers through Li's thin hair.

"I don't know..." replies Li, still coughing from the irritation brought to his throat by the waterboarding and the strangulation. "I can't breathe with my arms stretched like this. I'm an old man, you have to loosen up those ties," continues Li, trying to take advantage of Bianca's kindness.

"No way," replies Tiago. "I very much enjoy giving you a taste of your own medicine. I've been waiting to turn the tables on you for far too long, you sick old man."

"Look, I'm sure we can work a way out of this. Maybe we could loosen one of your four ties for each piece of valuable information that you are nice enough to give us. How does this sound?" asks Bianca.

Li's head lolls back. He breathes deeply staring at the ceiling. "Okay... I brought Phil to a small airport. I don't know where they took him," says Li with a few more desperate breaths, gasping for air with his lungs squeezed by the overextension of his arms.

"That's a start, yeah, you know that's very helpful," says Bianca while directing Tiago to loosen up the tie for one of Li's arms, which he does. Now able to bring his elbow closer to his body, Li is slightly more comfortable and can take a decent breath. "See, we can work together. Do you remember when we met in Australia? You also had me in an uncomfortable position hanging from the ceiling, and Phil ended up creating Equit for you. I'm sure we can collaborate again," says Bianca, with a hand on Li's chest to attempt maximum collaboration. "Now, what else can you tell me, so that we can retrieve Phil?"

"I remember when we met," says Li with a slight smile and his eyes closed, enjoying the peaceful moment with Bianca. "You're the only one that I never wanted to hurt; you know? I really didn't want to do this to you back in Australia but it was the only way to secure Phil's collaboration," whispers Li, faintly looking at Bianca with tears of pain rolling down the side of his head.

Bianca cringes, ignoring the tears. Did Li think this admission made what he did to her okay? How could he say he *didn't want to hurt her, but had to hurt her anyway so he could make money* and think she would understand and be okay with this?

"I know." She takes a deep breath, steadying herself. "But now, you really need to give me something else to secure *your* collaboration, otherwise Tiago is going to take over again. And I guess you guys have old scores to settle, so it's not like you would get a quick death, right?" asks Bianca in a soft voice.

"Alright, look, I only took Phil with me as a hostage the other night to make sure that you guys didn't start shooting through the containers. But hours later, I was contacted by Ernesto to deliver Phil to that airport for a large sum of cash. His guys took Phil. And I met Ernesto at Norrid's old office to get my money. It was a no brainer to me. I really don't know why these guys wanted Phil so much. I swear, I don't even care that you guys probably took money from me for God knows what reason. I'll just print some more..." explains Li as he closes his eyes with a faint smile, hoping to finally rest peacefully.

Bianca looks at Tiago with a puzzled look and waves for him to loosen up the ties for Li's other arm. Bianca wonders how Ernesto could possibly know that Phil had been captured by Li. And why would Ernesto, who was supposed to be behind bars in the U.S., would want to pay a ransom for Phil. "Keep an eye on him. No more torture for the moment," orders Bianca to Tiago. And she moves to the other room to work on Ernesto.

Ernesto is still asleep and producing a loud snore. He is fully dressed up in the suit and tie that he was wearing yesterday, with his arms and legs tied up at the four corners of the bed. Bianca looks at him in disgust. She remembers how he always wanted to look like the good guy, trying to facilitate good relations amongst everyone, even with Li's organization despite all the incidents of violence. But now she sees the real evil behind Ernesto. Full of anger and ready to make him pay for orchestrating the kidnapping of the man she loves, Bianca jumps on top of Ernesto, a knee on his chest, pulls on one end of his tie and squeezes the knot to tighten a chokehold.

"Urrrghh.. stop, I can't breathe," whispers Ernesto as he wakes up to the reduced air reaching his lungs.

"You're a real monster, you know. At least with Li, we always knew that he was malicious. Behind your nice suit and polite manners, there really is a monster ready to hurt people," yells Bianca while holding Ernesto's tie in a tight grip.

"Phil snitched on his family, we had no choice," says Ernesto slowly as if he's dying. Bianca releases the hold, removes the tie completely to let Ernesto breathe. She moves slowly to the side of the bed and sits down with her hands covering her face.

"Ernesto, you're absolutely disgusting. All that you're capable of is hurting people," says Bianca in a low and demoralized voice, then pauses to regain her composure. "Where is Phil?" continues Bianca, still sitting in the same position.

"I honestly don't know. And trust me, orders like that come from people way above my pay grade," replies Ernesto gently, still recovering from his near-death experience.

Tiago, who was observing both Li and Ernesto from the doorway in between the two connecting rooms, steps up near Bianca and motions to ask her to move aside. Then he stands on the bed on either side of Ernesto's body and grabs him by the belt as if it was a weight at the gym. This raises Ernesto's middle section upwards, stretching his arms and legs backwards in a painful position because his wrists and ankles are still attached to the corners of the bed. Ernesto winces from the pain.

"What were the next steps of your plan?" asks Tiago in a loud and commanding voice.

"Ehh..." starts Ernesto but stops for a few seconds, earning him enhanced stretching from Tiago. "Okay, okay, I was heading to California," says Ernesto with pain, his head swinging backwards. "I was going to meet people in San Francisco, who were assigned to handle Phil. They should have picked him up by now."

"Good. We're going with you to San Francisco," says Tiago as he releases Ernesto's body back onto the mattress. "You work for us now."

Tiago pulls out his phone and calls Agent Fuller. "Get the whole team onto the jet. And not a word to Agent Turner, if you want to remain healthy. Do the right thing for once in your life." Then, Tiago calls Sergio to fly everybody over to Kuala Lumpur.

Chapter 26

Tiago drives the car onto the tarmac, all the way to the jet to avoid that anyone sees him board Li and Ernesto onto the plane with their hands tied and a hood on their heads. For the safety of the team, Tiago wants to avoid that Li and Ernesto see their faces, especially Maria and Linda, who should still be completely unknown to the criminal organizations, so keeping the hoods on his prisoners' heads for most of the trip is imperative.

Maria is waiting impatiently for Tiago to come onboard to hug him tightly. While Tiago handles his prisoners, she looks at him with piercing eyes and with her hands on her hips as if she were going to scold him.

Moments later, Bianca watches as Maria inspect Tiago's body for any harm or injury, and smiles because that's exactly what she does to Phil after every time he leaves her alone to go off and do something crazy. She smiles to herself... Phil must be rubbing off on her, because she has just done something crazy. Thank goodness she's had better luck than Phil.

Maria notices that Tiago is tired and exhausted and places a hand on his face and rubs his forehead. "*Mi Amor*, you need to rest," says Maria softly. Tiago shakes his head and signals for her, Linda and Agent Fuller to remain silent. He wants them to remain completely unknown to Li and Ernesto.

With his prisoners sitting comfortably in the first row and looking towards the front of the aircraft, Tiago closes the door and goes into the cockpit to discreetly tell Sergio to depart for San Francisco. "Okay, but we'll need a refueling stop in Hawaii," replies Sergio.

Tiago cringes. That would waste a lot of time, but he understands that the plane needs fuel. "Do what you need to do, but we need to get to California as soon as possible."

He spins, leaves the cockpit and returns to the cabin. His prisoners sift uncomfortably in their seats. Li is shaking like he might be crying under that hood. Good. He deserves to be scared for once in his life. Then, Tiago addresses Ernesto sternly, raising his hood and handing Ernesto his phone.

"Call whoever you were supposed to meet upon your arrival in San Francisco and say that you're delayed a bit and you'll be there in approximately eighteen hours. And ask for Phil's whereabouts. Ask for a proof that he is still alive," orders Tiago. "You gotta sound casual. And no foul play, if you want to keep all your toes and fingers," whispers Tiago into Ernesto's ear to avoid Maria hearing him using these threatening words.

Ernesto, head down, looks at the phone for several long seconds, then at Tiago with pity eyes. They both remember the time when Tiago was protecting Ernesto. He would have taken a bullet for him. Ernesto makes a plea to Tiago with his eyes for a chance to escape this. Ernesto knows that he is stuck between a rock and a hard place. By going along with Tiago's plan, he will be ambushing the people that he is meeting in San Francisco, which will label him as a traitor. And if he doesn't, he knows that Tiago won't hesitate to use physical force to get what he wants. Ernesto looks down again and closes his eyes.

"Make the call. We both know that you're cornered. If you prefer, you can spend a painful eighteen hours with broken fingers or dislocated limbs with no medical attention, and still lead me where I need to go upon arrival," says Tiago, pulling Ernesto's hair to move his head upwards and gaze through his soul. Ernesto seems lifeless. Tiago lets go of his hair and squats down to adopt a friendlier style. "Look, I don't know how you got out of jail, but I'll help you get back in safely. I promise. This may save you from some of the pain associated with having helped us. I can even try to get you to a lower security prison with no former members of Norrid," continues Tiago, flashing his FBI badge to add credentials to his statement about returning him safely to prison.

"Interesting," says Ernesto, raising his eyebrows and moving his head back at the sight of the FBI badge. He moves his head to the left and notices that Li is sitting right beside him, then looks back at Tiago and tighten his lips. "Alright," continues Ernesto as he slowly dials up one of the contacts on his phone with his hands still tightly tied up. Tiago presses on the speaker phone feature before Ernesto has time to take the phone to his ear. Bianca is standing right behind in order to hear any details about Phil's well-being.

"Hi. It's about time you called," says the voice coming out of Ernesto's phone. Tiago perks up and looks at Bianca. The voice is strangely familiar to Tiago. It must be someone who was associated with the defunct Norrid.

"Hey Arturo, sorry I've been tied up the last few hours," says Ernesto, earning a dirty look from Tiago who is not appreciating Ernesto's choice of humor given the circumstances. But Tiago now recognizes the voice. Arturo used to be in charge of Norrid's street resellers in the U.S. "I'll be there in about eighteen hours. How's our prisoner?" asks Ernesto, as casual as possible.

"I don't know why you're asking this kind of question right now. You're breaking protocol," says Arturo, clearly unhappy with a question regarding the prisoner.

"Yeah, well, I need a current proof of life," says Ernesto with the hesitation of a teenager that just got busted, which Tiago perceives as risky, so he shakes Ernesto's shoulders and gives him a stern look. "I have my orders. Just do as I say, and keep him alive and well," continues Ernesto with more conviction.

"Fine, I'll text it to you. Give me a minute," concludes Arturo and hangs up.

Bianca stands in front of Ernesto with his phone in her hand, waiting for the picture. When it finally arrives, Bianca offers a faint smile with the relief that Phil is alive, sitting on a bed and holding a copy of today's San Francisco Chronicle. Her mood quickly changes to anger, however, when she zooms in and realizes that Phil's face is swelled up and bruised. With tears in her eyes and her lips shaking, she looks at Ernesto in disgust. And in an uncharacteristic act of violence, she slaps his face with the back of her hand, whipping his head against the headrest and causing a stream of blood to run from his mouth.

"I would have understood this kind of senseless torturing of Phil if it came from the piece of crap sitting beside you," says Bianca pointing at Li. "But after all we did for you, Ernesto…" continues Bianca but gets interrupted.

"I told you earlier, Phil became a dangerous snitch, which cannot be tolerated by our organization. I warned you guys to never turn against your family," says Ernesto with a soft voice, still wincing from the pain of the slap, and moving his jaw and cheeks in relief of the burning sensation.

"We never asked to work for you. You coerced us to commit crimes for Norrid's benefit. And you guys created a monstrous mess by going out to buy Goang. You blew the whole thing. We had no choice but to collaborate with the police, you idiot," yells Bianca, but immediately regrets sharing so much information in front of the team, and Li, still sitting quietly right beside Ernesto.

"Ok enough," says Tiago as he puts the hood back onto Ernesto's head, embraces Bianca into a hug to calm her down and takes Ernesto's phone to examine the picture of Phil.

Bianca collapses onto the plane's bed, crying heavily. Maria and Linda join her and the three of them hold each other tightly. "This is awful, how did we get ourselves into this mess? We need to get him back and disappear again," says Bianca, completely exhausted and barely audible given all of her weeping. Linda reaches for a wet cloth to place on Bianca's head to cool her off and help her fall asleep. Bianca takes a few deep breaths to calm herself down. She knows that she needs to be strong and more composed than what she just displayed. If the other girls also start freaking out, it may make it even harder to keep headed in the right direction and save Phil before it's too late… Bianca really wants to get her head back into the game.

While the plane is taking-off, Tiago's mobile phone starts ringing. He hurriedly pulls it out to silence it and avoid stressing out the ladies. It's Agent Turner.

"Yes sir, what can I do for you?" asks Tiago in an innocent voice, covering his phone with his hand and looking towards the window to avoid that the sound of the aircraft's engines reach through the microphone.

"Where are you guys heading to?" asks Agent Turner, visibly unhappy about something.

"Back to the apartment, why?" lies Tiago as he looks towards Agent Fuller with an accusatory look. But Agent Fuller raises his hands innocently to indicate that he didn't reveal anything.

"What is going..." starts Agent Turner but the reception is lost on Tiago's phone as the plane is already a few hundred feet in the air.

"It seems like he knew that we were flying out," says Tiago looking alternatively at Dr. Debo and Agent Fuller. "Could he be tracking us?"

"Possible. But it's also possible that he noticed that the jet wasn't in Singapore anymore, or tracked the jet with the air-traffic-control system," says Dr. Debo.

"I guess we may have FBI visitors upon landing in San Francisco," says Tiago as he picks up the intercom phone. "Hey Sergio, when we get really close to California, please change the landing site to a remote airport like Oakland or San Jose," continues Tiago, leveraging one of the careful lessons learned from Phil.

Chapter 27

Landing in San Jose, just 45 minutes south of San Francisco, ends up being the perfect way to escape the fifteen agents that Agent Turner has mobilized to greet Tiago, Bianca and the rest of the team at the San Francisco airport. The last-minute request to air-traffic-control for a change of landing location, however, raised alarm bells for the U.S. Customs and Border Protection ("CBP"). Sergio warns Tiago that a CBP officer would come in for a thorough investigation.

"Not a word out of your mouths, I'll do all the talking," says Tiago to Li and Ernesto, while removing their hoods, a few seconds before opening the cabin door.

"Good morning everyone," says the CBP agent as he boards the jet.

"Good morning," says Tiago, immediately showing his FBI badge to the CBP agent. "We have two fugitives on this plane with no travel documents. I am taking them into custody. You're more than welcome to review the passports of the rest of the passengers and crew, but please hurry," says Tiago as if he was conducting a military procedure.

"We were not informed that fugitives were being brought in today from another country. We have extradition procedures…" says the CBP agent but gets interrupted by Tiago.

"These men operate large drug cartels and money laundering operations. We never telegraph the movements of such dangerous men in advance. Plus, they have friendly operatives in this area, and we were informed that your agency might have been infiltrated by those criminals, so we couldn't risk announcing our arrival in advance. That is also why we changed the landing location at the last minute," explains Tiago, then pauses. "I respect that you have a job to do, so do it now, we need to leave in less than ten minutes," adds Tiago, earning a puzzled look from the CPB agent.

"I guess that makes sense," says the CPB agent as he moves through the aircraft, looks at the two prisoners with disgust and continues to check the passports of the other passengers.

Meanwhile, Bianca keeps a close eye on Agent Fuller, who has been nervously checking his phone every 30 seconds since the plane touched ground. After he also shows his badge to the CPB agent, it seems that Agent Fuller is about to type something on his phone, so Bianca gives him a nudge with her elbow.

"Don't do it. You're going to put Phil in danger again. Keep absolute radio silence," whispers Bianca as she snatches his phone from his hands.

"Agent Turner is on our side, we can trust him," pleads Agent Fuller.

"Really? Don't you find it odd that you guys have been sent to Singapore to arrest Li but Agent Turner has gone out of his way for that not to happen?" asks Bianca in a tone similar to a mother talking to her teenage son.

"Well, criminal organizations are complex. There are some very smart and experienced people leading the FBI operations," says Agent Fuller, but not very convincingly because he has also been wondering why the mission's ultimate objective keeps getting slowed down.

"Smart and experienced, huh? So smart that they needed Phil to help connect the dots between Norrid and KexCorp? So experienced that they needed Phil to join as an agent to help make Li come out of hiding?" asks Bianca sarcastically.

Curious about what the agents have been texting to each other, Bianca scrolls through the dozens of messages that Agent Fuller received from Agent Turner, who has been asking for a status report since prior to their departure from Malaysia. Given the repeated one-direction texting and querying by Agent Turner and the lack of answer by Agent Fuller's, Bianca feels confident that Agent Turner was not informed that they've landed in San Jose. Unless of course the FBI has a direct connection into the air-traffic-control system, which Bianca finds quite plausible. She knows that they really need to get out of the airport vicinity though. Bianca turns off Agent Fuller's phone to avoid possible tracking, and drops it into her purse, generating a soft resistance and an annoyed look from the agent. "Come on, can I get my phone back?" asks Agent Fuller, but Bianca brushes him off. Then, she puts some bright red lipstick and gets up to handle the situation with the CBP agent.

"Hey, do you need anything else? It's just that we're kind of in a hurry," says Bianca with a smile, showing her beautiful blue eyes, while rubbing the CBP agent on the shoulder. She thinks that the young agent could be easily influenced in order to let the group quickly get off the plane.

"Well, mam, humm…" says the CBP agent, thinking about an answer. "We need to bring the fugitives in for verification."

"Really? Didn't you already check the badges of the officers? Look, if this takes too much time, you may jeopardize these men's arrests over some procedures. And remember that we have evidence that someone in your office is dirty and will get these monsters back on the street. You wanna have that on your conscience after we've put so much effort into arresting them? Wouldn't you rather be one of the great civil servants that ensured that these bad boys are put behind bars?" asks Bianca, now with her hand on the CBP agent's forearm.

"Well, you know, it's just that…" says the CPB agent but gets interrupted by Bianca.

"I'll tell you what, take pictures of the FBI badges and the license plate of the car that we're going to rent with your phone. That way, if something goes wrong after we leave, the FBI will be able to track us," says Bianca with the utmost confidence.

"Okay, I guess that makes sense. But mam, who are you exactly?" asks the CPB agent.

"Oh sorry, I should have introduced myself. I'm an intelligence consultant and help the Five Eyes to find and arrest international criminals in my homeland of Australia. I'm sure you noticed my accent, right?" says Bianca with surprising credibility, still trying to soften up the CPB agent.

"Alright. Welcome to the United States. I look forward to read about all this in the newspaper," concludes the CPB agent with a smile before stepping off the aircraft.

As Tiago prepares to get off the plane with most of the team, he turns to Linda and Maria. "I need the two of you to stay with the aircraft for the time being to remain safe."

"But..." Maria starts.

Tiago holds up his hand. "No buts." He cups her cheek. "You are more important than anything." He places his hand on her belly. "You, and our baby." He turns to Linda. "Keep her safe for me."

Linda nods, blushing over the display. "Yes, of course."

Thank goodness they both looked like they would comply. "I also want you to continue to avoid visual contact with Li and Ernesto. I don't want them to be able to identify either of you when this is all over."

Linda places her arms around Maria's shoulder, nodding. "I absolutely understand." Then, to Maria, "Let's go get something to eat."

Tiago makes his way to the cockpit and looks out over the tarmac as he addresses Sergio. "I want you to fly the jet to a nearby unmonitored field without filing a flight plan." While this is unusual for a jet but possible nonetheless, Sergio understands the value of remaining under the radar, literally, of the US authorities.

Tiago makes his way back to the women and kisses Maria quickly. "I will see you soon." Then he quickly gets off the aircraft before she can object again.

As the rest of the team hurriedly heads over to the rental car agency, Bianca whispers to Tiago: "this CBP agent had such a weak mind, I'm starting to like this kind of quasi-military intelligence work." Tiago smiles and says "yeah, more like quasi-mercenary or vigilante," and keeps walking and looking straight ahead.

They quickly rent a minivan, allowing to fit Li, Ernesto, Agent Fuller, Dr Debo, Paul, Bianca and Tiago, and start driving to North San Jose. They need to find another car rental agency and switch to a second vehicle to make it more difficult for the FBI to track them down, especially that the CBP agent might have kept a record of the rental car from the airport.

Meanwhile, FBI agents are standing with an immigration officer of the San Francisco airport, who swears that the passengers of any private jet arriving from a location outside the U.S. must come through this area. The FBI agents impatiently look at their watches, waiting for the plane to land. After thirty minutes, with dozens of scenarios playing in their minds, the agents leave the immigration area and head over to the control tower. Slowed down by a few security guards who give way once they see the badges, they storm into the main area of the control tower, full of personnel busy with coordinating the heavy traffic of airplanes coming in to land. When the FBI agents are finally able to interrupt someone capable of helping them, they give the tail number of Phil's plane, only to learn a that it had filed a change of flight plan and landed in San Jose more than twenty minutes ago.

The FBI agents run out of the control tower while barking out instructions to other teams over radio to head over to San Jose's airport, and alert Agent Turner, who is sitting in a tight economy seat onboard a Singapore Airlines flight towards San Francisco. He is connected to the plane's Wi-Fi, so he sees the messages providing updates from his agents, and bangs on his tray table with his fist when he learns that the private jet landed in San Jose. The agent's anger generates distress from fellow passengers and stern looks from the cabin crew.

Agent Turner had calculated that he would arrive at San Francisco's airport shortly after Tiago and Bianca, who he was hoping would have been easily apprehended and put into custody, waiting for his arrival. He gets up from his uncomfortable seat and makes his way to the front of the plane to address the flight manager.

"Excuse-me, I need to talk to the pilot immediately," says Agent Turner while flashing his FBI badge.

"Sir, no passenger can talk to the pilots. Please return to your seat immediately," orders the flight manager.

"You don't understand, I'm in pursuit of dangerous criminals, we need to alter the final destination of this flight," says Agent Turner, raising his voice.

"Change the final destination?" asks the flight manager while raising her eyebrows. "I see... and I understand that this seems to be an emergency," says the flight manager as she takes one step towards the cockpit. But as soon as Agent Turner looks to his side to smile in the direction of the flight attendants sitting in the galley, the flight manager swiftly turns around and puts a handcuff on Agent Turner's right wrist. Then a security officer comes from behind, grabs Agent Turner's left hand and finishes to cuff him.

"Sir, I am the sky marshal on this flight and due to your suspicious behavior, I need to keep you restrained for the remainder of this flight and hand you over to authorities upon arrival," says the officer.

"I'm with the FBI, you idiot. I just needed to talk to the pilot to…" starts Agent Turner but realizes how foolish he is sounding. "Never mind."

Chapter 28

After the change of vehicle, Tiago drives a few blocks and stops on the side of the road. Bianca turns to Ernesto.

"Okay Ernesto, where are we going? You need to lead us directly to Phil," says Bianca sternly.

"We're all going to get killed if we go there, you know," replies Ernesto. Tiago looks at Bianca and raises one eyebrow.

"We'll see about that", says Tiago. "I promised you that I will personally take you back to prison if you were to collaborate. That is the best way to keep you alive. Otherwise, I'll drop you off right in the middle of the action, and sit back and wait for all of your old friends to take care of you. Or better yet, there is a nice National Park nearby and I hear they have proliferating and hungry mountain lions roaming around. Maybe I could leave you tied up to a tree over there," threatens Tiago and pauses to hear the reaction. But there is none. The man simply closes his eyes and slouches, wrinkling his already soiled suit. "Ernesto, tell us where we're going before I lose my patience."

Ernesto sighs, raising his chin. "Head towards the National Park that you were just talking about. An area called Calaveras Creek. Phil is being held up in a cabin over there," admits Ernesto followed by a another long sigh.

Li swallows hard under his hood, surprised that Ernesto is agreeing to lead Tiago to Phil's captors. He knows that this kind of treason will be very costly. Li also wonders whether Ernesto's collaboration and the potential ensuing rescue of Phil would offer him a chance to escape through the woods surrounding the cabin, result in him getting caught up in the crossfire or attacked by mountain lions in the forest of a land unknown to him. He feels a world away from his comfortable container in Singapore, where he was printing money and was surrounded by beautiful and willing women every night, and now he regrets having gotten involved in the middle of all this by delivering Phil to Ernesto. He could have been home free and gone back to business as usual. Now, he is hoping to live long enough to learn from this mistake.

Tiago is a difficult man to scare. But a cabin in an area called Calaveras, the Spanish word for skull, the most recognizable symbol of the festivities associated with the Day of the Dead, has a meaning for men of Latin American descent. Although considered by most as a day of celebration as opposed to mourning, Tiago is glad that Bianca grew up far away from where such festivities are common knowledge because he needs her to focus on the mission, and stay confident that they will find Phil alive. Dr. Debo, however, with his wealth of knowledge of various cultures, reacts with a frown and wonders whether they are about to step into a trap. Taking a hostage to a place named after a morbid reference sounds like more than a coincidence to him.

Agent Fuller is silently looking at how the situation is developing from the back of the minivan. Although he is not exactly the smartest tool in the shed, he realizes that the FBI's hesitations to promptly arresting Li have resulted in Phil being captured by people that he should have never come close to, given that Phil had been an informant for the FBI. Agent Fuller feels that, in hindsight, this was an avoidable situation and is starting to question Agent Turner's true intentions for the objective of the whole mission. As Bianca keeps saying, they were supposed to arrest Li and other criminals as soon as they would come out of hiding. Now that Phil is being held, and only a commando-style operation can strip him from his captors, Agent Fuller feels like he needs to help in any way he can.

"I suppose that you guys don't want me to call FBI reinforcements to help us to retrieve Phil," says Agent Fuller.

"You got that right agent. We're not sure who in the FBI we can trust at this point. We just barely tolerate you," replies Bianca, looking at the mountains in the horizon, tightening her lips and shaking her head while thinking about how Phil naively trusted the FBI. He'd let his guard down, and look what it had gotten him. In his line of work, with all that he'd seen over the years, Phil should have known better and be more skeptical.

"But I'm guessing we're going to need some weapons and bullet proof vests for the extraction mission that you have in mind, right?" The agent dabs his brow, visibly agitated. "There is an FBI office nearby, in Palo Alto. Why don't we stop by to retrieve some equipment?" suggests Agent Fuller.

And leave them wide open for the agent to turn the whole team in? That wasn't going to happen. "How about a proper and traditional gun shop?" asks Tiago.

"This is California, my friend. Buying guns and ammunitions is not as easy as you would think. We could be in-and-out of the FBI office in ten minutes," explains Agent Fuller.

"That's not a bad idea, but how do we know that you're not going to start mouthing around once inside the FBI office, and, as a result, screw up any chance we have of getting Phil back?" asks Bianca.

"Oh, he won't, trust me. I know that he wants to keep his testicles at their proper location instead of deep down his throat. Am I right, Agent Fuller?" asks Tiago with a half-smile while looking at him in the rear-view mirror. No one else is smiling in the minivan but they all turn to Agent Fuller to gauge his reaction, hoping that he agrees to collaborate to avoid having to witness the ugly images pictured in their minds after hearing Tiago's threatening words.

"Indeed. I want to keep all of my body parts in their rightful place. You can believe me. I want to help you get Phil back. Turn left at the next light, and I'll tell you how to get to the FBI office," says Agent Fuller.

It was risky, but it was their best option. One way or the other, they were about to find out if they could trust Agent Fuller. "I guess we don't really have a choice," concludes Bianca before waiving at Tiago to follow the agent's instructions. She is generally against weapons of all sorts, but she also believes that the end justifies the means. Rescuing Phil is the priority and the captors are probably well equipped. "Well, Agent Fuller, I hope you understand that this group has nothing to lose at this point, so for your own sake, you better be a man of your word. And why don't you come sit in the front passenger seat? It'll be more credible when we arrive at the FBI office."

The FBI office in Palo Alto looks more administrative in nature to Tiago as he pulls up in front of the security gates, so he frowns at Agent Fuller. "Don't worry, we're going to get what we need here," says Agent Fuller.

Under the agent's directions, Tiago waives at the guard and quickly flashes his badge, without coming to a complete stop, hoping that the guard will just raise the gate. Having to explain who is in the car might become a painful exercise and leave some kind of record with the FBI. Unfortunately, the gate doesn't come up. Tiago brings the minivan to a stop just in time to avoid hitting the metal pole and looks at the guard with an annoyed look and lowers his window by an inch, enough for Agent Fuller to yell out: "we're here for a meeting with the branch director." And the gate opens immediately. Agent Fuller sports a smile of success, happy to help to support the mission.

Once the van is parked, Tiago unbuckles and turns to Li and Ernesto to give them a stern warning that any attempt to evade will result in serious injuries, as he hands his gun and hunting knife to Bianca. She knows, however, that firing a weapon in the parking lot of an FBI building would be a big mistake. Li and Ernesto also know this and have known Bianca long enough to find it quite unlikely that she would use a weapon to hurt someone. So, they are both thinking about whether this would be their best chance to escape.

Tiago presses the child lock button to slow down the detainees in case they try to escape, and both he and Agent Fuller get out of the minivan and head towards the entrance of the building.

Ernesto and Li have had a hood over their head for most of the time since leaving Malaysia on the prior day. They have no idea what their surroundings look like. They assume that the FBI office is gated with a tall fence that would be very difficult to overcome with their hands tied in front of their bodies. Li prefers his odds of escaping once Tiago becomes busy with retrieving Phil from the cabin in the woods, so he intends to just stay still in the van. Ernesto, however, believes that gambling now is better than having his comrades realize that he led Tiago all the way to the cabin where Phil is being held captive. He is waiting for his best chance, perhaps in a few minutes after the other occupants have dozed off a little.

Once inside the building, Tiago and Agent Fuller attract a lot of attention from other agents that they encounter, equally due to their weird size combination, Tiago easily twice the size of his partner, and their dirty look, with greasy hair from almost two days without a shower. Agent Fuller knows where the weapon storage is located, so they just walk past everyone without paying attention to anyone.

"Good afternoon," says Agent Fuller as he walks up to the attendant of the weapon storage and shows both his and Tiago's badges. The attendant is an old man with reading glasses on the tip of his nose, probably in his last years with the bureau before retirement, seemingly unfazed about welcoming demanding agents. "We're from the Miami branch and are here to assist the LAPD S.W.A.T. on a classified mission. We need all this equipment," continues Agent Fuller as he hands over a list of items that make it sound like they're going into combat. The attendant raises his eyebrows.

"Are you guys heading to a war zone? I wasn't informed of this. Why wouldn't you source this from your own office?" asks the attendant, visibly annoyed with having to hand over so much dangerous and expensive equipment.

"We took a commercial flight to come here, old man. Did you expect us to board a flight with automatic weapons and grenades? Just mind your own business and do your job," says Tiago with fire in his eyes.

"Fine, but I'll have to send a notice to your office that we provided all this equipment," says the attendant as he turns away to find the items in the storage.

***

Meanwhile, Ernesto is sweating profusely under his hood as he gets ready for his escape. When he is confident that Tiago is far enough and inside the building, and the other passengers are succumbing due to their lack of proper sleep, he slowly removes his hood and, in a quick move, grabs the door handle, only to realize that the child lock is on, so he tries to jump to the front seat. Paul and Bianca quickly react and hold him by his belt. Ernesto pulls forward to free himself but his pants start to come down to his knees, and then to his ankles because his belt is firmly in the hands of Paul and Bianca.

"Ernesto, STOP!" yells Bianca but he still pushes forward, grabbing the steering wheel tightly. Bianca knows that Ernesto's help is critical to retrieve Phil, so she is not about to let him go. She also doesn't want to hurt him but maybe a slight puncture in his leg will be enough to discourage him. After battling with Ernesto for a few moments, Bianca wants to put an end to this. "Paul, hold one of his legs steady while I grab the knife."

"What? What are you going to do, you crazy woman?" yells Ernesto, now holding the driver's door handle, with his legs tied up by his own pants and held by Paul.

Li takes advantage of the diversion created by Ernesto to remove his hood. He surveys the area. No fence to slow down an initial escape and a large parking lot in the neighboring property, offering many ways to hide and maybe steal a vehicle to drive off. So, he also jumps to the front seat across Ernesto's body. Dr. Debo, who is best positioned in the back of the minivan, tries to hold Li back by his shirt collar but lacks arms' strength to slow him down. Li reaches for the front passenger door handle, swings his body forward on top of Ernesto's, opens the door and gets off.

"Oh, you're going to regret this Ernesto," shouts Bianca as she plants the hunting knife an inch into Ernesto's calf, who cries out in pain. He feels intense heat in his leg. "You better sit back here while I retrieve Li," says Bianca as she pulls the knife out, sending blood gushing all over the vehicle. She gives the knife to Paul and steps over Ernesto, who has given up his efforts given the pain, and she gets off through the door that Li opened.

Tiago and Agent Fuller come out of the FBI building at that exact moment. Tiago shakes his head when he sees Li awkwardly running to escape. "Hold these bags for a second, would you?" he says to Agent Fuller and starts running full speed towards Li.

"Wait a minute!" Fuller stumbles, nearly dropping the heavy bags.

Bianca sees Tiago running after Li, so she gives up the pursuit, and heads back to the car. She wasn't sure what she was going to do if she caught up to him, anyway.

Within seconds, Tiago catches up with Li and delivers a powerful tackle sending both men airborne for half a second. Upon connecting with the parking's asphalt, they land, Tiago on top, with Li's left side scraping the surface. His head, shoulder, hip and knees slide for at least a foot.

"You're a monster", mumbles Li, wincing and unable to move with probably a dislocated shoulder and deep burns and scratches all over his body.

"I was a linebacker when I played football, but I guess you probably don't know what this means. Anyway, monster will do as well. It's funny though, that's the word we used to describe you so many times," says Tiago as he gets back up, grabs Li by the collar and drags the partially numb body to the minivan.

"Ah, ah… it hurts, you big piece of gelatin brain. I'm sure that I have broken bones, you have to take me to a hospital," pleads Li.

"Maybe later. I can't believe your mouth is still running with insults after this. But don't worry, we'll get you care when we have time. I hope that this will teach you to stay put and follow directions. Now you'll have to suffer this for about ten hours. Or more. Maybe you could help Ernesto jog his memory in order to find Phil quicker," says Tiago with a smile.

An unknown FBI agent, presumably alerted by the parking gate attendant, comes running out of the building, unsure of what is going on.

"Are you guys ok?" asks the agent.

"Yeah… just dealing with an arrested suspect attempting to evade. Just one more charge to bring against him, I guess," says

Tiago with a laugh, as he puts Li back on his feet. Tiago's sweater was ripped as a result, exposing his left bicep and shoulder.

"Alright… wow man, what a tackle. You really should be playing professional football," says the agent while admiring Tiago's muscles.

"Ah, you know, I love the service. I wouldn't give up this job for anything in the world," lies Tiago with a fake smile. "But hey, thanks for coming out, things could've turned much worse, you never know what an old man like that could do to escape detention. I'm glad his hands were tied, maybe he would have given me a nasty stiff arm, or try to juke me," continues Tiago sarcastically. The agent offers a soft laugh and turns away.

Tiago opens the minivan's door and throws Li back in with no consideration for his injuries. Tiago quickly drops his smile however when he sees Ernesto with his pants down to his ankle, blood everywhere and his face as pale as a white bed sheet.

"What happened here?" asks Tiago, worried about losing the only person that can lead them to Phil.

"He was trying to escape, I was just trying to slightly cut his calf", replies Bianca in a panicked voice.

"Make a tourniquet with his belt below his knee and hold the wound tight, we're going to need to sew some stitches. How deep is the cut?" says Tiago with confidence. Ernesto passes out at the thought of getting stitches from one of these people without anything to numb him from the pain.

"About an inch deep and two inches wide," replies Bianca.

Tiago takes a deep breath. That is a big wound. This was more than any of them could handle. Luckily, they had someone with medical training on their team. "We're going to need Linda," says Tiago.

Chapter 29

"Have you guys departed from the San Jose airport?" asks Tiago as soon as Sergio picks up his cell phone.

"No, we're still evaluating where to go," replies Sergio.

"Perfect, bring the plane to the Palo Alto airport. We need Linda for a medical procedure," requests Tiago. "How much time before you get here?"

"Tiago, I already checked out that airport. We can't land the jet there. The runway is too short," says Sergio, bummed out that he can't easily help with the emergency.

"Arghh…" growls Tiago in annoyance.

During his time as a SEAL Team Six, Tiago made Navy and Air Force pilots push the limits of take-off and landing distances for the sake of dangerous missions. But he hesitates to make that request this time around, partly because Maria will be on the plane, but also, he wouldn't want to have difficulty taking off again in case they're in a rush to depart.

"Okay. Make Claudio and Linda rent a car and we're going to send instructions soon to meet us somewhere. Keep looking for a nearby place to take the jet and depart with Maria as soon as possible. You could get grounded by the FBI any minute," orders Tiago and hangs up.

Two hours later, after retrieving some key medical supplies for the required procedure, Claudio and Linda turn into the parking lot of a department store in nearby Sunnyvale, which is the place that Tiago had told them to go. Bianca is holding Ernesto's head upright, giving him sips of orange juice and trying to keep him awake.

"How is he doing?" asks Linda as she gets on the minivan and starts laying all the products on the floor.

"Seems like he's coming in and out of consciousness," replies Bianca.

"Keep the tourniquet on while I do the stitches," orders Linda as she removes the pieces of clothing that Bianca had wrapped around Ernesto's leg. "Gosh, he has lost a lot of blood. He might need a blood transfusion."

"We can't take him to a hospital until we retrieve Phil," says Tiago with a strict voice. Linda shakes her head as she pours disinfectant on the wound generating limited response from Ernesto. She quickly unwraps the suture needle and thread.

"Argh…" reacts Ernesto as Linda pierces his skin for the stitches.

"He's reacting, that's good. Keep feeding him that orange juice," orders Linda.

Fifteen minutes later, the stitches are in place and the bleeding has subsided. Linda breathes a sigh of relief and places a clean bandage over the wound.

"His colors are coming back. Let him rest for an hour. He probably won't be able to walk," says Linda.

"That's good actually. Thanks Linda. If these two clowns didn't try to escape like children in a schoolyard, they would still be perfectly healthy," says Bianca, giving a hug to Linda with her clothes full of Ernesto's blood. Linda looks up again and sees Li's clothes all ripped up.

"What happened to him?" asks Linda.

"Hard landing!" says Tiago with a proud smile.

"Let me fix him up a little," offers Linda. She uses the antiseptic to clean his face and the lacerations on different places on his body. "He's not going to be running any marathons any day soon, either," she says, pressing a bandage to the old man's cheek.

"That's also good," Tiago said. "It was fun practicing my old tackling skills, but I'd rather not get my clothes any dirtier than they already are." Tiago laughs to himself.

With both Ernesto and Li banged up and incapable of escaping, everyone relaxes a little bit. Every time Bianca thinks about Phil, who is probably tied up to something, hungry and hurt, she feels sick to her stomach and angry to the point of wanting to once again slap Ernesto violently. But she inflicted enough pain for today. She watches Linda slowly rub Li's skin burns, smiles at how caring she is, despite treating the worst monster in the world. Bianca feels the weight of her lids increasing and closes her eyes.

Once Linda is finished treating her patients, Tiago asks her to leave with Claudio and Dr. Debo and get back to the plane. Since the team is heading into a potentially physical and dangerous part of the mission, he wants to reduce the risk of casualties, and really doesn't see how Dr. Debo could partake and prefers that Linda is available to support Maria's pregnancy, as opposed to risking that she gets injured in a commando operation.

Sergio sends a notice to Tiago that he is moving the jet fifty miles east, on the other side of the mountains where Phil is being held. Consequently, Claudio, Linda and Dr. Debo have a longer drive to head back but Tiago is happy with this outcome. Having the jet stationed east of the mountains will allow better flexibility once they retrieve Phil from Calaveras Creek. It should be just a thirty-minute drive to get to the jet, with a lot less traffic than on the San Jose side.

***

Traffic is indeed horrible in Silicon Valley. Agent Turner learns that firsthand. After being humiliated by a sky marshal, paraded in handcuffs around the San Francisco airport and left in an interrogation room for thirty minutes, he finally gets released following intense pressure imposed by senior FBI officials on the Transportation and Security Administration. Agent Turner also receives an earful from his boss for what is referred as a complete failure to keep tabs on dangerous criminals. The agent is even denied a ride in an FBI helicopter, so he ends up in a painful bumper-to-bumper traffic situation while trying to head towards San Jose. At this point, he knows that trying to locate Tiago and Bianca is going to be like looking for a needle in a haystack. His only chance is to track Agent Fuller down but calls to his mobile phone keep going directly to voicemail. The phone is still safely stashed away in Bianca's purse. In fact, Agent Fuller prefers it that way because he doesn't get tempted to look and potentially react to Agent Turner's requests. Agent Fuller is really sold on helping Tiago and Bianca to retrieve Phil – for the moment. But then he needs to get back to business, and find out what is really going on and who he can, and cannot trust.

Chapter 30

The rolling hills of the State Park east of San Jose offer an interesting mix of trees growing in patches, but also open land with limited vegetation. Tiago worries that approaching a cabin without the benefit of hiding amongst large trees or dense vegetation might be difficult and present a high risk of detection. Perhaps the cover of darkness will help. The sun is already set when the map on Bianca's mobile phone shows that they are just a few minutes away from Calaveras Creek, so she tells Tiago to slow down, and orders Agent Fuller to remove Ernesto's hood.

"Okay Ernesto, where do we go from here?" asks Bianca. Ernesto slowly opens his eyes and studies the road for a good ten seconds to get his bearings.

"You will see a dirt road on the right in a few miles. Take that and the cabin will be less than 300 feet off the road," replies Ernesto, earning a frustrated look from Tiago, who would have preferred more than just than a few miles of notice, so he immediately stops the car to remain short of the dirt road and anyone's visibility while he prepares how to approach the cabin. "Don't look at me like that, you had a hood on my head," says

Ernesto, starting to be on the edge after being held captive for more than two days. And injured unnecessarily, in his opinion.

"Ernesto, would you tell us the traps and surveillance equipment that we will face as we approach the cabin?" asks Paul politely and softly, wanting to be helpful.

"I'm not aware of any surveillance equipment here. Just a few men armed to the teeth," says Ernesto before everyone turns to him, including Li who still has a hood over his head. "I told you this was going to be a dangerous endeavor. And unless you're ready to play Russian roulette with Phil's life, you won't be able to fire a single shot through that thin-walled cabin," says Ernesto while alternately looking at Tiago and Agent Fuller.

"But we have amazing hostages. Maybe we'll tie you both in front of the car and slowly drive towards the cabin. Do you think they'd shoot at us anyway?" says Tiago with a sadistic smile as he gets off the van. Bianca rolls her eyes at Tiago's comments. She senses the old vibes of Norrid when she hears him talk about gratuitous violence.

Ernesto is sweating bullets. For a man who was used to be in powerful positions during all of his years with Norrid, and, for most of the prior twelve months, after being incarcerated, leading groups of inmates that have an allegiance to the defunct Norrid, Ernesto now feels completely at the mercy of Tiago's desires. Ernesto's only chance of survival, whether in jail or as a fugitive, would be that Tiago pulls Phil away from his captors before they realize that he was even involved in leading him to the cabin. The faithful network of former Norrid operatives is still so powerful that someone would find and punish Ernesto wherever he ends up.

Tiago distributes bullet proof vests and helmets to everyone, including Li and Ernesto, and loads automatic weapons for Agent Fuller, Paul, Bianca and himself.

"This will shoot multiple rounds if you keep your finger pressed on the trigger, so keep the safety on, and only use it as a last resort," says Tiago to Bianca and Paul as he points out how to put on and remove the safety lever. "You two will remain in the car with our hostages while I will lead the way. Agent Fuller, you will remain in hiding about halfway between the minivan and the cabin with these night vision-goggles. Only I will go in for the rescue. We will keep radio silence, and absolutely no shooting by anyone until you can see that I have Phil, and you know for sure that we are nowhere near where you would be shooting. I will break radio silence with the word *'recovery'* if I have him and coming out potentially needing cover, or *'retreat'* if I am coming out empty-handed and we need to leave." Tiago stands taller. Looking each one of them in the eye. "In the unlikely event that I say, 'at will', you empty your magazine, because it means that I am confident that we won't be in your shooting lines and I need to disable the enemy quickly," explains Tiago, as slowly as possible so that everyone registers the instructions.

"Let's hope that we don't get to that point. We're not here to kill anyone," says Bianca, lecturing Tiago, as she always seems to be doing on matters of violence-avoidance.

"Yeah. And the gun shot would echo through the Valley, so our escape would become quite difficult, and we could face serious ramifications. At this point, we're acting more or less on our own account, the FBI won't defend us. Are we all clear on this?" asks Tiago, looking at Agent Fuller.

"Yes sir. I've assumed as much since we retrieved these weapons from the FBI office in Palo Alto," replies Agent Fuller with a hand on Tiago's shoulder, wanting to emphasize his support for the cause.

"Good," says Tiago with a friendly nod towards Agent Fuller, in a recognition of their first true moment of bonding. "Oh, and each one of you need to stick a few bands of this tape on your shoulders. You will appear brighter once Agent Fuller and I have the night goggles on." says Tiago as he finalizes the setup of all the equipment that he will have on him including knives, a tranquilizing gun with darts, a handgun with a silencer and an M16 rifle.

He looks at each one of them. They don't have the training he does. He hopes that they can all keep their cool. All of their lives might depend on it. For now, though, they'd done everything they can to prepare. Waiting would only make them more nervous. "Let's roll!"

Tiago drives the rest of the way on the main road and turns onto the dirt road that Ernesto indicated, then turns off the minivan's headlights and puts on his night vision goggles. When he sees the cabin at the end of the dirt road, he turns off the engine and lets the minivan slowly come to a rest, approximately 200 feet from the cabin. Tiago is quite happy that the cabin is surrounded by dense overgrown vegetation and tall trees. He lowers both of the front windows and signals to everyone to remain quiet.

"Agent Fuller, let's get out through the windows to avoid being heard. The noise from a closing car door can be heard from a distance," whispers Tiago. "We're going to crawl on the edge of the road. Stay on my six. On my signal, stop and hide in the bushes on the side of the road. Remain alert and limit your movements, there could be some hungry wildlife around here," cautions Tiago.

The road is sloping down, offering an elevated position to observe the activity around the cabin as they are slowly crawling down. Tiago's equipment hinders his movements and the pointy and sharp pieces of fine gravel pierce through the skin on his forearms every time he pushes forward. He carries through but finds this will not be ideal if he needs to make Phil crawl back up the road.

Tiago stops when he hears footsteps in the woods nearby and gives the signal to Agent Fuller to remain still. The goggles don't offer much peripheral vision, so he turns towards the woods. He sees a human shape nonchalantly walking in the direction of the cabin. The man is whistling faintly and seems to be zipping his pants up while trying to keep his balance, undoubtedly returning to the cabin after relieving himself. Tiago guesses that this is probably the product of excess drinking, which he considers as good news. If the men inside the cabin have been drinking for a while, they're going to be slow. "You're going to be my first casualty", says Tiago under his breath, wanting to take this opportunity to reduce the number of threats. He gives the sign to Agent Fuller to remain in his position, slowly removes the rifle from around his shoulder and hands it to Agent Fuller.

"Wait, you don't even know if he's with them," says Agent Fuller, but it's too late, Tiago is on his feet chasing the man as quietly as possible, his arm extended and pointing at the target with the tranquilizing gun. With less than ten feet separating the two men, Tiago shoots a dart in between his shoulder blades and catches him just in time to avoid a noisy fall.

Now closer to the cabin, Tiago knows that the risk of detection is greater and doesn't want to leave a body out in the open in case his fellow dirt bags peek outside and realize what happened. Tiago drags the body back into the bushes and removes the dart making it seem like the man was too drunk, stumbled in the woods and fell asleep. Tiago also searches the body and finds a finger-print operated device – the exact same that he used when he was part of Norrid's enforcement division. He used to leave those devices with important executives, to be activated in case of emergencies. Tiago finds it interesting that a guard would have one of those. And who would he call? Norrid's infrastructure is supposed to be dismantled.

Suddenly, a faint noise comes from a metal garbage can by the side of the cabin. Tiago freezes and turns to catch the glimpse of a bear cub sniffing the trash. At the exact moment when Tiago wonders how far a mother bear would let her cub adventure in search of food, he receives a violent paw swipe on the head knocking his night vision goggles ten feet away in the bushes and throwing him face down into the mud. Now in total darkness and shaken up, Tiago turns around to face the bear, standing on its back paws and emitting scary growls. The beast is massive. With mud limiting his vision and in total darkness, Tiago does not hesitate and shoots a tranquilizing dart into the stomach of the bear, generating even more roar, but no sign of taming the beast. So, Tiago reloads and shoots another dart, making the mother bear become visibly numb and falling forward. Tiago rolls to his side in time to avoid being the victim of a falling 750-pound mass, but his left foot gets awkwardly twisted and stuck under the animal, overextending the ligaments of his ankle. He winces but avoids any sound that could make him discovered and pushes on the animal's belly with his right leg to release his foot.

The pain is excruciating. Tiago can still move his toes, so he feels confident that his ankle is not broken or dislocated. But he worries that his ankle's ligaments are badly torn. He needs to immobilize his foot in order to continue the mission, so he comes on the radio with a faint "I need tape".

Bianca and Paul are perplexed when they hear this over the radio but go through Tiago's bag and find black electric tape. Bianca wraps it into a piece of reflective tape that Tiago had them put on their shoulders. Then, Paul pulls half of his body through the front passenger window and throws the roll of tape 50 feet down the dirt road. Agent Fuller sees the tape rolled down the road, retrieves it and starts crawling towards Tiago.

"What a beast!" whispers Agent Fuller, staring at the mama bear and handing the tape to Tiago.

"Thanks. Be careful, her cub is right there and probably looking for his mother," warns Tiago while pointing towards the cabin. "I only have three tranquilizing darts left, so I don't want to waste any on this cub" says Tiago, crippled by the pain, with blood rolling down his face from the bear's claw piercing the skin on his skull and jaw. "Do you see my goggles anywhere?" asks Tiago.

Agent Fuller looks around while Tiago tapes over his military boot and pants to create a sturdy resemblance of a cast. He doesn't find it ideal or tight enough to immobilize sufficiently, but removing his boot is out of the question for now, as it could result in major swelling. So, the loose taping will have to do until he can get back to Linda and some real medical care. It is okay, though. He'd been trained to suffer far more than this and still complete his mission.

"I can't find your goggles. Take mine," offers Agent Fuller.

"I'd rather you keep them to keep an eye on the surroundings and the minivan. There's probably light inside the cabin anyway. I'll make the rest of my way with this blue light," says Tiago as he turns on a small flashlight that emits low density powder blue light. "Move back to your position, I'm going in," orders Tiago as he stands up and starts limping towards the cabin.

Tiago remains at a distance and walks around the cabin to figure out the best way to enter. He grimaces from the pain in his ankle, now pulling through his calf and knee. And he feels dizzy from the blow to his head with blood still dripping down from his hair and on to the side of his face. As he turns the corner, Tiago sees light coming through a window on the other side, so he continues to slowly drag his painful foot over the tall grass. He's suffered through more pain than that over the years, so giving up on his mission at this point is inconceivable.

All of a sudden, Tiago sees something shining in the woods, across from the backside of the cabin. He wonders whether he is suffering from the effects of a concussion and perhaps seeing flashes. As he gets closer, however, he realizes that the light coming from the cabin is reflecting on an object in the woods. He approaches to find a car with no front license plate parked and almost completely hidden by the vegetation. Curious about why would a car be hidden that way, Tiago gets closer. His heart rate shoots up when he recognizes the vehicle's model. Now this is an interesting and not at all welcoming revelation. And the stakes just got even higher.

Chapter 31

A black unmarked Ford Crown Victoria can only be an FBI cruiser. Tiago is frightened by the meaning of this. What would the FBI gain from helping or orchestrating Phil's kidnapping, thinks Tiago. He already distrusted the FBI for their suspicious motivations but finds that cooperating with criminals to kidnap someone is on a totally different level. This new complication doesn't help Tiago's headache. He hopes that there is another explanation for the presence of this car.

Tiago decides to have a look inside the car to see if more clues could help understand the situation. However, the windows are dark and he can't see through, so he decides to test the driver's door. It opens and a light inside the car comes on automatically. Despite being limited due to his ankle injury, Tiago quickly reaches into the cruiser to turn the light off, painfully twisting his body to help himself land on the seat. He then looks at the cabin's window to see if anyone noticed the light from the cruiser.

No movement detected in the cabin, so he searches the vehicle thoroughly. His heart rate shoots up again when he finds a file in the glove compartment that includes printed picture profiles of himself, Phil, Bianca, Paul, Linda, Dr Debo and even Maria.

Tiago starts feeling cold sweats. Only agents Turner and Fuller would know the identity of the whole group, thinks Tiago. He cannot trust either of them anymore. Agent Fuller being out of sight at the moment, Tiago doesn't know if he's gone back to the minivan, putting the team in danger. With his head still sore, Tiago isn't even sure that he's processing all this information correctly and can't remember if he mentioned the new location of the jet in front of Agent Fuller. Although the agent's phone is still with Bianca, Tiago wonders whether he could somehow communicate with other agents, disclose the location of the jet and potentially endanger his beloved Maria. Tiago feels like he doesn't have a choice.

"Bianca, back the minivan up to the road and leave, head to the jet and depart to a new location," says Tiago on the radio, desperate to save the majority of the team.

"What?" asks Bianca.

"Do as I say. Leave Agent Fuller and I here," orders Tiago. Bianca slams the steering wheel in frustration but starts the car as she was instructed. She stares down the narrow gravel road for ten seconds, hoping to capture a clue or a slice of information of what could be going on for her to be ordered to abandon Phil, Tiago and Agent Fuller.

Agent Fuller looks on towards the cabin. He lost sight of Tiago when he walked around to the back. The agent is tempted to get on the radio and ask what's going on, but given the stern order to Bianca, he knows better than argue with Tiago, and remains silent.

Tiago folds the picture profiles into his pocket and waits to hear the ignition of the minivan in the distance, then comes out of the police cruiser. He loses his steps and falls to the ground, pushing the car door completely open and it swings back to close loudly. "Darn it, they probably heard this," mumbles Tiago under his breath as he starts to crawl towards the front of the cabin in time to see the door open swiftly.

"Johnny, is that you? What's taking you so long?" yells a man, with a shotgun in his hands, looking for the individual that Tiago tranquilized earlier.

Light is coming through from the open door, blinding Agent Fuller who is still wearing his night vision goggles but allowing Tiago a good view. The man walks directly in the direction of Agent Fuller, who remains completely motionless and still blinded. Tiago hopes that neither of them discharge their weapons.

When Tiago sees the man pull out a flashlight from his back pocket, he knows that this is trouble. He will be able to see Agent Fuller – or perhaps either of the tranquilized man or animal. Whatever he sees, this spells trouble. And what if the agent fires his weapon, thinks Tiago, it will break the precious silence that Tiago had been able to preserve thus far. So, Tiago decides to shoot a dart into the man's back, and he falls forward within seconds.

"Throw his gun into the woods," whispers Tiago over the radio, wanting to remove a threat from this potentially escalating situation, but also wants to test whether the agent was still following his orders.

Agent Fuller quickly removes his night goggles, and despite still being partially blinded, retrieves the shotgun as directed by Tiago.

"Can you see inside the cabin?" mumbles Tiago over the radio.

"Yep, the door is still open. No sign of any movement inside," says Agent Fuller after rubbing his eyes, still seeing flashes from the hyper exposition to light through his goggles.

"Good. Now, drag the body into the bushes," commands Tiago, wanting to avoid leaving any immediate evidence for anyone else coming out of the cabin. Agent Fuller sighs over the radio to express his disagreement with taking such a risk, exposing himself for at least twenty seconds, while dragging a 200 pounds man, to any other thugs walking out of the cabin. "Don't worry, I'll cover you, and keep the man's body in front of you as a partial shield as you drag him," says Tiago while moving back to an angle that would allow him a decent shooting angle to the door in case someone else shows up. Tiago finds the risk acceptable because the next guy would only start worrying about his comrades after at least a few minutes, not twenty seconds.

Tiago continues to be troubled with the thought that an FBI agent is probably inside the cabin. He wishes that he could torture Ernesto right at this moment to make him explain how and why the FBI is collaborating with former Norrid operatives. He is disgusted at the thought of having helped these agents, just to find out that they might have been in cahoots with Ernesto and others all along.

Once Agent Fuller completes his body dragging duty, Tiago painfully approaches the cabin, his ankle almost completely numb, and stands by the door, ready to tranquilize whoever comes out next. He decides to text Bianca: *'FBI unmarked cruiser here. Possible connection with Ernesto. You and Paul get some info out of him'.*

Bianca's phone's flashes with the message but she doesn't see it. She is furiously driving to the other side of the mountains, with Sergio ready to take-off as soon as she arrives with the rest of the team. She is following mindlessly the directions being provided by the car's navigation system, her mind preoccupied by what could have panicked Tiago to order that she leaves with the rest of the team. She wonders whether there is a real threat, or if he was just trying to shield her from an ugly scene involving Phil. But most importantly, how will Tiago, Agent Fuller and hopefully Phil be able to leave that place without transportation?

When they arrive at the Livermore airport, Bianca parks near the plane and helps Paul move the prisoners inside the cabin.

"Where are Tiago and Agent Fuller?" asks Maria firmly as she grabs Bianca's arm to lead her towards the cockpit for a discreet conversation.

"They are still working on the rescue. Tiago told us to come back here and move the aircraft," replies Bianca with tears in her eyes. Sergio comes out of the cockpit in time to hear Bianca talk about moving the aircraft.

"What? And how are they going to get out of there without a vehicle?" asks Sergio.

"I don't know. Tiago was being cryptic," says Bianca, nervously pulling her phone out of her purse, only to realize that Tiago had texted. Her face turns to anger when she reads about the presence of an FBI unmarked cruiser at the cabin. "Get everyone on the plane and close the door. Fly us somewhere discrete. Now!" orders Bianca to Sergio, who nods gently.

Bianca walks towards Ernesto and removes his hood. He grimaces from the pain and discomfort of his calf injury. Linda was just about to check on the stitches but she sees the anger in Bianca's eyes, so she takes a few steps back.

"What the heck is an FBI unmarked cruiser doing at the cabin?" shouts Bianca, sending drops of saliva flying into Ernesto's face. Everyone else gather near Ernesto, surprised and stunned by this new development.

"I tried to warn you guys that going to that cabin was like jumping in the lion's den," replies Ernesto without even opening his eyes.

"You better tell me," says Bianca as she pulls out the same knife that she used on his calf a few hours ago. "Or I'm going to help you with that plastic surgery that you always wanted," continues Bianca while placing the blade of the knife on Ernesto's cheek.

"I'm so tired of this. You want to kill me, just go ahead, you, crazy woman," yells Ernesto earning a slight movement of the knife from Bianca, drawing some blood from his cheek, right below the jawbone. "Ouch! You're really out of your mind. You really want to know what's going on? Fine. The FBI sent me to Malaysia to retrieve Phil and put him on a plane back to the U.S. to lock him up in one of Norrid's hideouts. I didn't even have a choice. They sent me to do their dirty work," says Ernesto, while intensely looking at Bianca's face expression turning from anger to extreme sadness.

"YOU'RE LYING," shouts Bianca directly in front of Ernesto's face and slaps him with the back of her hand. Then she turns to Paul. "He's lying, the FBI can't send him to retrieve Phil, it can't be true, right? That's not possible," continues Bianca unconvincingly, as tears fill up her eyes.

As much as Bianca doesn't want to believe that the FBI would carry out such diabolical plans, she knows deep down that it is making perfect sense, especially that Ernesto was freed up from jail to fly to Malaysia. She suddenly feels lightheaded, drops the knife to the floor and starts falling backwards from the dizziness. Paul catches her just in time before she hits the ground.

"We're not safe here. Agent Fuller knows where we are," says Bianca faintly, holding onto Paul's shoulders. "Sergio, fire up the engines and let's get out of here."

"Yes mam," replies Sergio.

Chapter 32

Standing by the door of the cabin and waiting to tranquilize the next occupant to come out of the cabin, Tiago realizes that it might now be clear for whoever is left inside that something is wrong because the two operatives that ventured outside haven't returned. No one else is crazy enough to step out.

This is bad news. If there is indeed an FBI agent inside the cabin, he is no doubt calling for reinforcements, thinks Tiago. So, he pulls out one of his knives, extends the blade and holds it in front of the cabin to use it as a mirror to get a glimpse of what is going on inside. No apparent movement.

Tiago believes that a low entrance might be his best chance to safely get into the cabin and hide behind a sofa near the front door. He crouches down, with pain shooting throughout his injured leg, takes a deep breath and pushes his body inside by rolling on his shoulder. He lands on his behind with limited noise. "Back to original plan. Keep your position," whispers Tiago over the radio, hoping that Agent Fuller will continue to cooperate, irrespective of who Tiago is about to dig out of the cabin.

Except for a distant muffled cough every few minutes and the buzzing of insects that are starting to fill the air, Tiago hears no sound throughout the cabin. He decides to crawl towards the back side of the structure, tranquilizer gun in one hand, sliding his body on the floor with his other hand, and making himself less noticeable by making sure his boots don't touch the ground. He breathes a little more easily. If he's being honest, this is easier on his injured ankle as well.

Suddenly, a car can be heard driving on the gravel road leading to the cabin. This can't be good, thinks Tiago as he tightens his lips and shakes his head. He assumes that this is the reinforcement that was called from inside the cabin. He uses the distracting sound, however, to move quicker in order to cover more of the cabin's surface. Nobody in sight, but Tiago notices a door, presumably leading to a basement, so he places his body on one side and slowly opens the door.

"Hey Johnny, is that you?" says a man from downstairs, walking towards the staircase to see who's coming, and making Tiago believe that reinforcements weren't actually called. And whoever is downstairs doesn't know that his buddies have their faces in the dirt outside the cabin. Wanting to take advantage of the element of surprise, Tiago turns towards the bottom of the stairs and launches himself face forward with his arms in front, with each step of the stairs painfully hitting his elbows, chest, hips and knees. When the man looks up the stair in stupefaction, unsure of who is sliding down, he doesn't have time to react or pull his weapon. Despite his unstable position and rough ride down the stairs, Tiago extends his right arm and shoots a dart into the man's leg, right above his left knee. The man immediately pulls the dart out of his leg, seemingly before the drug could completely enter his body. He takes a few steps backwards, stumbles slightly, either from the pain of the dart's needle or some of its effect and attempts to reach for his gun.

"I wouldn't do that if I were you," says Tiago, already on his feet, pointing his gun at the man, who immediately raises his hands. Tiago notices Phil in the back of the room, tied to a chair with tape over his mouth. "Get over there and untie him. SLOWLY! I want to see your hands at all times," orders Tiago, pointing at Phil while pulling his silencer from his pocket.

"Thank you, brother," says Phil once the tape is removed from his mouth and the ties are removed.

"Of course, my friend. Search him really quick and take his weapons," Tiago orders Phil. "*Clear and recovery*," says Tiago over the radio, in accordance with the agreed terminology with Agent Fuller.

Phil finds two Glock 19 pistols on the man. The same type that was issued to Phil and Tiago when they became part of the FBI. Phil looks at Tiago and back at the man.

"What the heck? Are you with the FBI?" asks Phil. But obtains no answer.

"No time for this. He's most likely with the FBI. I found an unmarked police cruiser outside the cabin, and an extensive file with all of our photos. We…" starts Tiago while pulling the papers from his pockets to show to Phil but stops when he hears a car door closing. "Shhh.. put tape on this guy's mouth and hold him at gun point," whispers Tiago as he puts zip-tie handcuffs around the man's wrists and a longer one around his neck. "Agent Fuller is outside, hopefully he'll handle the situation with whoever arrived quietly."

Tiago and Phil hear footsteps on the gravel approaching the cabin, then Agent Fuller's voice in the distance: "Agent Turner, what are you doing here?", some more footsteps, and a faint conversation. Agent Fuller seems to express his disagreement or disappointment with something but their words are inaudible.

"Great... Agent Turner is here now. Something is definitely fishy between the FBI and the guys that abducted you. Agent Turner's magical appearance here is absolutely evidence of that," whispers Tiago.

"Seems like a lot has happened over the last few days. And... where are we exactly?" says Phil, looking a bit disoriented.

"A few klicks east of Silicon Valley," replies Tiago in a military language that means kilometers. Phil raises his eyebrows. He knew that he had been on a plane but is surprised to be 10,000 miles from where he was captured. "Hide below the stairs. Let me handle the conversation with Agent Turner," orders Tiago.

Tiago grabs the man, who he assumes is a dirty FBI agent, by the tie-wrap around his neck and moves him like if he were administering a tough discipline to an unruly dog.

Agents Turner and Fuller enter the cabin together and slowly make their way downstairs. When they turn towards the main area of the basement, they see Tiago pointing a gun at them and holding a man in front of him by the collar.

"Drop your guns on the floor and put your hands up. Both of you," yells Tiago with no place for negotiations. The two agents comply promptly. "Kick your guns towards me and put these on. Slowly," commands Tiago as he throws zip-tie handcuffs to them.

"You're making a big mistake Tiago," says Agent Turner. "We're here for the same reason as you. I'm glad you were able to free Phil."

"Agent Fuller was here to help me. At least, I think... You, however, you're just a dirty cop," says Tiago but Agent Turner shakes his head. Tiago tightens his grip on his gun. "Really? So, how did you know that Phil was being held up here?" says Tiago.

"Tiago, you're making a big mistake. Why would you think that I am dirty? We've been with you on this from the start," asks Agent Turner.

"Let's see. First, you went out of your way to make sure that we don't arrest Li at every single chance we had, almost handing Phil over to the criminals that had every reason to hurt him. But let's start with this simple question: how did you know of the existence of this cabin? Or where we were?" asks Tiago.

"I didn't know about this cabin. The clerk from the Palo Alto FBI office called to inform me that you guys had taken a bunch of equipment. So, we just activated the GPS trackers in the bullet proof vests that you guys are wearing," replies Agent Turner calmly as Agent Fuller touches the front of his vest to see if he can feel the GPS receiver. "About Li's arrest, those are the orders that I received. I was told to hold off on Li's arrest until more high-profile criminals from his entourage show up. If we moved in too quickly on Li, the others would have stayed in hiding for a long time," says Agent Turner calmly, then pauses. "Now, why don't you put the gun down, Tiago," pleads Agent Turner. Tiago starts lowering his weapon, but still holds on tightly to the unknown man by the tie-wrap collar.

"What about this guy? Isn't he FBI?" asks Tiago while tightening the collar.

"I have no idea who that is, Tiago. Did you try to confirm his identity? This is not really how we taught you to make an arrest," says Agent Turner.

"He had two FBI issued Glock 19's on him. But let's see," says Tiago.

Tiago sits the man violently on the chair on which Phil was being held up, removes the tape over his mouth, and pulls back hard on his hair.

"What's your name?" Asks Tiago, but the man remains tight lips. "I can have a very bad temper, you know. I usually don't give second chances," says Tiago as he tightens his grip on his hair and readies to smash the back of his head against the concrete wall.

"Okay, okay," says the man with a Hispanic accent. "I'm Agent Mudor, and I was put on a mission to infiltrate Norrid six months ago. These guys trust me. Now, you might have blown my cover."

"Norrid? Norrid is done, what are you talking about?" asks Phil, back on his feet and in Agent Mudor's face.

"Norrid is well and alive, I guarantee you that. They've been fully operational for almost a year," says Agent Mudor.

Phil walks towards Agent Turner, grabs him by the collar and points his index finger at his face.

"You knew that when you recruited us, didn't you? You needed my help again to dig out these criminals. You just couldn't do your own job," says Phil with a disgusted look. After a few seconds, Agent Turner looks away, unsure what to respond, and closes his eyes.

"Tell me that's not true... is it?" asks Agent Fuller, looking intensely at Agent Turner, who is still has his eyes closed. "I trusted you. We took a lot of risks out there. You withheld valuable information from the people conducting this mission. You put us in harms way," continues Agent Fuller.

Crickets chirp outside, answered by a few frogs. But still no answer from Agent Turner.

Tiago turns to Agent Mudor and cuts off his zip-tie handcuffs. "Go! Start writing your report, and we'll be in touch," orders Tiago. Phil hands Agent Mudor his service weapons back, and the agent walks out of the cabin. Fifteen seconds later, he drives off quickly.

Still in the basement, everyone continues to look at each other in silence. Just the noise of the car driving away through the fine gravel can be heard.

"Wait," says Phil. "Did you say he had an FBI unmarked cruiser?" asks Phil.

"Yeah... the standard Crown Victoria that all the FBI agents drive," replies Tiago.

"Well, there is absolutely no way that he would try to infiltrate Norrid with such an obvious FBI car. We were taken for a ride by this guy," says Phil. "He's either not FBI or a dirty cop working with Norrid. No agent would be stupid enough to drive a police car while infiltrating a criminal organization."

Chapter 33

"Hi baby," says Phil as soon as Bianca answers her phone.

"Oh my..." reacts Bianca while sobbing slightly. "I'm so happy to hear your voice. Are you okay?"

"Just a few scratches and bruises. I was asleep for most of the time, probably thanks to some special cocktail from Li's gang," explains Phil with a tired voice.

"The cocktail could be from other sources. Ernesto pretends that he was sent to Malaysia by the FBI to retrieve you, so be careful with Agent Fuller by your side," says Bianca.

"Yeah... we also just had a weird encounter with the FBI. We got both agents Fuller and Turner handcuffed in the back of Agent Turner's car. We're heading your way," says Phil.

"Good. Well, we moved the plane to Sacramento, so you'll have to drive a little further," says Bianca.

"Alright. We'll stop by a motel to sleep for a few hours and meet you in the parking lot of the U.S. Department of Justice in Sacramento at eight o'clock sharp in the morning," orders Phil. "Once you get there, stay in the car. We'll come to you to retrieve Li and Ernesto."

Tiago gives Phil a sharp look when he mentions sleeping in a motel and continues to wince from the pain to his left foot every few seconds. He grabs a few pain killers from his vest's pocket and shakes his head as Phil's words sink in some more. Tiago is not convinced that discreetly bringing two handcuffed FBI agents into a motel room – and keep them there for the night – is as easy as it sounds. Also, Tiago knows that holding two agents against their will with limited evidence of crimes could turn against Phil and himself very quickly.

"Tiago, can't you see that I've supported you in every way I could over the past few days? Why do you assume that I'm in cahoots with malicious minds in the FBI? I'm on your side man, I wanna help," pleads Agent Fuller, attempting to distance himself from whatever suspicions Phil and Tiago have about Agent Turner or other people at the FBI.

"I know you've been good," acknowledges Tiago while nodding in Phil's direction.

"I have no idea why you think that either of us have anything to do with your kidnapping, Phil," says Agent Turner. "I was getting orders from my superiors at the FBI to keep Li on the loose until more Norrid leaders come out of hiding. We were there, trying to assist, when Li's guys took the container that you were in."

"You were at the shipyard?" asks Phil.

"Yes, they were there," says Tiago. "Not sure if they helped though. They appeared at the scene all guns blazing, to borrow Bianca's expression. They might have spooked Li and taken away our ability to take action immediately," explains Tiago. Phil closes his eyes to try to evaluate all this information.

"Why were you hiding from us the fact that Norrid was alive and well? Especially when you showed up in Columbia to recruit me," asks Phil while turning to look at Agent Turner, who is sitting on the back seat.

"I wasn't necessarily hiding it. But my mission was to ensure that we could enlist you as an agent to help dry out the money laundering schemes. Remember, all I asked you to do is run a surveillance operation from a Singapore apartment. I never asked you to independently start following people around and pretend that you're some secret agent. You guys decided and came up with the plans to follow Li to his hideout," claims Agent Turner.

Phil slightly nods in approval. He realizes that he didn't notice any form of collusion or complicity, let alone any knowledge of each other, between agents Turner and Mudor when they met in the basement of the cabin. Despite the now obvious and suspicious intentions of some people at the FBI, Phil finds it plausible that Agent Mudor was under the orders of different people at the bureau and was acting independently from Agent Turner. If Norrid is truly back on its feet, it is conceivable that various departments of the FBI are investigating or trying to infiltrate it, believes Phil.

For his part, Agent Fuller has appeared completely innocent to Phil since they first met in Miami, when Agent Fuller found out about Tiago's exceptional strength and fighting abilities. Aside from being proud of his position with the FBI and his failed attempts at trying to impress the ladies, Agent Fuller just seems to wear his heart on his sleeve and stands ready to follow his superiors' orders without questioning them too much. Agent Fuller even appeared gullible or naïve at times, which makes Phil believe that his ability to design deceptive plans would be fairly limited.

On the side of the highway, they finally stop, in the pouring rain, at a motel and check into one room equipped with two double beds. Quite cozy for four grown men to share. Phil figures it will be easier to closely watch the agents and they're only there for a short nap. After locking the door and securing it with a sofa, Phil grabs one of Tiago's knife from his pocket.

"Alright Agent Fuller, I think that you're innocent," says Phil as he cuts the agent's zip-tie handcuffs. "Agent Turner, I'm sorry but we're going to have to keep you cuffed, both wrists and ankles, until the morning," continues Phil, followed by a long sigh from Agent Turner. "Don't worry, it's just a few more hours. We'll set you free when we arrive at the DOJ, and if you help book Li and Ernesto, we won't share our suspicions about you with the Department. Deal?" asks Phil.

"Pfff... I can't wait to prove to you that we're on the same team. You know, if you had followed your mission, maybe we'd be done and back home by now. Anyhow, you were probably in much harsher captivity conditions during the past few days, so if it can soothe your mind to keep me cuffed for a few hours, go right ahead," says Agent Turner with another sigh, while lying down on the bed and easily offering his ankles for Tiago to tie up.

Minutes after the lights are off and silence fills the air, Agent Turner starts snoring loudly. Not just heavy breathing, more like heavy farming equipment noise. "I guess the cuffs are not too much of a discomfort after all," says Phil under his breath.

Phil experiences limited shut eye and alternates between lying down, looking at the ceiling and standing by the window, hypnotized by the heavy precipitation flooding the parking lot of the motel. He thinks about his beautiful Bianca, who must have been so worried over the past few days. He wonders whether she's holding up or about to have a nervous breakdown. And will she and the rest of the team be able to bring Li and Ernesto to the DOJ without further incidents?

Tiago, also unable to sleep, stands, limps a few steps, his ankle now really stiff, and joins Phil by the window.

"Who do you think we're up against this time?" whispers Tiago.

"It's plausible that the FBI was conducting an operation to discreetly get closer to Norrid executives, which would also partially explain Ernesto's sudden appearance as some sort of double agent. But using a Ford Crown Victoria seems like a risky move for an undercover agent," says Phil.

"The car wasn't completely visible, but also not really well hidden. I could see reflections from the cabin's light on the car's bumper and windshield. And, if an FBI agent was just infiltrating Norrid, why would he have pictures of all of us?" asks Tiago.

"Being able to identify us in order to rescue me might have been part of their mission. But you know, it's also quite possible that a mix of criminals with unlimited resources are after us again, and they've enlisted corrupt officials," replies Phil. "Keep an eye on them, I'll shower before we get back on the road. I've been in the same clothes for a couple of days," says Phil as he taps Tiago's shoulder.

Chapter 34

Parked on the street in front of the DOJ's building in Sacramento, Phil is nervously tapping on the car's dash. It's eight fifteen and there is no sign of Bianca and the rest of the team. Phil dials up her cell phone. No answer.

"We should have met them at the jet. What if Li and Ernesto resisted or escaped?" asks Phil with both hands on the back of his neck.

"I doubt it, they're both pretty banged up," says Agent Fuller with a congratulating tap on Tiago's shoulder, who looks away.

"What have you done to our prisoners?" asks Phil.

"The prisoners attempted an escape." Tiago Shrugs. "One can never know what will happen while attempting to get away from an All-State Linebacker," replies Tiago while wiping his sunglasses with his shirt. "I did what I had to do. Li will live." He smiles. "Your girl did more damage to Ernesto. She has a bite that our former friend will not soon forget."

When Tiago places his sunglasses back over his eyes, he looks into the rearview mirror and notices a Toyota Prius with heavily tinted windows slowly pulling up behind. "Is this Bianca?" asks Tiago noticing long blond hair in the front passenger seat. Phil turns around and moves his head for several seconds, trying to make out with difficulty who is in that car. The door opens and Bianca steps out quickly.

"I love you so much," says Bianca to Phil as she jumps in his arms with her legs wrapped up around his body. "Sorry we couldn't rent a car this morning, we had to use a ride-share."

"No worries. Are Ernesto and Li in there?" asks Phil followed by Bianca's quick nod and smile. "Perfect, get in this police cruiser and don't move." Orders Phil as he lands Bianca back on her feet.

Phil approaches the Prius and opens a back passenger door to let Li out. Despite still hurting from yesterday's vicious tackle by Tiago, he is quite agitated and belligerent because he knows exactly what he is facing: the first imprisonment of his life. Phil holds him as best as he can while Tiago is cutting Agent Turner's zip-tie handcuffs.

Just as Phil seemed to lose his grip on Li, Tiago grabs him by the neck tightly.

"Where do you think you're going boy?" asks Tiago with a scornful smile.

"Agent Turner, read this man his Miranda rights and take him inside with Tiago," orders Phil.

Meanwhile, Paul is helping Ernesto get off the other side of the car. Ernesto is grimacing heavily and can barely put any weight on his injured leg. Phil comes around the car and asks Paul to wait in the police cruiser with Bianca. "Lock the doors and don't open to anyone", commands Phil.

"Ernesto, we meet again. I honestly thought that the extent of our communications would be the postcards that I was going to send to you for reading pleasure in your jail cell," says Phil with sarcasm, one arm around Ernesto's back. Agent Fuller is waiting a few feet away, letting these two reconnect.

Ernesto's hair mat against his brow. His injuries and lack of proper sleep make him look partly incapacitated and much older than he is. Barely moving his heavy skull, he motions his eyes up with a fake pity look. "Phil, I always treated you with respect and never harmed you in any significant way. I treated you like a son. And I helped Tiago find you in that cabin so you can be saved and be back to your normal life. Tiago promised me that he would discreetly return me to jail. It's not safe for me here. Norrid has well placed informants in the DOJ," pleads Ernesto.

"We have no choice. We need to leave you here – for your own sake, actually. Did I hear correctly that you retrieved me in Malaysia under FBI orders? If you're so worried about how you will be perceived by fellow Norrid thugs, why would you collaborate with the FBI?" asks Phil. But Ernesto lowers his head again and offers no answer. "Let's go inside," says Phil.

Once inside the DOJ building, Phil requests to meet with a U.S. Attorney to process the arrest of dangerous criminals, pointing at Li and Ernesto. The guard at the front desk moves one of his eyebrows up while looking and at the two men, crippled by their injuries. "Dangerous, hey? What'd they do? Steal bingo cards in a nursing home?" says the guard while looking at his screen to find someone to call for this matter. "Have a seat over there. Let me look into this."

"Phil, it's quite unusual to bring suspects directly to the DOJ," says Agent Turner after sitting on lobby sofas.

"I don't know who to trust at the FBI anymore. At least with the DOJ, there are some elected officials that we could embarrass in the media if criminals aren't handled as they're supposed to. Plus, we need to send the DOJ looking into Agent Mudor's actions, in a sort of internal affair review. No better place than the DOJ to do that, right? I don't suppose that FBI agents would investigate each other with much seriousness," says Phil, quickly regaining his fiery style.

"I guess… let's see what happens," says Agent Turner.

After more than an hour waiting in the lobby, everyone is led into a plush office by an executive assistant.

"Can I offer you some coffee or water?" says the assistant looking at Li and Ernesto's bloodied clothes in disgust, worried that the expensive furniture will be ruined. She also briefly places her hand over her mouth and nose due to the men unpleasant body odors.

"Coffee would be lovely," says Agent Turner, not accustomed to operating on an empty stomach.

A moment later, a tall skinny man in a tightly fitted dark suit enters the room and introduces himself as U.S. Attorney William Knoter.

"Good morning Mr. Knoter, I am Agent Turner with the Miami Branch of the FBI. I am here today with my associates, also with the FBI and two suspects," says Agent Turner while displaying the four FBI badges on Mr. Knoter's desk.

"Interesting. But this is the DOJ, not the county jail and…" says Mr. Knoter but gets interrupted by Phil.

"Sir, we understand but we have an unusual situation that needs the direct attention of the DOJ," says Phil while intensely looking at Mr. Knoter, who opens his palms towards Phil to invite him to share his concerns. "You see, we were sent to Singapore on a mission to find dangerous criminals subject to international arrest warrants, including smuggling of narcotics into the U.S. and money laundering involving American institutions. But for reasons unknown to us, the FBI wouldn't let us proceed with the arrest of Mr. Li, which contributed to a series of event that resulted in me getting kidnapped by these men, tortured and injected with various substances to transport me back to a cabin near San Jose," explains Phil, pointing at Li and Ernesto, causing Mr. Knoter to put on his reading glasses and pull out a pad to jot down some notes.

"Please go on," says Mr. Knoter.

"Well, when I found out that one of my captors was an FBI agent, who claimed to be undercover, I started to wonder whether the FBI had a role to play in all this," states Phil, as if he dropped a heavy sledgehammer on the glass table by his side.

"Now I understand why you wouldn't follow standard FBI procedures. But first, let's get these men in proper detention cells, they shouldn't listen to this conversation," says Mr. Knoter as he picks up his phone and calls for agents to take Li and

Ernesto away. Everyone remains silent until Li and Ernesto are brought by the security personnel.

"Lots of good and honest people at the FBI have spent countless hours building cases against these dangerous men," says Agent Turner in support of Phil's efforts. "We're counting on you sir to ensure that they be taken off the streets," continues the agent as Li and Ernesto are taken away.

"If the evidence is there, rest assured that we won't disappoint you and your teams," says Mr. Knoter as he turns towards his desktop. "You got me curious about this mission in Singapore. I'm wondering under what kind of jurisdiction you were hoping to make arrests in a foreign country. Show me your badges again, please," requests Mr. Knoter, extending his hands towards his visitors.

Mr. Knoter spends several minutes to type a series of data points and scroll through multiple screens, and intently reads some material, raising his eyebrows on a few occasions. Then he turns back to his visitors and slowly places his hands on his desk.

"Gentlemen. I happen to be very familiar with our international missions and the records that we keep in our systems. You see, the FBI's ability to make arrests on foreign land is limited and would need special approval. I cannot find any record of such approval for yourselves or anything whatsoever going on in Singapore in the recent past. This alone could explain why you incorrectly believe that someone at the FBI was trying to slow you down or not let you make arrests. Your mission might have been lost in the complicated bureaucracy of the bureau or not sufficiently formalized for actions to be taken. What concerns me more, however, is the lack of any trace of yourselves even going to Singapore. We normally have a record of all agents deployed internationally in case we, or the Department of State, need to intervene in the event of a mishaps. I'm sure you know what I mean by that," says Mr. Knoter calmly, looking into each of his visitor's eyes, one-by-one for a few seconds, seemingly trying to register their reaction.

"Sir, with the amount of resources that we deployed in Singapore, I can assure you that our mission was duly authorized and sanctioned by the bureau. I am not sure why your files are not showing the records," argues Agent Turner.

"Alright, well, I guess we'll have to look into that," says Mr. Knoter, turning back to his computer to type a few words. "It looks like the suspect by the name of Li is indeed wanted for many crimes. That's a good catch. Hopefully you arrested him lawfully. The other man's name was Ernesto you said?"

"Correct. Ernesto Guero," says Phil.

"Let's see," says Mr. Knoter, still typing. "Ah, okay, yes that's him. Well, no arrest warrant. He's out on special unescorted prison furlough. Interesting. He is permitted to be out for another five days. We will have to release him. Unless of course he committed another crime."

"He absolutely did. He participated in my kidnapping," says Phil. "Why was he on furlough? This is completely reckless. It is making me even more suspicious of the FBI's actions."

"His file doesn't say. I wouldn't yet use the word suspicious. Perhaps unusual would be better. Well, if you say he kidnapped you, we will need your deposition right away. Otherwise, we'll have a smart criminal lawyer getting him out of here in a New York minute," says Mr. Knoter in Phil's direction.

"Absolutely, sir," replies Phil.

"Oh, and also, you might be interested to know, that I just saw that a complaint has been filed against the two of you," says Mr. Knoter while pointing at Tiago and Agent Fuller. "For allegedly interfering with an undercover FBI operation. This case is getting more interesting by the minute."

Chapter 35

Back to the jet, safely parked in a hangar at the Sacramento airport, everyone is in a happy mood, being back together after many moments of angst. Sergio even brought in a few bottles of Champagne.

Phil and Tiago are sitting on the front most seats of the cabin, with Bianca and Maria on their laps. Phil recounts what he remembers seeing in Li's container, the printer and the women, before being violently hit by one of them.

Agent Turner settles into one of the seats, looking comfortable despite his toils over the past day. Odd, how he is able to come back smiling, despite the fact that the team distrusted him so much. Phil isn't sure if he really trusts Turner yet, but at the moment everything seems fine. With the impending accusations against Tiago, they need a friend on the inside, and for the time being at least, Turner may be all they have.

Bianca lays her head on Phil's shoulder, horrified about the events of the last few days but happy that Li is finally facing justice. "I tell you; it's comforting to think that we've finally dealt a major blow to Li and his organization," says Tiago with a victory smile. Phil is not as convinced as everyone. He wants to see Li properly sentenced and Ernesto back behind bars before letting any celebratory thought enter his mind. And the investigation into the actions of certain people at the FBI could take months. Phil doesn't know who can be trusted in the meantime. But he doesn't want to ruin the moment, so he goes along with a festive drink as Sergio passes by with the glasses.

"Leave the bottle right beside me, my good friend," says Tiago still wincing every few seconds. "I'll have to remove that boot and I need some alcohol numbing. You shouldn't mix throttle and bottle anyway, so I'll just take your share, Sergio," continues Tiago grabbing the bottle with a smile in Sergio's direction.

"Oh dear, what happened now?" asks Maria with a serious look, examining Tiago's taped boot.

"Nature at its best, honey. Hunter and prey. The roles reversed a few times in a manner of seconds. No worries though, nothing broken," says Tiago with half a smile as he starts removing his boot. Maria puts her hands on her face when she sees Tiago's swollen ankle looking like it had been painted with blue and green colors. And she waves for Linda to assist.

"We need to ice this right away," says Linda as she grabs the container full of ice that Sergio had brought in for the Champagne and slowly immerses Tiago's foot into it. "We should go to the hospital for an x-ray."

"It may not be wise to step outside at his point. Sorry my friend, you'll have to wait until tomorrow," says Phil with his hand around Tiago's shoulder. "We're going to need to ask you to tough it out."

Tiago nods in approval.

"Phil, we're too many to hunker down in the jet for more than a few hours," whispers Bianca in Phil's ear.

Phil agrees that the jet is overcrowded but doesn't want to risk leaving anyone behind for the moment. Who knows what Agent Mudor and his accomplices in the FBI are capable of doing at this point? By lodging his complaint about Tiago and Agent Fuller's presumed interference with an FBI operation, Agent Mudor gave a solid indication, in Phil's mind, that he wanted to obscure any DOJ investigation into his acts.

With enough seat belts on the plane for everyone, Phil asks Sergio to get them into the air, while he's evaluating their options.

"Where are we going?" asks Agent Turner, generating a few laughs from the team.

"We never know before hand," says Tiago loudly with a smile. "But don't worry, we have parachutes on board if you're unhappy with the destination." More laughs break out throughout the cabin.

"Hey Phil, do you mind dropping me off near New York City?" asks Agent Turner, lowering his voice while bending down near Phil. Still sitting on Phil's lap, Bianca tenses up and grips Phil's hand tighter when she hears New York. She recalls the dangerous mission that Phil had to complete before joining the team in Grand Turk.

"That's not how this works. Our destination is never known until we're high up in the sky. But, out of curiosity, why do you need to go to New York?" asks Phil.

"I need to find out why our mission wasn't showing as sanctioned in the DOJ system. I want to confront my boss directly at his office at the Federal Plaza in New York," replies Agent Turner. Tiago overhears the agent's explanation and looks and nods at Phil to indicate that his reasons seem legit.

"I'll keep that in mind when forming our itinerary. Now please take your jump seat and buckle yourself in for takeoff, attendant Turner," says Phil with a smart tone of voice, as if he was commanding the flight attendants from the cockpit. When Agent Turner looks confused by the instruction, Phil points to the uncomfortable metal seats that the flight crew typically uses for takeoff and landing. Bianca and Tiago laugh slightly when Agent Turner turns to look at the seat. "What can I say? On this plane, you have no seniority," continues Phil, then closes his eyes to indicate to Agent Turner to leave him alone.

Twenty minutes into the flight, Phil looks out the window and sees the Pacific Ocean and a clear sight of the coastline, with the plane heading North towards Oregon. Phil figures he should give Sergio a destination, so he stands up, passes by Agent Turner with a smile and enters the cockpit to give instructions. When Phil emerges again, the agent turns to look at him but Phil just keeps walking all the way to the back of the plane to chat with Dr. Debo.

"What an adventure. I'm glad you've come back safe and sound Phil," says Dr. Debo with his usual soft spoken and precise words.

"You bet. I tell you; it almost seems to me like the authorities just let these criminal organizations thrive," says Phil, rubbing his temples.

"Perhaps. Your friends really came through for you on this. We witnessed *The Rise of Bianca!*" says Dr. Debo with a proud smile. "You should have seen her. She really took charge, and everyone listened to her without question. You would have been proud." He glances at her from across the plane. "And Tiago's plan to retrieve you was nothing short of a commando mission with military precision."

"I know. You guys were all amazing." Although scared as all get-out, Phil knew in the back of his mind, that as long as his team worked together to find him, that they would get him out for that very reason. Split up, they were a mess, but jointly they meld and form a cohesive unit to be reckoned with.

There were still some strings left unattached in this quilt, though, and Phil needed to find the answers.

Taking a deep breath, he looks back to Dr. Debo. "Hey, there really seems to be foul play by the FBI in this whole thing. Why and who at the FBI would have an incentive to mess around with our mission, get me kidnapped, transported to the U.S. and held in captivity in that cabin?" asks Phil.

Dr. Debo takes a sip of his drink, then scratches the back of his head, as if thinking. "The same reasons that drive the whole economic system: greed and fear. If Norrid is truly back on its feet, they could be bribing or threatening dozens of people at the FBI, the DOJ or any other government official that can make a difference," explains Dr. Debo.

This is certainly not ideal. Phil had hoped he'd seen the last of Norrid. "Do you really believe that Norrid is back to life? How could it be re-formed if KexCorp and the Boldwell Foundation were unwound and blown into pieces?" asks Phil with mounting fear accumulating in his mind, almost knowing the answer before Dr. Debo even replies.

Dr. Debo sighs and places his glass on the table beside him. "The pieces can always come back together. Different legal entities, different chains of command, but over a long period, as I told you a few times when we were working on stabilizing Equit, the same actors come back and carry the workload," says Dr. Debo.

"Scary to say the least. Last question: what do you think about agents Turner and Fuller? Trustworthy?" asks Phil.

"Agent Fuller is harmless. I don't think that he has the intellect or the wit to design criminal schemes," reasons Dr. Debo. Phil nods. He had the same gut reaction to the guy.

"Moreover," Dr. Debo continues, "he's been following Tiago like a puppy dog the past few days, so I guess he has probably proven his worth to the team." He looks across the plane, to where Agent Turner is twisting in the flight attendant seat, trying to figure out how the seatbelt works. "As for Agent Turner, I'm not sure. He is definitely smart and savvy. You've turned him into a celebrity when he arrested Henry, so would he have incentives to make another run at fame and glory? And perhaps cheat or make up a few things along the way to ensure maximum star power when he gets in front of the press for having resolved the greatest mystery of the world?" He shrugs. "I definitely see this as a possibility," says Dr. Debo.

"Interesting. Would he go as far as faking a whole mission to Singapore? But to what end?" asks Phil.

The doctor's eyes widen. "You have to be kidding. He wouldn't…" says Dr. Debo, stunned by Phil's comment.

"Well, according to the DOJ, our mission wasn't sanctioned," explains Phil.

"Interesting… Unless it was somehow erased from the system, Agent Turner had to know that the required bureaucracy was not on file for the mission. He had to produce something to get me pardoned. There must have been some paperwork that explained the mission that I would be joining," whispers Dr. Debo.

Phil frowns. The idea of the mission being real at first, but then the details of the operation erased from the FBI system had never occurred to him. But who would do such a thing. And why?

Chapter 36

Looking through the window nearby his uncomfortable jump seat, Agent Turner sees the Manhattan buildings in the distance when the jet initiates its final approach. Phil sees him look nervously at his phone a few times, frustrated to still be out of cellular service.

"Everything okay Agent Turner? Trying to reach someone?" asks Phil.

"Yeah, just waiting for cellular service to contact an agent to pick me up," replies Agent Turner.

"We'll be on the ground soon, don't worry. Relax a little," says Phil in a playful tone, still trying to read the agent's mind.

"You're right, I got a bit of time. And Teterboro airport is so close. I'm sure that I'll be in Manhattan in just a few minutes," says Agent Turner referring to the airport in New Jersey that is often used by executives shuttling to New York City.

"Well, we're landing in New Jersey but not exactly where you expected," says Phil with a wide smile, prompting the agent to look through the window again, only to see the famous skyline and boardwalk of Atlantic City. "Too much traffic around New York. We had to come down here and land in Atlantic City," continues Phil, still gauging every bit of reactions from the agent. In fact, Phil wanted to avoid the obvious airports around New York, which Agent Turner might have filled with agents to arrest members of the team.

"Phil, what are we doing in Atlantic City? You're putting me on a three-hour drive to New York," says Agent Turner with a sigh as he turns back to his phone, texting furiously, seemingly now with cellular service.

Phil gives a stern look towards Tiago across the aisle. He tightens his lips and shakes his head. Something is definitely off about Agent Turner, thinks Phil. Tiago immediately understands Phil's concerns. "I got it," whispers Tiago.

After several minutes of taxiing to the terminal, the plane finally comes to a stop. Tiago quickly stands up to retrieve a bag in the back of the aircraft. Then he makes his way back to the front of the aircraft to address Agent Turner.

"It was a true honor to work with you on this mission, Agent Turner. I learned a lot, thank you. I wish we could have done more drying of these thugs together. Maybe next time," says Tiago as he hugs the agent and slips a small device in his pocket.

"It was quite an adventure indeed. I'm sure we'll have other chances. You guys still work for me, so I'll see you at the office in a few days," says Agent Turner with a smile, knowing that after Phil's experience, the chance of keeping them as agents is limited. "Alright Agent Fuller, let's get on the road," commands Agent Turner.

"Well, if that's ok with Phil, I'd like to stick around the team for a couple more days until we all get back to work in Miami," requests Agent Fuller.

"Fine with me, you're welcomed to stay with us for now," answers Phil, somewhat surprised by the request.

Agent Turner gives a puzzled look to Agent Fuller and quickly deplanes. Once he is 50 feet away from the plane, walking to the terminal, Tiago wraps his arm around Agent Fuller's shoulders.

"My friend, now is time to prove your value to the team," says Tiago, holding the agent tightly with their bodies side-by-side.

"Of course, I'd be happy to," says Agent Fuller, pumping his chest and smiling at Bianca, Linda and Maria. "How can I be of service?"

"I just dropped a tracker in Agent Turner's pocket. This receiver needs to be within five miles of him for us to hear him and see where he is," says Tiago as he hands a small black box with a digital screen to the agent, who immediately realizes the high risks of the task. He suddenly drops his shoulders, crushed by the notion of having to tail his boss. "Needless to say, that he absolutely cannot see you while you're tailing him."

"I'm not sure that I..." starts Agent Fuller but stops mid-sentence.

"We're counting on you," says Bianca with a flirty smile, followed by nods from every other member of the team.

"Alright. Will you guys also see his movements?" asks the agent.

"Yes. And hear all of his conversations. We'll let you know if he said something that would lead to your discovery," explains Tiago.

"Where do I meet you after?" Asks Agent Fuller nervously.

"You know we can't reveal that in advance. We'll be in touch. We won't let you down," says Phil trying his best to offer a pep talk to the agent. "Hurry up now, you'll need to jump in a taxi right after he does."

Agent Fuller slowly gets off the aircraft, sad to leave a team with which he was starting to bond with, looks back to wave at them and enters the terminal. He sees Agent Turner in the distance talking on his phone as he hurriedly moves towards the taxi line.

"What are you up to Turner?" mumbles Agent Fuller under his breath and watches from inside the building while Agent Turner gets into a taxi. Agent Fuller snaps a picture of the license plate and rushes outside and also jumps into a cab. "Follow that car," he says loudly to the driver, who speeds away.

Worried about any leak of their presence in Atlantic City to malfeasant FBI agents, Phil orders Sergio to take-off without filing a flight plan and remain relatively close to New York City at an uncontrolled airfield. Perhaps nearby Wildwood, New Jersey, Phil suggests, then closes his eyes, resting comfortably for the first time in weeks, surrounded exclusively by his trustworthy friends.

Bianca sits beside Phil, holds his hand, and rests her head on his shoulder. Her beautiful blond hair tickles his cheeks, so he delicately moves them behind her ear, enjoying every small movement that they make towards each other. While they were holding Phil captive, making Bianca worried and devastated about his disappearance had been so much more agonizing to Phil than the physical pain that his captors inflicted. "I promise to be more careful in the future, baby," says Phil. Bianca squeezes his hand tightly.

"You have to be less naïve about the FBI's intentions," warns Bianca.

Of course, she is right. But Phil isn't quite ready to close the book on all of them. "I'm still hoping that this is all just a misunderstanding inside the FBI. If it weren't, then why would Agent Turner even show up at the cabin. If he was there to collaborate with these thugs, I would have heard or seen him, right?" asks Phil.

"Hey, not for nothing, but how did Agent Turner even know about the location of the cabin? He arrived in California after us and couldn't possibly find us that quickly," says Bianca.

"The bullet proof vest had trackers. Speaking of those vests, they're on board, so we need to get rid of the trackers, otherwise we'll keep providing our location to the FBI," says Phil as he looks towards Tiago. "Hey Tiago, can you get the vests, remove the trackers and destroy them." Commands Phil.

Tiago feels the material of one of the vests to find a hidden tracker. After a few minutes, he gets frustrated and uses his knife to gut open the dark fabric that covers the protective kevlar. Still no device.

"Crap. He lied to us about how he found our location," says Tiago, fuming and brandishing a tight fist.

Phil's chest tightens. If Turner lied about that, what else had he lied to them about?

Chapter 37

Parked in a quiet corner of the Cape May Airport, minutes away from the famous Wildwood beach in New Jersey, Phil is glued to the screen of his laptop to follow the location of Agent Turner as he is approaching New York City. The tracking pauses when Agent Turner's taxi enters Manhattan through the Holland tunnel. Phil dials up Agent Fuller.

"Are you following him through the Holland tunnel?" asks Phil.

"Yes sir. He's about 200 feet ahead of me," replies Agent Fuller.

"Good. You might need to follow him closer and keep a visual once you're in Manhattan. We must absolutely know which building he enters. If you can, take a video for us," requests Phil. "And, if you're stopped in traffic somewhere, take the opportunity to switch to a yellow cab, you'll be more discreet."

"Sure thing," says Agent Fuller and hangs up.

Dr. Debo approaches to watch Agent Turner's movements in Lower Manhattan from over Phil's shoulder. Phil is sweating profusely as he is attentively studying every movement on the map.

"What's in Lower Manhattan that could be of interest for Agent Turner?" asks Dr. Debo.

"The FBI office at Federal Plaza, for one thing. So, he could actually be heading to his boss' office as he told us," says Phil, scratching his head.

"Don't they have metal detectors at the entrance of federal buildings? The tracker and microphone will most likely get exposed," says Dr. Debo.

"You're right, that's not good. And then we'll have no idea what he's up to," says Phil while turning his head to Tiago, who nods in agreement. "The offices of KexCorp were right around there as well," continues Phil with a trembling voice, then clears his throat. He is distraught with the thought that some remains of KexCorp might still be alive.

"Interesting… but Norrid people are smart. They wouldn't setup shop where KexCorp used to be," advises Dr. Debo.

"True, but if Norrid survived, don't you think that parts of KexCorp could still be alive and collaborating with Norrid again?" asks Phil as he turns towards Dr. Debo with fear in his eyes.

Phil's phone vibrates at the same moment. When he unlocks the screen, a video message from Agent Fuller appears. It shows Agent Turner getting off from the taxi and entering the Metropolitan Correctional Center.

"What is that? Where is he going?" asks Bianca pointing at the screen.

"That's a prison in lower Manhattan. Who could Agent Turner possibly be visiting there?" asks Phil.

"Could the DOJ have transported Li and Ernesto there already?" asks Bianca.

"Unless they immediately boarded them on a flight after we left the DOJ office in Sacramento, it's almost inconceivable that Ernesto and Li have already been imprisoned in New York," says Dr. Debo.

Heavy doors, clicks, buzzers and security systems can be heard on the radio transmission as Agent Turner makes his way through the building. "I'm here to see this inmate," Agent Turner can be heard. Then more doors and buzzers. Phil is rubbing his forehead forcefully, waiting to find out who this mysterious prisoner could be. Finally, a conversation can be heard to reveal this enigma.

"Good to see you," says Agent Turner.

"You are the most incompetent corrupt cop that I've had to work with. All you had to do is wait for someone to take care of him out there in Asia," says a low voice, that Phil immediately recognizes.

The cocky and arrogant voice that Phil once found inspiring, and supportive of all the supposedly great things that KexCorp was accomplishing around the world, is now synonymous with dirty business. That voice sounds so diabolic now. Henry has crept back into Phil's life, now using Agent Turner as his puppet. Phil grabs the back of his head, puts his feet on the seat under his butt and rolls himself into a tight ball. He just realized that he has been duped by a corrupt FBI agent under Henry's control.

"Did you at least bring me back my half of the money from the drying operations?" asks Henry.

"I had to leave everything in Singapore and rush back to California when Li and Ernesto got kidnapped by Tiago. I'll get you your money, I promise," says Agent Turner in an apologetic tone.

"Right, just like you said you'd get Phil taken care of. Well, you better bring me my money, I need to pay a pretty penny to whoever I can find to frame Phil and get him into a prison cell," says Henry with a laugh, implying that Agent Turner hasn't been able to do that. "You know, I really have to do everything for you. I would have gotten you rich with my plan to get Phil to dry up Li's operations, and now I have to clean up after you," says Henry, savoring his brilliance to have seemingly gotten Agent Turner to recruit Phil to dry up Li's operations in Asia.

"You're a real pain in the butt, you know. I had a perfect record and a promising career at the FBI before you started to black mail me with your made-up stories. Now I've got the DOJ looking into our unsanctioned mission to Singapore," says Agent Turner.

"Be careful with the way you talk to me. I still control a lot of what's going on outside. And remember that most of your glory and fame was built on my demise, so count your blessings. And just be more careful next time. You brought all of this onto yourself with your incompetence. Take Agent Mudor, for example. He went in for his mission and when things turned sour, he bolted unscathed. And he didn't even cost as much bribing as I've given to you," says Henry.

"You haven't even given me any money, you, old sap," replies Agent Turner with tight lips.

"You got half of the drying money. That was your bribe," concludes Henry, as he stands up with a smile, proud to have found a system to bribe cops from his prison cell without even having to touch the money himself. The fruit of the drying operation ends up in dirty cops' hands. So brilliant and perfect.

Tears are running down Bianca's cheeks. She knows that a normal life is now further away. She places her hand on Phil's head and slowly massages his temples. "Honey, we gotta go. We're not safe in the U.S. The dirty cops are going to try anything they can come up with to frame you." Phil thinks of the irony of having helped gather the funds in the drying operations, which were used to make Agent Turner dirty, and are now going to be used as a payoff to frame Phil himself. He raises his head, nods gently to Bianca, stands up and walks to the cockpit. Minutes later, the plane is taxiing and ready to depart.

A text message from Agent Fuller shows up on Phil's phone. Phil thinks of what to tell Agent Fuller, for whom they unfortunately cannot wait to get back in the air. Phil unlocks his phone as he thinks about the right words to break the bad news to the agent. But he freezes when he sees the text from the agent: "the DOJ just let Li walk based on insufficient evidence."

Made in the USA
Middletown, DE
09 November 2022